A TORTURED PEOPLE

THE POLITICS OF COLONIZATION

HOWARD ADAMS

THEYTUS BOOKS LTD.
PENTICTON, BC

Canadian Cataloguing in Publication Data

Adams, Howard, 1926-
  A tortured people

  ISBN 0-919441-77-7

  1. Native peoples--Canada--Government relations.* 2.
Native peoples--Canada--Ethnic identity. 3. Indians,
Treatment of--Canada. I. Title.
E92.A32 1994   323.1'197071   C94-910782-4

Primary Editor: Linda Jaine
Secondary Editor: Greg Young-Ing
Design & Layout: Marlena Dolan
Cover Design: Marlena Dolan & Greg Young-Ing
Typesetting: Sherri Slobodian and Lutcya McCormick, Arbutus Secretarial Service,
Vancouver, BC, Regina Gabriel, En'owkin Centre, Penticton, BC

THEYTUS BOOKS LTD.
257 Brunswick Street., Penticton, BC, V2A 5P9

Printed in Canada

Acknowledgements

This book was written over a long period of time. Many ideas emanated from experiences of life and struggles in halfbreed colonized communities. As a result, it includes many years of documents and letters that I have accumulated through my experiences as a student, professor and activist leader in the struggle against racist and colonial oppression. For this reason, the book is one of the first to apply an Aboriginal perspective to a socio-political analysis to colonization in Canada. It is an attempt to provide a new perspective on Metis and Indian life and culture. In addition, a hope is provided that it will stimulate other Aboriginal intellectuals to explore and analyze colonial notions from this point of view.

Additional ideas arose out of the mass movement activities of Indians and Metis during the political movement of the 1960s. Analysis and interpretations were made from the conflicts and situations within their context at that particular time. Therefore, they served as notions of decolonization.

Certain theories are based on research from California Indian reservations on political culture, which was conducted while I was a professor at the University of California, Davis. In these studies much credit goes to a graduate student, Hazel Brandt, for her superior work and insightful collection of relevant data.

Valuable assistance was also provided in the early stages of organizing and planning of the volume by Rose Klinkberg.

However, Heather Prime must be singled out for her special contribution. This book could not have been completed without her diligent efforts. She assisted in editing and writing of most chapters. In addition, Heather provided an authentic insight and analysis that was consistent with the Aboriginal perspective. As an editor, her contribution was exceptional and outstanding.

Thanks to the excellent work of Sherri Slobodian and Lutcya McCormick of Arbutus Secretarial Service. Also, a special thanks is due to the superb work of the staff of Theytus Books.

Howard Adams

Table of Contents

Introduction

This book developed out of concern that eurocentric history and the politics of colonization are not widely understood by many Canadians, and particularly by Aboriginal people. Since there is a serious lack of knowledge about Canadian colonialism, the book is written to cover several aspects of colonization and the role of governments in maintaining it.

I have attempted to analyze the relationship between the history and political culture of Canadian Aboriginal people and their colonization. The essays examine how eurocentric historical interpretation of Indians, Metis and Inuit are used to justify, conquest and to camouflage government mechanisms in maintaining oppression. The authentic history of Indians and Metis has been hidden or falsified by establishment academics who use distortions and stereotypes to obscure the harsh political and colonial practices of the state.

After five hundred years of colonial oppression, Indians, Metis and Inuit have internalized a colonized consciousness. The colonizer's falsified stories have become universal truths to mainstream society, and have reduced Aboriginal culture to a caricature. This distorted reality is one of the most powerful shackles subjugating Aboriginal people. It distorts all indigenous experiences, past and present, and blocks the road to self-determination.

Honesty for Indian and Metis history and culture is more than a quest for decolonization and a national identity; it is a pursuit to transform imperial structures of the state. History, as told by authentic Aboriginal historians, does more than retell establishment history. It explains the struggles for self-determination and promotes efforts to overcome present colonization. Indian and Metis liberation is not possible if eurocentricism is not terminated.

The format of the book consists of a series of related essays divided into four sections. Section I combines narrative and analysis of the politics and history of colonization from a subjective Aboriginal point of view. Section II explains eurocentricism, and analyzes the histories of Indian, Metis and Inuit people written by white supremacist historians. It deals with history as a contest between two different civilizations in which the white supremist/militarily superior nation conquered, plundered and enslaved an indigenous communal subsistence society and its people. The unfolding of western imperialism is debated. A critique is made of European thought and tradition. In other words, it is a de-Europeanization of the political culture and history of Indian and Metis peoples. By explaining imperialist culture as ideology, it gives an understanding of colonialism and eurocentricism as political phenomena. It can be seen how imperial culture and ideology fit together as colonizing logic. Chapters in this section serve as a demystification of the early history and happenings of Indians and Metis in their relationship with European intruders.

Section III is a condensed narrative of historical struggles of Metis and Indian people against European invaders over the last five centuries. It lays bare the dehumanized underpinnings of imperialism and mechanisms that facilitate its functioning. Contrary to establishment historians who study Indians and Metis as 'simple primitives' of 'semi-stone age', the book deals with them as intelligent human beings in a developed civilization who fought heroically to protect their homes, land and resources. They are not naive and passive victims of ruthless invasion. They are relentless fighters in the struggle against foreign predators.

The focus of Section IV is neocolonialism, discussing the civil rights movement of the 1960s that became struggles of liberation in the early 1970s against restructured neocolonial governments. The content examines the fundamental character of neocolonialism as it pertains to Metis, Inuit and Indians. An analysis is made of the rise of the Aboriginal comprador regimes in neocolonization and the functions they perform in collaboration with the multinational corporations and governments in maintaining oppression of the mass of lower class Natives. It shows how indigenization of Aboriginal organizations and programs has deepened impoverishment and subjugation of Metis, Inuit and Indians. Neocolonialism has resulted in maintaining the old colonial structures and institutions, rather than change to a new socio-economic system. The new 'ruling class' Natives have become an integral part of the structure of imperialism. At the same time, governments have developed a neocolonial conservative ideology among the young Aboriginal people through university education, training programs of administration and managers of small businesses. The struggle for self-determination for Native people is no doubt a long haul. Not only are the forces of neocolonialism powerful and resilient, but the mass of Third World people are slow to develop the necessary counter consciousness and essential political movement.

Each topic, could have constituted its own book. However, I have tried to develop an historical interpretation that explains the politics of colonization. The book combines academic research with personal experience as a Metis peasant and activist. Most orthodox historians would argue that their history is 'value free'. However, I share the view of a prominent Canadian historian that "no historian is free of bias, no history is capable of presenting only the facts."[1]

No one book can provide a complete discussion of the state's system of colonization, but I hope this book will challenge as well as illuminate and clarify many dimensions and mechanisms of colonization imposed on Metis, Inuit and Indian people. I also hope that this book will encourage Aboriginal intellectuals to reclaim their history, and culture, in order to conduct further research, and write history from an authentic indigenous perspective. I hope they will explore more extensively the issues in the book. My objective is to provide a theoretical framework for analyzing Aboriginal history and culture. The past not only explains the present, it is also a source of power and provides a sense of direction to the future for Indian, Inuit, and Metis people engaged in current struggles for self-determination.

Part One

The Local Nature of Colonization

Chapter One

Colonization in Our Backyard

I am a halfbreed and grew up in a halfbreed ghetto. In Canada's racist society, I learned and felt the politics of colonization in its reality. In a white supremacy society, the values and standards of the middle class are taken for granted as the norm for all society. It is automatically accepted as politically and culturally correct. In this way, it has a moral value. There are rewards for conforming and punishments for non-compliance. For the colonized, however, there is much more: economic poverty, political coercion, and cultural distortion. Through the politics of colonization, we were socialized to the image that we were inferior, stupid, lazy. The list of stereotypes are well known. It is natural that self-hatred should follow. I soon became to hate myself—for how I looked, behaved and spoke. Such indoctrination is as powerful and pervasive as the catechism of any religion. In school I was taught that we were retarded. I believed that I was dumb, in comparison to white students; and that I was low class, crude and dirty. Is it any wonder that we became shy, submissive and socially crippled? The aspects of the 'apartheid middle class,' although not spelled out, exploit and mangle us. They are the odious underlying principles of a colonial society. As Natives, we are marginalized and victimized by these Arayan middle class charades. We are not the 'ordinary'; we are the targeted people, the village idiots. How do we know? As a child in the ghetto, I knew my shame by looking 'Indian,' by living in a log shack, by eating bannock and lard.

Hostility and violence emerged with self-hatred. The fact that I could not play on the village baseball team or hockey team because I was not white stung me deeply. Teenagers were invited into white homes for games and parties, but the door closed when I was about to enter. Because self-hatred had no more space, I made excuses to myself. I was ragged, uncouth and I stunk. I did not belong to the level of the 'nice, proper, elegant' middle class. There were reasons, I told myself, why I should be treated differently. I lived in a low class colony. I did not speak the 'Standard English.' I was socially awkward in a middle class house with polished furniture in a decorated room. I could not look a white person in the eye and say with confidence "I have the right to be at the party, or that I have the right to play on the ball team." Instead, I felt ashamed and guilty that I was a halfbreed peasant. But, is there any other class of halfbreeds, other than the underclass?

White people are not aware that they are the pace-setters for the racist cultural standard of mainstream society. It is taken for granted without sensitivity. Racists whites are the dominant 'ordinary.' No one ever talks about the ugliness of racism and the politics of colonization. Instead, the masses speak about racial minorities, multiculturalism, and appropriation. We should be talking about racist education, theft of land, Mohawk style revolt, imperial bureaucracy and Davis Inlet soweto. But, I am reminded that my language is too political, pejorative and rhetorical. I do not apologize. My language is in harmony with my race/class and colonization. Behind my back, I hear the whites whisper in mockery, 'He's a Red Power radical.' All my credibility is destroyed, and I am reduced to an over politicized halfbreed.

Eventually, I tried socially, and linguistically, to edge into mainstream. But I could not change my pigmentation and colonial politics, so the stereotype images shadowed me. Eventually I grew impatient with the hypocrisy and self-righteousness of middle class society. It was keeping me in the grip of a mythical facade. It prevented me from thinking critically and politically in order to decolonize myself. Although our ancestors had been conquered by a superior military, in the long run it was the weapon of a political culture that kept us perpetually in a state of subjugation and exploitation. I reconciled with my race/class and colonization and made it a characteristic part of decolonization. To my way of thinking Western European culture has a predatory conquest thrust, combined with superiority, dispossession and violence. British and French colonizers in their 400 years of constant warring and terrorizing of Indians demonstrated this vicious contempt. The invasion and capture of Metis/Indian territories in the late 1800s by the Ottawa Regime with its thousands of mercenaries, cannons, machine guns, and latest killing weapons revealed the vilest of Euro-Canadian imperialism. Public scaffolds in the city streets of Regina and North Battleford that snapped the necks of several Indian and Metis heroes had to be the most extraordinary acts of violence, terror and perversion. How long were the colonized victims expected to willingly submit to brutality, starvation and torture? The killing of white oppressors under such conditions is not murder. It is an act of heroism. A Jew who shot Adolf Eichmann would be a hero! In the same reasoning, Wandering Spirit of Frog Lake reserve was a hero. He has always been my hero. I am outraged that his body is buried far down in the desolate bush at the base of the Saskatchewan river in an unmarked grave, while a mile high on the adjoining hill is the pompous spectacle of the Mounted Police fortress and the glorious imperial museum.

European interlopers claimed that it was their birthright to conquer and possess whatever land came into their vision and imagination. As Lords of a visionary empire, the Hudsons Bay Company officials gave themselves "possession of all the lands within the drainage basin of the Hudson Bay— which included the greater part of all prairie provinces, as well as the tundra of the north."[1] "These English 'noble-pirates' who had never travelled to North America obtained a charter from the King of England that gave them nearly half of the land of Canada."[2] Europeans, according to their philosophy had the right to invade and plunder all indigenous lands and claim them as sovereign territory. No land was foreign to them. As recent as 1992 Quebec businessmen invaded the cemetery land of the Mohawk Indians at Oka and tried to claim it as sovereign land for a golf course. Nothing is sacred in imperialism!

Imperialism changed barbarianism into civilization according to white historians. At conquest and invasion most Indians were either slaughtered or made slaves. "The [Europeans] have so cruelly and inhumanly butchered, that of the three million people," wrote de la Casas in 1600, "overrunning cities and villages where they spared no sex, nor age; neither would their cruelty pity women with child, whose bellies they would rip open, taking out the infant to hew it to pieces."[3] This was typical behaviour of the 'civilized' European explorers and missionaries that eurocentric historians have been boasting about for the last 500 years. Long before Columbus brought mercantilism to North America, Indians of the Northeastern coast of America were part of the international trade route with the Mediterranean ancient civilizations. "The ancestors of the Micmac Indians were familiar with metals, and employed the same hieroglyph [writing] for [trading] silver and gold as were used by the ancient Egyptians." "It is evident that the Micmac hieroglyphs were already transmitted to North America more than 2000 years ago, when they were still in use in Egypt."[4] Thor Heyerdahl proved the fact of this ancient ocean travel in 1972 when he sailed in a reed RA II boat from Gibraltar to America.[5] 'Discover' is one of the greatest con-game concepts in the imperial vocabulary. Why was Marco Polo's visit to China in 1295 not a discovery? 'Discovery,' obviously is only a notion of European imperialism, and which applied only to vulnerable indigenous countries. Wandering European pirates encroached upon any foreign land they sighted and plundered the homes of indigenous citizens. Although colonialism may have provided some material benefits at the beginning, such as guns and kettles, in the long run the political culture of imperialism destroyed indigenous institutions and processes of democratic collective governments that were in harmony with nature, animals, resources and environment.

European colonizers saw themselves as grand organizers. Only they could bring 'civilized order to primitive chaos.' They never admitted that order already existed in prevailing Native civilizations and had for thousands of years. The British boasted about English law being based on ancient Roman law. In pre-imperialism, Europe copied words and terms from ancient civilizations that advanced its purpose, but, in imperial expansionism words were selected to suit that specific purpose. Imperialist law and bureaucratic logic is characteristic of modern white authoritarian governments. The Indian Affairs Department manages Indian reserves as oppressively and rigidly as maximum security prisons. Colonizers are still using the old system of 'divide and rule.' Immediately comes to mind the conflict in South Africa between Mandela's ANC and the Zulus; as well as the war between the Tamils and Hindus in Sri Lanka and tribal civil wars in Rwanda and Somalia—to name a few. Most Third World nations are ruled by military dictatorships of co-opted Native leaders who are manipulated by an imperial nation, usually the United States. Countries such as Chile, Argentina and Brazil are controlled by comprador regimes, their military and death squads. "These countries received $2.3 billion in military aid and arms credits from the United States. In addition, these nations bought a staggering $13.7 billion worth of US arms."[6] Such massive military arms are used for internal use to control the Native people in the interests of the imperial corporations. Thus the colonizers make profits from the sales of armaments to both sides, while keeping the Aboriginal people divided, weak and colonized.

Indians, Metis and Inuit of internal colonies are not beyond a type of Third World tribal conflict. In March, 1994, an experienced and seasoned collaborator leader pushed his way into the national leadership of the Non Status Indian organization. "Just hours after he was elected president of the newly named Congress of Aboriginal Peoples . . . he signed a political accord with the federal government."[7] One does not have to be paranoid to be suspicious of the political corruption that underlie the actions of this old comprador leader and the Chretien neocolonial government. As the mass of underclass Natives, we need to mobilize as a political force to stop the collaboration and exploitation by such comprador rule. The move for so-called self-government can be a dangerously oppressive and reactionary move.

The consciousness and behaviour of Native collaborator leaders have sharpened since the rise of neocolonialism. They do not only identify with the oppressor, they have actually become the new Aboriginal oppressors. With the support of governments and multinational corporations, they have become much more brutal and vicious than white imperial rulers. As Metis, Inuit and Indians, we should not kid ourselves that such type of rule happens only in Third World colonies. This type of suppressive rule is very possible in internal colonies in Canada. In fact, since the mid 1970s it has become the typical form of rule on reserves and Metis colonies. The colonizer was eventually successful in stopping the radical Red Power movement for self-determination.

This collaborator class created by massive government grants has taken over leadership of major Indian, Metis and Inuit organizations, as well as the communities. The purpose is to maintain suppression over the quasi-liberation movements that flourished in the 1960s. As a result, the last thirty years has resulted in increased political turmoil, excessive corruption, deepened ghettoization and increased colonization. The politics of colonialism has the specific aim of managing the resistance of the oppressed, resulting in schemes of manipulating and co-opting the victims. Most, Metis, Inuit and Indians have been socialized and partially integrated into the imperialist system as supportive members. They have harmonized their lives and goals to the political culture of the colonizer.

As Aboriginals of internal colonies we have to give careful attention to tribal divisions, mechanisms and names that foster internal tribal conflict. Conflict can flare up over matters as simple as unequal funding to different tribal groups. Status or treaty Indians seem to be inclining towards exclusiveness and primacy, atop the Non-status Indians, Inuit, and Metis. The term, First Nations, is racist in tone. It assumes there are second or lesser nations. Furthermore, First Nations is part of the imperial vocabulary. It was through the emergence of distinctive nations that imperialism flourished. Finally, the term First Nations does not indicate anything indigenous or democratic, such as Inuit which means people. Metis, Inuit, and Indians are kept in a constant state of oppression and impoverishment where jealousy and chieftain power-struggles ignite easily. Internal conflict is fostered regularly in many different channels that brings agitation to the threshold of potential flare-up. The collaboration and double-dealing of governments, Aboriginal puppet organizations, and multinational corporations are cunning and corrupt because they have access to the structures of power. If the local Metis and Indians do not come to terms with the subtleties of power negotiations, they will fall into deeper colonization and exploitation. The only strength of Aboriginal communities against imperial forces is 'people power,' including environmentalists, unions, women, elders, students and others. Our struggle is similar to that of the Mayan Indians of Chiapas, Mexico. As a result, our methods of decolonization may need to be the same.

The world is awash in low-level wars today. There are almost 100 wars being fought around the globe that involve indigenous peoples, their nations and resources. Imperial nations, especially the USA, have crucial interests in every one of these conflicts.[8] Inuit, Metis and Indian colonies have important similarities and relevance to these low-level conflicts because they contain vital rich resources, such as uranium, oil, gas, water, timber, etc. Despite the publicity of enormous aid to Third World countries, the First World (G7) takes from the Third World in raw materials twice the amount it sends in as aid. Furthermore, the debt and interest payments paid by Third World countries are three times more than all the aid they currently receive. In 1990 they paid $52 billion in debt repayments to the monetary agencies of the First World.[9] As indigenous nations we need to recognize that the rich G7 nations are suppressing and exploiting Third World nations more than ever. They are parasites on our people, blood-sucking the few necessities we have for mere survival.

The European ethic, according to Ani, "is to create an image that will prevent others from anticipating European motives."[10] In other words, the intent is to promote European interests by defrauding or cheating other people. This characteristic is very obvious in the treaties which the British made with the Indians. An example of this swindling is shown in *Treaty Number Six* made with the Cree Indians of Saskatchewan in 1876. Governor Morris in addressing the Indians, said, ". . . we wish to give you as much or more land than you need . . . and that no one will interfere with you. I see Indians receiving money from the Queen's commissioners to purchase clothing for their children; I see them enjoying their hunting and fishing as before."[11] However, when the final agreement was made and the document signed, it stated, "I do hereby cede, release, surrender and yield up to the government of Canada forever, all their rights, titles and privileges whatsoever to the lands included, that is to say, . . . the tract embracing an area of one hundred and twenty-one thousand square miles."[12] Indians were left with only a few acres of poor land that formed a reserve, or rural compound which they could not leave without first obtaining permission from a white security guard. The money promised to Indians turned out to be five dollars a year. One cannot disagree with Ani when she claims that hypocrisy is a crucial ingredient of European culture.[13] Rhetoric and hypocrisy are natural components of imperialism. The word of the colonizer is only empty rhetoric. The words have no relationship to the deed. When Indians accuse the whiteman of speaking with a 'forked tongue,' they are, indeed, accurate.

There is a common settlement pattern in each colonial nation. Despite the fact that Metis, Inuit, and Indians are scattered in isolated pockets throughout Canada, which are similar in socio-economic conditions, they are administered by a single government department. The same type of Native settlement exists in New Zealand, Australia and South Africa. This was the typical colonial settlement pattern for British imperialism. Although other European nations had slightly different settlement schemes, the final results for all indigenous people were the same: dispossession, subjugation, cultural and political division, and severe colonization. In spite of checkered isolation and slight diversity in colonization Natives embrace a certain unity as a race/class of colonized peoples. We sink or swim together. As indigenous peoples however, we constitute the majority of the world's population. Of the approximate 5-1/2 billion people in the world, approximately 3-1/2 billion are Third World Natives. Yet, we talk of Third World people as 'racial minorities.' Why? Seemingly, the G7 nations control not only the military and financial power of the world, but also the language and public information. Furthermore, they distort it to suit their interests and purposes. In all countries indigenous peoples suffer the greatest economic disadvantage. They are on the lowest rung of the ladder in every area of living conditions.[14] It seems fairly obvious that as Aboriginal people, we are still deeply colonized and politically unorganized, otherwise why would we prolong this atrocious hell? We seem to have forgotten that a small 'primitive' nation (Vietnam) with 'barbaric' weapons defeated the strongest nation (USA) in the world with the most advanced military weapons, including nuclear and napalm bombs. From this convincing victory of the heroic Vietnamese people we must take strength and hope. We now know that the greatest power of imperialism is not beyond defeat by a small indigenous nation.

Chapter Two

The Poverty Grip on Metis

Welfare payments to Indian and Metis families were cut off almost every spring. The government bureaucrats and politicians boasted that it was the only way to force the 'shiftless' Natives to get jobs. It was a nightmarish and repressing measure, which could mean death for Natives in Northern Canada. The government ignored or simply didn't care that there were no jobs in what is one of Canada's most underdeveloped regions. After 300 years of the fur trade, when all profits were shipped to London and Paris for investment, Northern Canada was a wasteland. Once plentiful with fish and wildlife, it was reduced to a sterile hinterland plundered by reckless tourists and logging and mining companies. The Natives had undergone a terrible process that gradually undermined or, in some cases, completely destroyed the indigenous economy, cultures, and political systems, in spite of their struggles for improvement. However, if they criticized the local governing councils, e.g. tribal councils, or white village councils, they were immediately stripped of their welfare, even in the dead of winter, and harassed into submission. Underdevelopment and dirty, low-paying jobs under these circumstances created a dispossessed, powerless, and hungry Indian and Metis population.

Poplarville, a typical Metis colony, was a tortured community located at the edge of a swamp. It seemed to be the most desperate place on the face of this planet. Its people were regularly rounded up like slaves and forced to take on menial and lackey jobs, such as picking roots, stones, and sugar beets. When the dilapidated buses commandeered by Indian Affairs officials arrived, Indians and Metis of all ages were abruptly herded, without choice or recourse. They were abducted to perform the most dehumanizing, back-breaking work in Canada.

Charles Joseph and his wife Marie described their job of picking roots for a southern farmer. They worked from sunup to sundown, clearing one acre at a time. It was heavy work, packing armfuls of roots through soft, dusty fields. In 1969, they earned $4 per day for this work. Beet workers were housed in abandoned horse stables and given only enough provisions to keep them working. If there was bad weather or a worker became ill, his or her pay fell below the cost for 'room and board.' On average, one month's work, providing it was long and good work, paid $100. Many did not make enough to pay for their return fare. Some escaped by hitchhiking or walking the 600 miles back home. The Josephs knew it was virtual slavery, chain-gang work, but they stuck it out. There were no other jobs, and if they didn't take this job, they would not get welfare during the winter. With every step they took, their deep-seated agitation stirred.

In spite of the atrocious working conditions, rumors spread among the mainstream communities that the Aboriginal 'ingrates' refused to take 'good' jobs at the beet fields, where they could earn as much as '$100 per day'! This proved, the whites insisted, that Indians and Metis were lazy and naturally prone to lying about and boozing. If Natives could refuse such 'fantastic jobs and big pay, the whites persisted, then they deserved to starve. As far as the whites were concerned, they had proved that Aboriginals could not be made into responsible workers. Their 'proof' fuelled their tireless, racial slurs: 'They always want handouts' or 'They never come back to work after pay-day,' and 'the only good Indian is a dead Indian.' Such falsehoods, distortions, and stereotypes keep Natives oppressed. Contrived racist stereotypes always violate Aboriginal dignity.

Our oppressors continue to give us only enough to survive. They refuse to invest in our communities; banks seldom provide loans to Aboriginals. Moreover, Indians and Metis do not have rights to the resources on their reserves or colonies: "The Federal Government has exclusive jurisdiction over Indian reserve land and resources."[1] Where private enterprise has managed to develop, the majority of positions go to outside white workers. The state's policies are unimaginative, unbending, and, except for the token Aboriginal civil servant, strictly prevents regular employment and economic development.

Racism imprisons most Aboriginal peoples to the lowest levels of Canada's society. How many Aboriginal workers do you see in administrative jobs or in the public realm such as sales clerks, bank tellers, bus drivers or postal workers? Employment officers relegate Indians and Metis to labour, janitorial, and domestic positions. Regardless of training, education, or skills, our racial appearance determines our reception and job opportunities. If we are lucky, we may get some sort of casual or seasonal work, dead-end jobs that force us to live day-by-day. Unemployment among the Indians and Metis hovers steadily between 50 and 90%.[2] We are prevented from establishing a home or financial security. Our only reward is hopelessness, frustration, and hostility.

Approximately one half of Metis families before 1970 lived in rented accommodation, typically shacks without indoor plumbing. In many cases,

Metis were clustered into ghettos or shantytowns lacking proper facilities. Approximately 20% of Metis families lived under the same roof with at least one other family. It was not uncommon for as many as ten people to live in as few as three rooms.[3] And yet, the Metis and Indians were forced to pay excessively high rent.

During a trip to Northern Saskatchewan in 1966, I visited many Metis brothers and sisters. I was startled and outraged by some of the situations and conditions I encountered. However, it was clear that the local people were uniting against brutality, discrimination, and hunger. A fresh and defiant hostility was emerging to challenge state oppression.

Ron Thompson, the regional social worker, took me for a coffee at the cafe, but he hesitated, wondering if we would be served. Ron had a genuine compassion for Indians and Metis. His concern brought him to Northern Saskatchewan where he hoped to do meaningful work. As he slowly stirred his coffee, he said softly, "Isn't it horrible about poor little Laureen Fontaine? She was such a lovely child." He made it sound so final. With surprise and curiosity, I asked, "What happened to her?" Ron replied, "She starved to death."

Starvation is a harsh, cruel finality. It is an agonizing parting. For the colonized, it is a tortuous end to a struggling existence. It may be easy to define, but it is painful to explain. Why do masses of visible minorities, not white Canadians, live close to starvation? Are the white immune to starvation? Probably, their surest protection is an imprisoned buffer zone of the oppressed and abused. The Aboriginal peoples of Canada are as vulnerable to starvation as those in Somalia. One only need examine Canada's backyards, e.g. Davis Inlet, to realize this Canadian reality.

I pressed Ron for details about Laureen's death, "How do you know that Laureen actually died of starvation?" He described the situation slowly and precisely. He had followed the Fontaine case closely for some time, but not because they were different from other Metis families. Without welfare, or even with welfare, every Indian and Metis family was pushed to the edge of starvation. The paradox, however, was that there were no jobs to be had in the region. It was not a matter of choice; it was a matter of surviving on whatever could be salvaged from the surrounding woods.

There were six children in the Fontaine family. They lived in a two-bedroom, tumble-down shack. They only had the most basic necessities: a small wood stove, boxes for chairs, and some bedding. Laureen, at one and a half years, was the youngest. According to Ron, Mr. Fontaine had probably tried harder than most men to find odd jobs to keep his family alive. But, as usual, he was rejected everywhere. And as if that wasn't enough, the local lake no longer contained fish, and the woods had been cleared of all game, including rabbits. As a result, the Fontaines were reduced to eating one meal a day. Those who did not get that much ate chunks of bannock and lard, and little of that, to ease their hunger pangs. Although families shared what little food they had with others a community can do little, if anything, to aid the needy when all are equally desperate.

Ron had visited the Fontaine home one week before Laureen's death. She was in a dreadfully weakened state. He managed to get her admitted to the hospital in spite of the nuns' strong objections. According to the sisters, they could not take in every starving Metis child—the hospital would be filled within hours. The sisters argued that the hospital was neither a home for the poor nor a restaurant. However, when pressured, they agreed to take Laureen in for a 'check-up' and 'clean-up.' To Ron's dismay they sent her home the next day, claiming she did not suffer from a specific disease.

Laureen died two days later. She was a pitiful sight of fleshless bones. Her emaciated remains were the indelible, unmistakable proof of deprivation and colonization. Dr. Schneider, however, listed Laureen's cause of death as the 'flu.' Although he acceded to Ron that she had died of malnutrition, it was a regular practice among doctors to not report that an Aboriginal child had died of starvation. Such honesty would contravene their unwritten policy, their vow of silence, not to mention the fact that it would undermine Ottawa's 'initiatives' for promoting universal equality and justice. The more I learned about Laureen's case, the more I understood its similarities to the situation of South Africa's black people. In colonized societies, officials, privileged members of a white supremacist system, live handsomely off the misery and death of the colonized. A Canadian doctor is part of the state officialdom that buries the truth under the state's racist policies. Why should he disrupt the system? Indian and Metis lives are cheap. It was rumoured that Dr. Schneider was the highest paid doctor in the province. Would he have provided better treatment to a white child? The answer was so obvious there was no need to ask the question. In hushed tones, we talked of mobilization and protest.

To counteract the 'flu' decision, Ron kept a detailed journal and organized potential witnesses. Laureen's death provided factual evidence that an Aboriginal person had actually died of malnutrition in Canada. Her death stirred long-suppressed rumblings in the village. Racial antagonism that had smoldered for years finally flared into a colonial bonfire. Her death was the central issue to ignite action and impact our civil rights struggle. It sparked the beginning of a struggle to decolonize Aboriginal peoples. It generated an intense and extended controversy about Aboriginal economic oppression and poverty.

The Hudsons Bay store locked its door, protecting itself against the anticipated outrage, as Laureen was buried in a tiny grave marked with a crude stick. Laureen's sinking pine box stirred painful feelings in me. We resolved that someone would have to pay for this crime. To let people starve to death when the storehouse is full, is murder. In my mind, we had the right to raid the Bay's storehouse after centuries of exploitation and subjugation.

A colonized society is structured by the state's control and management of indigenous people. Perhaps the easiest way to oppress the colonized is by keeping them weak, too weak to upset the system, but strong enough to fulfill their lowly role as menial workers to support the economy of corporate rulers. As long as the government provided welfare cheques, it provided the necessary relief to prevent mass unrest. In the small, backwood towns of Northern Canada, this meant that profits went to the Bay and crumbs went to our people. The Bay, which operated the post office and, therefore, controlled the welfare cheques, eventually received all the Aboriginals' monies. In most cases, one family member signed the cheque and then gave it directly back to the Bay clerk.

How well I remember the humiliation my mother suffered at the colonizer's store. Our welfare cheque, as small as it was, never failed to arrive. And just as consistently, my mother was deliberately and callously treated like a beggar. Shopping for our groceries was a painful ordeal in which we regularly paid a high price with what little pride we had left. Although she shopped within the welfare regulations, she was routinely treated as a suspicious vagrant. The shame and disgrace crushed her, and created a damaged state of mind that infected our entire family. We suffered physically, mentally, and spiritually. Like Laureen, we inherited the legacy of British colonization. The colonizers seemed to enjoy inflicting pain, and they rejoiced in our broken spirits and defeat.

Welfare assistance is one of the most effective ways of controlling the oppressed, who represent a threat to society's order. However, once people are forced to live on welfare for a while, they develop a dependency that soon encompasses their entire lives. The structure for maintaining Aboriginals under the welfare system extends through numerous state institutions, such as the police, schools, and the church. The result is a highly sophisticated and efficient mechanism for making the poor fearful, intimidated and, most importantly, subservient. There are alternatives the state could use to care for its unemployed and indigenous people, but they would not have the same controlling force as welfare. Would the liberation revolution never come?

In July 1969, a group of unemployed Indians and Metis in Northern Saskatchewan wrote a letter to the province's Minister of Welfare, Mr. MacDonald, describing their predicament:

> There are little jobs here and just a few men are working. It is very hard for us to support our families. There is no fishing on this lake because there is no fish. It's not because we are lazy. It's because of government people . . . come and see a lot of poor Indians . . . there's no food for children. This welfare man is helping some Indians with ten dollars no matter if he's got nine kids, that's a month. Right now they have nothing at all at home.[4]

They argued that they also required "public washing facilities for ourselves and our clothes. The government provides this for [white] tourists at Lac la Ronge but carefully segregates it from [Aboriginal] residents."[5] These Aboriginals understood that the state was to blame for Canada's apartheid policies and Aboriginals' extreme poverty. They promised that "in the next election many will vote for anyone except those presently causing our children to starve."[6] Minister MacDonald suggested educational upgrading and training programs as solutions, but the politically smart Aboriginals responded that "starving people can't learn what they need to learn."[7] The Metis pressed their complaints logically and simply, "At best, welfare is a tragic way of life. But, to deny welfare to starving families who cannot get work anywhere is a mortal crime against humanity."[8]

The Aboriginals responsible for this letter clearly understood that colonialism had locked them into a life-threatening situation. There were endless examples illustrating how cruelly they were treated.

> Mr. Veronique says that on one occasion he asked the social welfare worker in the local area for help for himself and thirteen men who were trying to make a meal from one rabbit because there was nothing else available, and they were denied help.[9]

A few weeks earlier "he was able to get a loan of $2 from the Hudsons Bay store to buy some food for his family . . . I suspect there may be present problems of malnutrition in other children which may result in other potential cases of TB or [death]."[10] When the colonized are degraded so severely, they feel treated worse than most animals. One report spoke of a home where six children were trying to eat out of one dish. The Aboriginals lacked food, furnishings, and decent clothing. Medical care was too costly as well. The local Catholic hospital required $6 for each admission. How could poverty-stricken Aboriginals ever pay $6?

Again, Aboriginal activists focused their blame on the political leaders, and stated that they "believe that the men guilty of the worst child abuse in Saskatchewan are Welfare Minister MacDonald and Premier Thatcher."[11] Dissatisfied with the Liberal party, the Aboriginals placed their support behind the Conservatives. This is how a two-party capitalist state works. When frustrated by one party, discontented voters turn to the other in hopes that their problems will finally be resolved. However, mainstream parties are profoundly capitalistic and function almost identically when it comes to Aboriginal policies. The other party continues, if not enhances, colonialism. Unfortunately, our civil rights movement never advanced far enough to deal fully with this issue. Native leaders made a terrible mistake by not going beyond racial and nationalist themes to promote a liberation movement.

When the struggle, of the 1960s and '70s faded, so did the media coverage. Once again, the Metis became forgotten people. Writers and reporters returned to old practices, suppressing the real news of the Metis struggles. Historians continued to write racist, eurocentric interpretations of Aboriginal peoples, just as they have been doing for centuries.

Part Two

Sources of Colonization

Chapter Three

Eurocentricism: Myths of Aboriginal History

Emasculate Aboriginals; that is the function of eurocentricism. In other words, white supremacy begets intellectually crippled Natives who bare their inferiorization and subservience. They look up, pathetically with reverent awe to the 'glorious' Anglo-European colonizer. Our obvious dependence and supplication are indications that we have been suckered into eurocentric culture. Years later, I can still repeat the patriotic poem from grade school:

> England with all thy faults I love thee still
> I like the freedom of the press and quill
> I greatly venerate our recent glories
> And so God save the Regent, Church and King
> Which means that I like all and everything.[1]

Even worse, were the nauseating racist poems of Rudyard Kipling.

> Blessed be the English and all that they profess.
> Cursed be the savages that prance in nakedness.
> Blessed be the English and everything they own
> Cursed be the Infidels that bow to wood and stone.[2]

In my 'slow halfbreed mind' frantic as it was I could not understand how this delusion of grandeur fit-in with living in a delapitated log shack half starving on bannock and lard. The 'Bible' of our history course, *A History of the World* declared that "The Anglo Saxons made tremendous progress during the six centuries they had been in England. From Anglo Saxon culture would come the system of law and justice and the triumph of the rule of law. Eventually English common law would come across the oceans to become the proud inheritance of people of many lands, including Canada."[3] In the classroom, these passages were more of a prayer than a discussion. As oppressed Aboriginals who lived under ghetto justice of rigid Mounted Police rule, this was pure catechism. The local jail was filled with Metis and Indian citizens.

These egotistical ramblings of eurocentric history and literature created puzzled notions of learning for Aboriginal people who lived beyond the margins of the glorious British Empire, 'where the sun never sets, and the blood never dried.' What relevance and value did the racist poems of Rudyard Kipling and the grotesque stories of King Henry VIII chopping off his wife's head have to do with our schooling and intellect? Most of us could not even read, except for the Eatons catalogue. Our vocabulary was limited to the language of Michif and to the slang of the 'King's English.' Eurocentricism taught us to be stupid. Instead of developing, it fossilized our brains. Eurocentric culture was intended to arouse the sting of racism and colonization, and to socialize us into white bourgeois mainstream society.

Precisely, what is eurocentricism? It is the view that Europeans' have of themselves as being culturally and politically superior to all other peoples in the world. Europeans have long believed they possess a superior civilization, and they have long believed indigenous civilizations to be subhuman and inferior. Imperial Europe viewed Aboriginal societies according to its white supremacist ideals, not in terms of Aboriginals' own socio-economic cultures. Indians of North America were seen to be the opposite of Europeans. European scribes created mythical images of Native peoples, images that denigrated Aboriginals' appearances, behaviours, and cultures. For example, it was not unusual for Europeans to describe an Indian as "a wild man that was hairy, naked, a club wielding child of nature who existed halfway between humanity and animality. Lacking civilized knowledge or will, he lived a life of bestial self-fulfillment, directed by instinct and ignorant of God and morality."[4] As a result of these gross fabrications, Indians and Europeans were forever established as opposites—the oppressed and the oppressor. A Manichean civilization—two separate societies—was created even before contact. Eurocentricism assumes that there is only one view of human reality: the 'self-evident' superiority of European culture. Since the European invasion of North America, eurocentricism has come to dominate Aboriginals' consciousness, and affects the way they perceive, understand, and theorize about the world.

Eurocentric history is a political interpretation of the world based on Christianity, exploitation, profit, and Western Europe's blind faith in its superiority. Eurocentric history embraces the myths of Indian inferiority (a myth that encourages Aboriginals' complicity in their own oppression). Although white historians claim that their versions of history are objective and correct, their perspectives are in fact biased and the result of tunnel-vision. According to these historians, Indians, Metis, and Inuit have no history because almost nothing is known about them before European conquest. Eurocentric historians aggressively seize Native intellectual space and claim it as their own in much the same way as imperialists seized and occupied

Native land. This displacement does not allow for the recognition of Aboriginal thought and history.

Eurocentricism, as an ideology, is the major contributor to the continuing devastation and suppression of Aboriginal civilizations. It has progressed unchecked and has flourished through the imperial control of all media forms and, therefore, popular opinion. As a result, the culture of the Western world is best known from the eurocentric perspective.

Eurocentric history and culture developed gradually over many centuries, and eventually took specific shape with the rise of mercantilism and territorial expansionism in the early 1500s. Eurocentricism's development is distinguished by a patchwork of myths and historical interpretations designed to prove Western Europe as the supreme civilization. Early eurocentric theories pointed to ancient Roman and Greek civilizations to explain Western Europe's self-proclaimed 'advanced' development. Western Europe saw itself as the product of a rich heritage, beginning with Greece, "the mother of rational philosophy."[5] This undue and distorted emphasis on these early civilizations waned with the advent of Christianity and capitalism.

During the Renaissance, three forces, mercantilism, Christianity, and racism, combined to form a powerful myth—European supremacy. Although historians traditionally interpret the Renaissance as the pivotal period that ushered progressive and rationalist philosophies into Western culture, in reality, it marks the birth of a colonial and white supremacist ideology that formed the foundation of European imperialism. Eurocentricism emphasized rationalist explanations of history. A narrow perception of the world distorted Western thought to the extent that "social theory produced by capitalism gradually reached a conclusion that the history of Europe was exceptional. . . because it could not have been born elsewhere."[6] Eurocentricism formed the ideological basis of a methodical system of colonial and economic dominance of Native nations that created the most horrific human disasters in every conquered land. In other words, European states conquered and devastated indigenous societies, and established a system of oppression that remains to the present time.

Modern eurocentric interpretations of history are rooted in the Spanish, Portuguese, Dutch, French, and English explorations and subjugation of indigenous nations throughout the colonial world. Armed with gunpowder and military technology plundered largely from Asia and the Mediterranean, Europeans seized Aboriginal land. Britain and France, for example, conquered and oppressed Aboriginal peoples with military force as a matter of policy. When Natives served no economic purpose, the Europeans slaughtered whole populations—such was the fate of the Beothuk Indians in Newfoundland and Tasmania's Natives.[7] Imperialism was the vicious destructor of everything Aboriginal; its weapons were Christianity, political subversion, violent repression, and germ warfare.

All European colonial powers "espoused the same basic goals to justify the exploration and settlement of the New World."[8] The imperialist nation-states mutually agreed that the "cross and crown, gold and glory constituted the legitimating symbols in Europeans' eyes for the invasion and takeover of the Americas."[9] While missionaries were undermining indigenous civilizations in the name of God, European merchants were accumulating "private and public wealth, through trade and the enhancement of national and personal prestige and glory through colonization."[10] In fact, the ideals and interests of the missionaries and private profit seekers were one and the same; "Religion subdued the Natives . . . economic advantages paved the way for national expansion."[10] The missionaries, protecting their own profit, spread propaganda to enhance national glory and convince Europeans to promote the imperial system. At the same time, they were deepening oppression of the Native population. European documentation from that period is nothing more than fictional messages designed to justify the Europeans' brutal actions. The colonizer claimed his actions were humanitarian and divinely ordained—that was the myth used to camouflage, as well as rationalize, the conquest, dispossession, and oppression of Aboriginal peoples.

To ensure that God's, that is the Church's goals were protected, the 16th century saw priests design colonial charters, royal edicts, and colonial public law. The Europeans set up a quasi-legal system allowing them to commit atrocities against Aboriginal peoples with impunity. This sham has evolved into today's racist judicial system that continues to deal unjustly with Aboriginal peoples. The Aboriginals had no legal recourse to protect their land or their homes from European plunderers. According to the Europeans, Aboriginals were subhuman, so indigenous occupancy did not constitute human residence. The Europeans claimed they had 'discovered' vacant land that they were free to claim as their own. "If Native Americans challenged such a white view of their ownership and economies, white laws, customs and courts existed to prove them wrong and decide the matters of emptiness and title in favour of the invaders."[11] The political structure was designed to place all authority, privileges, and even the most basic human rights exclusively within the colonizer's domain. Short of warfare, the Aboriginals had no options; however, the ruling imperialists were allowed to use violence freely. Public violence could now only be used by the colonial authority. It embodied the public interest. All other violence was private and illegitimate. This state policy has continued to the present day.

European imperialism relied on two distinct forms of racism-vulgar and cultural—to uphold white supremacy. Vulgar racism was especially prevalent during the early period of colonization when dubious physiological science claimed that Indians had smaller brains than Europeans. Anthropology, "a child of Western imperialism,' supported the so-called need for aggressive colonialism."[12] Begun as a crude, home-grown 'science' anthropology labelled coloured people as primitive, savage, and heathens. Cultural racism, on the other hand, was, and still is, a more sophisticated and insidious form of eurocentrism. It is the degradation of and prejudice against Aboriginal life styles, including language, dress, food, and traditional social mores. Unlike the more obvious biases and gross errors that typify vulgar racism, cultural racism is more vague and flexible to suit new generations and is, therefore, harder to dispel from the mainstream's consciousness.

During the 19th century, when Western European colonial activities sharply increased, cultural racism became more entrenched and pronounced in academic literature of the social sciences. Western publications were based on colonial assumptions using Western European philosophy as the norm. Thanks to the unethical and imperial practices of European scientists and academics, indigenous peoples have been stereotyped as 'backward and lazy Natives' or, more generally, of static or stagnant non-European cultures devoid of civility or creativity. These stereotypes have been used to exploit Aboriginal workers and reduce them to slaves. These stereotypes persist today, deep within the fabric of Euro-American society.

Eurocentricism, as an instrument of camouflage and exploitation, is still alive and doing well in the Western world. In fact, one could argue that it is practiced more extensively, albeit more covertly, than it was one hundred years ago. Eurocentric writings stress 'universal truths' and obscure concepts that are misleading and of little analytical use. Popular texts concerning North American Aboriginals exhibit a crass eurocentricism, betraying ignorance of the effects of political and social structures on economic behaviour. Because eurocentricism advocates competition and individual achievement, it is not surprising that the mainstream propagates the myth that Native people prefer to live on welfare.

Consistent with the self-image as 'world conqueror' is the European self-proclaimed mandate to save the world with is somehow 'special' superior qualities and knowledge that oblige it to shoulder the burden of guiding those less fortunate. This is the arrogant presumption in the European self-image.[13] Today, eurocentricism serves as the ideological basis for maintaining white supremacy and justifying the continued oppression of Aboriginals through the promotion of the mainstream economy and culture. The current work of Euro-Canadian academics and journalists serves the Establishment by upholding the eurocentric tradition with racist and distorted interpretations of history. The proliferation of academic publications sustains a widespread eurocentric bias in the production and dissemination of distorted history.

Eurocentricism is not a departure from the historical process; it is the result of the establishment's efforts to convey through a multitude of agencies, and it is deliberately intended to create a consensus. That is, a consensus in the validity of the free enterprise ideology, and the racial stereotypes and distortions used to secure the positions of the upper class. It is, in other words, an interpretation of Indian, Metis, and Inuit peoples designed specifically to belittle them. It denies them their own history and their participation in a transformed Western society. Euro-Canadian academics treat the Aboriginal population as marginal, and thus do not recognize their contributions to the development of Canadian society. For example, Indians and Metis, together with European farmers and workers, played an integral part in the growth of Western Canada, but the state is silent on Indian and Metis contributions.

Aboriginal history cannot be understood without understanding 'white settler' colonialism and its relationship to Aboriginals. British colonizers, using the imperial state, were instrumental in shaping Canada's demographic development to their political and economic advantage. As a rule, the British assigned a large population of European immigrants to Canada, thereby ensuring imperialist development. The Canadian industrialists and the British imperialists developed the colony through immigrant agriculture. The Canadian government also received preferential treatment in the form of British capital. During the latter part of the 19th century, Western Canada became an agricultural economic region. To expand the agricultural means of production, land was required for incoming white settlers, who served as markets for British industrial products. The homestead scheme was enacted, and the Indians and Metis, whose livelihoods depended on the soil, were driven from their land. With the death of the fur trade economy, Native labour was no longer required, only their land and resources. Aboriginal peoples were suddenly no longer needed in the growing, fast-paced industrial economy. Thus, British and Canadian troops, with the state's authority, took offensive action, confiscated the Aboriginals' land, and almost annihilated the Metis nation in the process.

Eurocentric historians usually claim to have studied previously unexamined documents when researching to write their books, but one does not require much historical knowledge to realize that most government documents are far from objective accounts. They are professed to be reliable if one chooses the selected information and opinions of imperialist officials and bureaucrats. The establishment requires documented 'proof' that corroborates its prejudices and upholds the dominant Euro-American ruling-class perspective. Academics discredit Aboriginals' historical perspectives as 'myth' or 'advocacy', and thus denigrate the works of Indian and Metis historians. White historians are obviously unaware of their rampant biases and subjectivity. They are, without exception, the strongest advocates of capitalism.

In distorted historical writing, the Metis uprising at Batoche in the 1800s, is said to be due exclusively to Riel. Such theorizing allows the authors to select their personal aversions for historical treatment while ignoring the essential imperialist dynamics that shaped history. Such is the stuff of academic eurocentricism. By failing to locate the rebellion in its proper colonial context, academics neglect the central economic and political issues that led to Batoche. Twisted interpretations deflect attention away from the facts concerning expanding imperialism in the Northwest and the exploitation and oppression of Indian and Metis peoples. Instead, eurocentric historians portray a narrow segment of history in isolation. And generally, coupled with this blatant error or deceit, they fail to link Aboriginal peoples and their livelihoods to the prevailing economic structure during the late 19th century. Consequently, such authors have little, if any, understanding of Metis' social consciousness, making it that much easier to distort and manipulate the facts, and to interpret history for their personal gain and justification of the state's repressive policies.

In eurocentric societies, racist theories constitute the official criteria to determine the 'objective' situation. Historians working within the Euro-Canadian system do not have to prove Western superiority; it is taken for granted. This assumption remains implicit in their historical analysis, particularly those of indigenous populations. Mainstream academics claim that oppression of the Metis, however severe, was not enough to require an armed uprising against the state.[14] This sort of opinionated statement has no historical value. Instead, it legitimizes the policies and structures of the white supremacist state. Most academics are not interested in analyzing the dynamics of economic production that led to the uprising at Batoche. Because racial minorities were segregated and detached from society's material base, this does not mean that they were economically static, nor does it follow that

Aboriginals were politically and intellectually stagnant. Nevertheless, the predominant mainstream notion of the Native periphery was one of a closed society that had one of two options: assimilation or death.

Racist works exploit the issues likely to draw heat and generate media coverage, promotion, and, of course, revenue. These works are also stepping stones for reviewers to further spread and augment eurocentric biases. Reviews praising white supremacist platitudes protect eurocentric writers and academics within a system that "has produced intellectual freaks; a kind of lumpen-intellegenstia more engrossed in its own psychodramas than the concrete: best known for its verbal ferocity which is intended to foreclose further argument rather than to promote discussion."[15]

Perhaps the most crucial issue one should realize about eurocentric publications is the support and encouragement they receive from government institutions and the media to fulfill their role as falsifiers of Aboriginal history. The eurocentric power structure, made of governments, universities, and the media, clearly believes that it is in its best interest to not only sustain but deepen Aboriginal oppression. When the Establishment attacks Native people, it encourages racism and eurocentricism.

Most fellowships and private foundation grants are inclined to support academics who uphold the dominant ideology and the stereotypes of racial minorities. Likewise, academic journals usually give uncritical reviews of eurocentric publications. At the same time, very few grants are given to indigenous scholars and teachers who produce publications that contain an authentic Aboriginal perspective. This may not be a startling revelation about Canadian society, but it does suggest how eurocentricism is supported, and at the same time how Metis and Indian society is denigrated and stereotyped.

Racism is certainly not new to the Canadian establishment, but it is disappointing to see the *Western Producer*, a small Saskatchewan press, join its ranks. *Western Producer* was once a progressive publisher for Aboriginals, farmers, and the working class. But today, in a period of ultraconservatism and racism, it is a suboppressor of the same people it championed only a decade ago. This transformation is consistent with what is happening with many Canadian journals and magazines today.

The state ensures its supremacy by preventing anti-establishment historians, especially Indians and Metis, from initiating or developing alter-Native interpretations or explanations of the past or present. Canadian publishers readily provide establishment historians with a forum to twist history and fabricate racist anecdotes to obstruct an empirical analysis of Aboriginal history. Unfortunately, racist writing appeals to Canada's average white reader because it harmonizes with the racist stereotypes he or she holds. The publishers know which side of their bread is buttered; for the most part, they will not alienate their white audience by challenging the familiar stereotypes of Aboriginals that keep whites comfortable. Fortunately, there are a few small publishers that do not follow this practice. Indigenous scholars of newly independent Third World countries, such as those in Africa, were the first to challenge eurocentricism. Gradually the Aboriginal people of Africa took control of their lives as well as their past. The European imperialists' histories of African people were not only irrelevant, but also gross distortions of the Aboriginals' heritage and cultures. Primary documentation once thought to be pure, unvilified sources of history have slowly lost their authority. This process is only beginning in North America.

Although academia is slow to re-examine what has been accepted for centuries as authentic historical sources, many sources are now being critically scrutinized. For example, the Jesuit Relations diaries, which were portrayed for centuries as unquestionable 'deified' statements, are today regarded as little more than myth. The Jesuit Order was a unique ecclesiastical class that had enormous vested interest in successful colonization. In addition to their owning approximately one million acres of land grants, being half of the entire land available to the ten Roman Catholic orders, they were deeply involved in the fur and slave trades. The Jesuits were also paid substantial sums by King Louis XIV of France for their diaries. Under those conditions, primary documentation is not infallible evidence proving eurocentric philosophies; rather, such documents are carefully constructed myths.

These myths have been so deeply ingrained in the people's psyche that even Aboriginals will have to go to great lengths to rid themselves of colonial ideologies. Eurocentric interpretations create a false consciousness among the colonists and the colonized. Eurocentricism does not allow for alternatives and thereby deceives Aboriginal peoples into believing that their history can be acquired only through the colonizer's institutions. Rather than critically attacking their oppressor's dogma, indigenous elites have accepted historical distortions to an alarming extent. Many Aboriginals are intellectual captives and have become part of the colonizer's regime. Some Aboriginal academics write Indian and Metis history from a strictly eurocentric and racist interpretation.

Criticism of the colonizer does not occur spontaneously. Instead, many of the oppressed elites want to be like the colonizer, or even worse, they wish to be the colonizer. In some cases, this desperate desire leads Aboriginal people to become more passionate eurocentrics than the average white supremacist who takes his or her privileged position for granted. Unfortunately, a tendency to uncritical imitation pervades almost the whole of the intellectual activity in Aboriginal countries. Many of our Aboriginal intellectuals collaborate with the oppressor. Often, they do not offer new insights into Aboriginal history; they instead tow the line, entrenching their own subjugation and colonization. Not surprisingly, their racist publications are made highly visible by the academic community, which endorses these works with little, if any, critical examination. As for the Aboriginals who do contradict the accepted version of history, they are ignored or publicly discredited as being advocates or Marxists.

Ideally, Aboriginals, not Euro-Canadian academics, should research Aboriginal culture. Indigenous institutions must be staffed by Native scientists who grew up in Aboriginal societies and, therefore, identify themselves with the future well-being of Aboriginal nations. This, however, is no small task. Canada is imbued with quasi-apartheid philosophies that make it difficult to develop a counter consciousness. Aboriginals have to dispel the pervasive stereotypes and destroy all encrustations of colonial mentality that repress them. This must occur before they can develop new interpretations and foundations for a new indigenous nation. It demands a calculated process of analysis that emphasizes Aboriginal consciousness, life experiences, and struggles of resistance.

As an Aboriginal historian, I am deeply concerned by the incredible lack of authentic Aboriginal historical writing. By muffling the voices of protest or simply by ignoring them, the establishment hopes to keep Aboriginals out of sight and out of mind. Our histories are dismissed or marginalized by not including them in most bibliographies and reviews. This tactic is extremely effective; our work is obscured from the white population as well as from the indigenous people. Of course, white historians offer several excuses for dismissing Aboriginals' work. The most common argument is that Aboriginal writing lacks documentation, authenticity, or methodology, and, therefore, credibility. State functionaries also accuse Aboriginal writers of sloganeering of radical political dogma. Although they will not admit it, the true reason is that Aboriginal writers, free to write from their own consciousness and perspective, will challenge and eventually succeed in sidelining eurocentrism.

White academics, primarily historians and anthropologists, have owned the past, particularly that of Aboriginal nations for far too long. Although the military was the initial force to conquer Natives, the continuing psychological processes of dehumanization and humiliation ensure Aboriginals' colonized status. Therefore, it is from that base that Aboriginal decolonization

'e racist pattern established by the first colonizers will be bro-
he colonized reclaim their history. Third World scholars who
ing their history demonstrate that Aboriginal history can be
preted by Aboriginals only. Other scholars and authors do not
inderstanding and the ability to express the authentic socio-political
orientations, and social consciousness of Aboriginal societies. Only an
inal who has experienced colonization can intimate the nuances of
Native customs, spirituality, and traditions, all composed of unspoken
assumptions and symbolic meanings that permeate Aboriginal communities.

Metis and Indian history is both a movement and a discipline challenging eurocentricism. Intrinsic to our history is our people's sense of resistance
and struggle that emerges from a growing counter consciousness and realization that we have suffered injustices and oppressive inequalities because of
our race and colonization. As a movement, authentic Aboriginal history
attempts to confront the inequalities in the justice, economic, and political
realms; however, in order to do this it is first necessary to examine the
processes and structures that promote and house racism.

In certain countries Aboriginal historians, humiliated and dissatisfied
with eurocentric history, are beginning to write history from an indigenous
perspective shaped by an Aboriginal social environment, political consciousness and nationalism fundamentally based on liberation. In Canada, Metis
history is much more than Riel. Finally, there are Aboriginal accounts of the
Metis' positive contributions to Canada's development. But unfortunately,
their work has so far failed to alter the distorted interpretations of the mainstream, of the state, and certainly not those interpretations of white supremacist historians.

Eurocentric history is more than a glorification of Western Europe's past
and a denigration of Aboriginal people. It is another aspect of imperialism-
cultural imperialism, a mechanism designed to suppress resistance and to prevent the indigenous population from developing a counter-consciousness to
the mainstream culture. Within the context of imperialism, Indians and Metis
are unique in that we are a distinct class/race nation of indigenous peoples
within a capitalist state, and we deal directly with its centre, Ottawa.
Eurocentric history and culture serve to hide this fact, as well as our historical claim to our territorial possessions and the right to govern our internal
affairs without external interference. Indian and Metis history has been principally that of nationalist liberation struggles for land and autonomy; written
history should reflect the reality of our continued fight for self-determination.

Chapter Four

Mainstream Ideology: The Control of Colonized Minds

In any nation, a single system of beliefs and values dominate. Historically, this ideological system develops during the period of emergence of nation-state capitalism. As a result, the basic system of beliefs and values is capitalistic. This condition first developed in Western Europe, where imperialism originated. European conquest and domination of indigenous civilizations led to colonialism and the rise of a specific ideological system in the 'New World'. In the process of colonialism, Native populations gradually accepted the belief of European bourgeois ideology which, over time, became part of the Aboriginals' own system of beliefs and values. The importance of this colonial ideological process is that it became and still is one of the major tactics used to control and oppress Aboriginal people.

Ideological domination is the primary means by which the state maintains control over its citizens. The state, such as the U.S., has established and maintains an elaborate socialization scheme to control the masses. Ideological authority is thought control; the manipulation of one's consciousness, and thus, of one's entire belief system. The aim is to maintain the status quo—the corporate ruling class society.

Consciousness is one's knowledge of what he or she is thinking, feeling, or doing. It is having an awareness of what exists and how one relates to his or her immediate social environment. Consciousness is total, or all-pervasive, affecting every waking moment of an individual's life. It is comprised of the sum total of a person's experiences and constitutes a person's unique sense of reality. An individual's consciousness is a reflection of the particular social milieu in which he or she lives. For example, Indians who grow up on reserves develop a consciousness unique to their socio-political environment and class/race position of a reserve ideology. Indians and Metis recognize that their belief systems are somewhat different from the mainstream's. An Aboriginal consciousness is determined by the objective reality —life experiences—of the reserves and Metis communities. Racial stereotypes also play an important role in shaping a Native's consciousness. Subjective feelings, such as inferiority, are an integral part of consciousness, and work together with the objective reality of poverty and deprivation to shape a Native's world-view. Society's ideological system determines one's viewpoint and shapes one's consciousness—most often, for life.

The term ideology is often used to mean a system of ideas and political values. In Canada, as in much of the world, the state's ideological system is based on capitalism, and the system's goal is to indoctrinate the public with these values. The state's system of beliefs and values is not judged on the basis of whether it is true or false, or good or bad. Instead, an ideology is valued according to its ability to bind different groups of society together in mainstream to serve as an efficient means of uniting the masses for the ultimate 'good' according to the ruling class notion. The ideology must be capable of organizing the population and shaping the citizens' specific belief to the system and participation in the society. To succeed, this total ideology must become part of the nation's common sense or natural order of things. The masses, including Metis and Indians, must willingly accept it and internalize it as their own views and values, otherwise military force would be necessary to control the population. The state's prescribed ideology, as distorted as it may be, becomes the citizens' own sense of belief and rightness.

By accepting the ideology of the dominant class as their own, the subordinate masses not only submit to it, they also legitimize the rule of the establishment. In this way, ideology oppresses the masses. The ideology becomes a moral faith, and the people accept it and conform to it as if it were true and good in the ethical sense. In fact, the state ideological system can be compared to religion, in that it is not subjected to scientific, or objective analysis and is put forward to be accepted on faith. Most people do not realize that they are bound within a deliberately constructed bourgeois ideology.

Why do citizens so willingly accept and consent to an ideology that subjugates and exploits them, particularly the Metis and Indians? Simply, they have little choice. They are born into the Canadian culture and it automatically becomes part of their consciousness. Socialization is aggressive. There is little chance for someone to develop a different belief system because one cannot get outside, or beyond the prevailing ideological structure. An eminent professor claims that state structures "are institutions for indoctrination, for imposing obedience, for blocking the possibility of independent thought, and they play an institutional role in a system of control and coercion."[1] Although Metis and Indians are contained in sub-culture, they are still subjugated to the state's theological system.

By controlling the mental means of production, the state maintains and enforces the capitalist ideology; for example, through T.V. and newspapers. The state influences a nation's entire population, regardless of ethnic background, class or race under a single ideology through subtle means of coercion and domination. Because society is diffused, the state is able to oppress its citizens quite effectively, and with relative ease. Ruling class power depends on public legitimation; that is, the citizenry believing they are free to dissent, but, in reality conform to the socio-political system, and thus in their own subjugation.

However, when the oppressed people oppose the state, violence is a likely result. This is a well-known fact; one only has to think of what the Mohawks went through in Oka during the summer of 1990. The Mohawks refused to accept and behave according to the state's ideology and social values—they had their own unique beliefs that contradicted the establishment's. When people recognize that they are being manipulated and suppressed, the situation can lead to state violence, as it did in Oka, or against the Metis in 1885. However, each time that the corporate class reveals its violent and repressive methods of domination, it demonstrates the true nature of society and the fact that the public's right to protest and challenge the status quo is not allowed. Indians and Metis found this out during their liberation struggles in the 1960s.

Within the capitalist world-view, certain concepts, such as private property, are included in the numerous state institutions that help shape social behaviour and relations. Ideological principles are usually reinforced in the religious, cultural, educational, judicial, and political sphere. For the Native people the most powerful sphere was the missionaries. State ideology is developed in relation to the economic base. This means that components of the state ideology, such as culture, education, and politics, are determined to a large extent by the nature of the economic system of livelihood. For instance if the economic system is free enterprise, then the ideological system will be capitalism.

Considerable emphasis is placed on political socialization. "The political system provides a flow of information and continuously creates deep feelings of loyalty and obedience for its basic forms of socialization."[2] Political parties, such as Liberal, Conservative and NDP adhere to and represent the market economy system. The masses believe that by voting for different parties the system will change, but the only things that change are the names and faces in Parliament. This misguided thinking is encouraged, because it obscures the actual power relations of the corporations which control the government.

Organizations such as religious groups, trade unions, and Native organizations also embody the ideology of the nation. These organizations play an important role in socializing its members and thereby sustaining the state's ideology. The judicial system is an important agency of indoctrination. To preserve the state, the public's belief in the law and the courts is absolutely essential, especially Indians and Metis who constitute the majority of the prisons' population. Yet, this same system is one of the most discriminating structures used against the subordinated masses, and particularly the Aboriginal people. The fact that most people conform to the law, and accept it as being fair and just proves the coercive power of the ideological system.

Although the judicial system seriously discriminates against Natives, many Indians and Metis believe the courts are fair and even express a certain loyalty to judges. But, Canada's judicial system is racist. The case of Donald Marshall is one case in point. "Despite a police investigation that involved perjured evidence, a trial where vital information was withheld from Marshall's defense counsel, and mounting evidence that pointed clearly to the real killer, Donald Marshall spent eleven years in prison." [3] A Micmac Indian, Marshall was wrongfully convicted of murder because he is Indian.

The education system is another powerful indoctrination tool. The curricula teaches children the importance of submitting to the establishment. All schools share the common goal of socializing children to the capitalist ideology and preventing the development of counter-beliefs. The greatest part of class time is devoted to this goal, under the guise of learning. All learning is oriented to the market economy. Children are rarely, or never informed about the reality of poverty, war, multinational corporate power, or state violence. They are seldom taught about racism and colonization.

The school reinforces a process that actually begins at home. As early as three years of age, parents are socializing their children to become positively oriented toward political authorities. The child enters school with strong positive emotions about political leaders, but very little knowledge about the political world. Canadian children begin school believing Canada is the best and most beautiful of all countries, and the school's job is to reinforce this belief. This is taught in spite of the fact that Native people's quality of life is as low as the poor Third World people.

By age thirteen, children are fully indoctrinated to the capitalist norms that govern the political state.[4] Peer groups at school also reinforce the capitalist message. Even if some children become disenchanted later in life, a strong residue of capitalist thought always remains. A renowned educator concludes: "It is now a possibility that this undemocratic pattern of our schools is not a random or haphazard phenomenon but it is in reality functional; that is, it is important for an ideological conservative state to train its citizens to accept authoritarian regimes in case they are needed to maintain order."[5] This is bordering on a semi-fascist ideology.

The education system reproduces and legitimizes social inequalities. Metis, Inuit and Indians have had the lowest quality of life since the Europeans arrived. Schools play a key role in passing the establishment's ideology onto the next generation. The mental framework of one's analytical capacity to understand the existing political system is fixed, to a large extent, by the school. According to Chomsky, "They are institutions for indoctrination, for imposing obedience, for blocking the possibility of independent thought, and they play an institutional role in a system of control and coercion."[6] Together with the family, the school bolsters the ideological hegemony by socializing children to develop an uncritical perspective of the world. The classroom creates a state of passivity and submission; the children readily accept and consent to the state's belief system. Without realizing or having a choice in the matter, students internalize the establishment's systems of beliefs and values. It is an unconscious process that has profound effects on one's consciousness and perception of society.

Ideological hegemony is an obstacle to critical analysis of capitalism. It encourages apathy, deactivates political action, and produces unthinking people who passively perform suffocating daily tasks with a sense of gratitude. Ideological hegemony results in a standardization of thought and intellectual production. This is even true for academics. The nature of the capitalist ideology—the glorification of competition, individualism, greed, and the pursuit of power and wealth—is rarely explained or analyzed by establishment academics and intellectuals. The capitalist ideology breeds a politically conservative population. It is camouflaged, obscured, and mystified to prevent the masses from detecting the clear connection between the ideology and their subordinate positions. For instance, if Native peoples understood the cause of their subordination, they would go against the government. This does not mean that all individuals in the nation think exactly alike, but the few who develop alternate views rarely have access to the levers of power, and are not sufficiently united to challenge the corporate class. This is one of the reasons that Aboriginal peoples are kept divided.

As colonized peoples, we internalize much of the state ideology and its ethnic, class and race dynamics which perpetuate our subjugation and repression. We adapt considerably to the structure of the dominant ideology and become resigned to it. As a result, a certain sense of self-denigration and personal contempt develops within our consciousness. The belief of white supremacy is so pervasive, it is impossible to avoid internalizing it. By accepting common racist views, believing we are 'ignorant, worthless cheats', we submit to our own oppression. We are inclined to reject or disregard our own traditional Aboriginal ideology and value system. Subjugation within a capitalist system has cost us much of our traditional values and spirituality. We are losing our Aboriginality. Our authentic indigenous beliefs are polluted by the nation-state's production of caricatured Aboriginal culture.

However, Aboriginals have not always been swallowed up by capitalist socialization. Historically, our ancestors were forced to live in isolated colonies and reserves, segregated and disconnected from the dominant ideology. At one time they were denied any communication with the white population. A semi-apartheid system contained them in their colonies and prevented the exchange of ideas with those outside. Natives were unable to receive news or learn about mainstream society and the way it functioned. This situation existed until the 1950s.

As a member of a Metis colony, I spent most of the first twenty years of my life isolated from mainstream society. Our community was confined primarily to our local indigenous culture and beliefs. Our lives were determined largely by a Native cultural ideology (tainted by racism, colonization and low class) that made us uniquely indigenous. We associated mostly within our subordinated Metis community. Hence, our Aboriginal orientation and values were consistently reinforced. At the time, our oppressor did not perceive us a threat and therefore did not need to devote much time or money to brainwash the Metis with the state ideology. The only exception to this situation was the state's practice of shipping Indian children to residential schools. There, the priests exposed the Native children to the capitalist ideology, but the brutality and perversion of the schools prevented the priests from changing the traditional ideology of the majority of the children. The church's cruel treatment overrode its attempts to 'convert' the children to the state's beliefs and social values.

Although missionaries had been in North America since the 17th century, it was not until the mid 1800s that their services were recruited by Anglo-Canadian imperialists for systematic colonization. The Hudsons Bay Company and the British Colonial office brought in both the Anglican and Roman Catholic churches to the Northwest Territories during the period of serious working class agitation against the Hudsons Bay Company. The main function of these churches was to help maintain economic and political control within Ruperts Land. The churches, in an aggressive manner brought to the entire Aboriginal population ideological colonization. There is no question that these churches played an important role in indoctrinating Indians and Metis to subordination and inferiorization. Also, they helped to stabilize the nuclear family as the basic unit of society. Families were needed to create more workers for the fur trade's labour pool. Furthermore, the churches helped to keep the Metis business class subservient and loyal to the European bourgeois class. At the same time they served to divide the working class from the business class on religious ground by separating French and English halfbreeds. It was with the churches' ideological colonization that Indians were influenced into signing treaties that dispossessed them of their lands. Christianity fostered excessive methods of exploitation and oppression of Indians and Metis, yet, at the same time promoted the notion that Christianity was a stepping stone to civilization. Although these churches held considerable power over Native communities for many years, their influence has been seriously weakened in recent times.

Since most Indians and Metis grew up in segregated colonies, and most of their time was spent in these colonies, their consciousness and socialization was determined by their local Aboriginal relationships. Metis were essentially peasants. Our connection to the marketplace was limited and therefore had little influence on us. The radio was our main exposure to mainstream ideology, but even that had little impact as we had no world-view consciousness and little political awareness.

But this does not mean that we managed to escape racism and state ideology. Indians, Metis, and Inuit grow up on the fringes of a bourgeois class system, but state racism still has a profound effect on our collective consciousness. The white supremacist ideology banishes us to a subordinate situation, and we are surrounded by repressive beliefs. It is almost impossible not to develop feelings of inferiority and inadequacy. Racism contributes greatly to our oppression, as Aboriginals are bombarded by debasing stereotypes. Negative perceptions reinforce feelings of inferiority. It is not surprising that our behaviour is inclined toward apathy. The ideology of the dominant society quashes any potential for developing positive and strong ideology in our Aboriginal communities. The nation's racist ideology can cause us to hate ourselves as intensely as bigots and racists hate us.

Since the 1960s, the state has made significant efforts to assimilate Indians, Metis, and Inuit to the capitalist ideological hegemony. The corporate society is extremely efficient in manipulating the oppressed Natives for its own survival. The education system, including universities, is whitening the Aboriginal consciousness. Educational institutions are infecting Aboriginal students with petty bourgeois concepts. Television has also had a profound effect on altering the Aboriginal consciousness. The multinational corporations have discovered that the valuable resources, i.e. water, timber, uranium, etc. are in Aboriginal territories.

Today, most Indians, Metis, and Inuit are subjected to the influence and socialization of the ideological hegemony. It is quite impossible to live beyond its influence. Nevertheless, there are varying degrees of adherence to the nation's belief system. Certain individuals, particularly collaborator leaders and elites, have adopted the colonizer's ideology. These persons want to resemble their oppressor, and to believe in and to follow his ideology and socio-economic beliefs. The Native petite bourgeois have internalized the consciousness of the colonizer as their own consciousness. They attempt, however, to keep one foot in traditional indigenous culture, and the other in the oppressor's culture. Two-timing Aboriginals participate in traditional Indian/Metis rituals and ceremonies, but are not sincere in their beliefs. These Aboriginals prefer cultural imperialism to counter-consciousness. Indians and Metis who participate in pseudo-traditional ceremonies serve the colonizer's interests by supporting and reinforcing the ultra-conservative ideological hegemony and encourage other indigenous people to do the same. These Aboriginal leaders and elites do not understand the full reality of oppression. They see the possibility of reforming, not transforming colonial oppression within the system. They are unable to distinguish between repressive and liberating ideologies.

Collaborator leaders and their organizations, the Assembly of First Nations, the Metis National Council, the Native Council of Canada, and other Native organizations promote the state's colonial aims and ideology. The colonizer rewards Aboriginals who conform to mainstream and the oppressor's purposes. A glaring example is the appointment of the Aboriginal leader Yvon Dumont to the position of Lieutenant-Governor of Manitoba. It is highly unlikely Dumont will demolish the imperialist institution of the Lieutenant-Governor or any other imperial structure. If he does not, he then is a direct oppressor of his own people. As Lieutenant-Governor, he is a prominent symbol of the colonizer's structure and the ideological hegemony of white supremacy and imperialism.

Since the original conquest period, Aboriginals' unique consciousness has gradually intertwined with capitalist ideology. This has led to great confusion for our people, and as a result our goals have become difficult to determine. As a result, we waste much time and energy trying to achieve the unachievable. Some try in vain to prove to the colonizer that they are equal to the white man and indistinguishable from white society in the goals and roles that they seek. The more we assume of the bourgeois ideology, the more the state controls our minds, and the more we accept its dominance. Ideological hegemony creates a colonized consciousness in Natives. Because we have low self-esteem, we are driven beyond the ordinary to prove our abilities and efficiency to our oppressor. This is why Indian and Metis police officers in Native communities are sometimes dangerous to their own people. Aboriginals who adopt the colonizer's ideology become the cruelest oppressors of their own people.

For Aboriginal people, ideological domination is serious repression. If we perceive ourselves, our status, and our future in terms of the mainstream free enterprise system, then we have completely abandoned our Aboriginal consciousness for a false one. This does not free us; in fact it oppresses us more than ever. It makes our claim to Aboriginality a sham. An authentic Aboriginal consciousness can not be a facade; it is an intrinsic or inner essence that lies somewhere between instinct and intuition, and it evolves from the humanness and spirituality of our collective, Aboriginal community. Without an indigenous consciousness, Indians, Metis, and Inuit peoples only claim to Aboriginality is race and heritage. That is not enough to achieve true liberation. To accomplish self-determination, we need more than racial pride. We must have Aboriginal nationalism, an understanding of the state's capitalist ideology and its oppression, and, ultimately, a counter-consciousness.

The state attempts in many ways to prevent the development of this counter-consciousness. One of the important methods used in enforcing Aboriginal people into the ideological system of the state is through Indian and Metis petite bourgeois class and collaborator organizations. By taking control of this class and these organizations and their leaders, the government has been able to manipulate their operations, crush the counter-consciousness of our people, and bring them back into the capitalist mainstream ideology.

Chapter Five

Indian And Metis Slavery in New France

Slavery is the most heinous holocaust of imperialism. Arrogant and aggressive European colonizers seeking greater greed, power and territory cannibalized almost every non-white nation throughout the world. In their plundering for gold and gems, Europeans devastated and enslaved continents of innocent and defenseless indigenous peoples. During the long painful centuries of slavery rivers of Aboriginal blood flowed continuously through the New World. In the early years of Canada, the Indian and Metis were also treated like slaves.

As a young Metis looking for work, I was always terrified by the attitude and looks of a powerful Arayan boss as he cautiously eyed me up and down. He took control and paralyzed my confidence. I felt so meek, docile and stupid. He reduced me from man to beast. "Could I stay sober for a week," he roared. In a very submissive and downcast manner, I answered, "yes sir." I felt like a slave on the auction block.

Although slavery in Canada was abolished 150 years ago, its remnants were still rooted in the institutions, structures and attitudes of Canadian society. I was fully aware that ten generations earlier my ancestors had been whipped slaves of these arrogant Franco slave masters. Somehow that ancestry seemed to linger forever. Do slave genes last for ten generations? Are there such genes? Unquestionably, slavery idiosyncrasies remain embedded in the deep ravens of the socio-economic system. "Canadians took sharp slave-selling practices to a high level in New France"[1] claimed a French historian. "Buying a slave required as much care and attention as buying animals. A buyer would be very foolish not to examine the merchandise." My ancestors had been creature slaves of the humanless Europeans. My mother's heritage from the Lavallee and Lepine families had been tortured beasts of burden to white slavers. It is a pride of my heritage, and not a shame that my ancestors were owned, driven and brutalized as stubborn mules. They were chattels bought and sold as private property. More importantly, however, they were continuously courageous, and fierce fighters of resistance to slavery, oppression and inhumanity through ten generations—right down to the 1990s.

Euro-canadian academics readily admit that black slavery existed in New France, but most steadfastly deny that the French enslaved Indians. The few who admit to Indian slavery insist they were only used as occasional domestics. To keep up this charade, popular historians like Garneau and other racist historians have misquoted the colony's laws and policies that permitted Indian slavery. Canada's standard histories have masqueraded, glossed over, or simply omitted the subject of Indian slavery from discussions. However, it is known that "At least 4,000 slaves have been identified in French Canada. Roughly 1,500 were Black, the other 2,500 were Indians."[2] There is considerable evidence demonstrating that Indian and Mixed-Blood slavery existed, in New France. This fact was emphasized by an English historian in 1906. "That the blot of slavery existed at one time in Canada is a fact mentioned by a few of our historical writers. Some gloss over the fact, others allude to it in a most casual manner, others are silent."[3]

It is difficult to determine exactly when Indian slavery began in New France, but it is clear that it was started by the colony's shortage of cheap labour. In 1607, more than one hundred years before Indian slavery was legalized, colonists like Poutrincourt, the founder of Port Royal, captured Indians for slave labour. The demand for Indian slaves increased during the late 1600s because France's manpower was tied up in King Louis XIV's imperial wars in Europe. Colonists complained that it was impossible to operate businesses and the seigneurs criticized government officials for not providing them with enough workers, adding that "most of the censitaires [serfs] escaped from the farms for the fur trade activities."[4] A seigneur complained that cheap labourers were badly needed. "Workmen and domestics are such an extreme rarity and so expensive in Canada that they ruin those who attempt any enterprises."[5] The Catholic church and the bishops put their weight behind the cause, insisting it needed more workers to spread God's word. As a result, an Intendant recommended to Louis XIV's royal government that "the people of the Indian nation are necessary to the inhabitants of the colony to assist them as labourers on their farms."[6]

Responding to the colonists' vocal complaints, the King of France released a decree in 1709 which stated that: "we ordain all the Indians and the Negroes who have been or shall be purchased shall be the property of those who have purchased them and they shall be held as their slaves."[7] This ordinance provided the colonists with a legal basis and moral justification for enslaving indigenous people, a formality that recognized a growing practice. This relieved whatever guilt white slave owners may have had about the use of slaves. Every Indian on the continent became a potential victim of bondage, forced labour, and the humiliation of becoming someone's chattel. ". . . slaves were imported and held for domestic and agricultural purposes is amply proved. Also that Panis and other Indians were captured and sold or bartered on the shores of the St. Lawrence for purposes of slavery is an undisputed fact." [8]

The Pawnees, also known as the Panis, who were located in the southwest corner of Missouri, were the primary victims during the early stages of the French slave trade. They were targeted because the French believed that "the people of the Panis nation were . . . more docile, more susceptible of becoming useful labourers."[9] Essentially, the Pawnees were thought to be 'comparatively safe people to attack and kidnap.' Another significant factor that worked to their disadvantage was that the Pawnees were located far away from New France, which meant escape attempts would be few and far between. Distance was like a prison wall; it made escape difficult thereby protecting the colonists' investments in slaves. Furthermore, local Aboriginals were less likely to assist 'foreign' Indians.

It was consistent with policies of slavery that neighbouring indigenous people were not enslaved, thus slaves were not taken from the Iroquois, Hurons, Ottawa or Ojibway. "Our slave population generally came from very far away"; *wrote an official* "it was an added guarantee for the slave-owner."[10] This was the general practice of slavers in the 1700s, and was necessary as far as slave owners were concerned. It made slaves foreigners in their new residence where they were unfamiliar with the territory and with local indigenous people. In turn, resident Indians would not recognize these strange Indians and would, therefore, be suspicious of them and unlikely to befriend them. This made escape difficult, if not impossible. This method of enslavement copied the practice used in capturing slaves in Africa. In Canada, a few slaves were seized from the Sioux, Fox, Assiniboine, and Cree. Later, more distant nations, such as the Natchez and Shawnee, were plundered. It was cheaper to capture an Indian slave, regardless of the risk than to buy a Black slave. A Black slave cost 900 livres, whereas an Indian cost only 400 livres. One reason for the difference in price was 'that it was generally understood that there was a plentiful Indian supply close at hand.'

Indian slaves were captured through warfare, raids, kidnapping, and trickery. Each method, however, was embroiled in violence and bloodshed. The military, fur merchants, and missionaries organized fiendish raids on Indian villages. Imperialists raided unsuspecting Indian settlements and kidnapped men and women of young ages. In one incident more than 500 warriors and 300 women of the Fox nation locked themselves in a fort, but were eventually forced to surrender to white slaver, Louivigney, a French military commander. The raids were massive, war-like operations often involving hundreds of Aboriginals. According to Trudel, in one instance: "[A]fter a victory over the Sioux, the number of slaves was so great that according to the account and description of the savages, in their march they took up four acres of land."[11]

In some instances, the Indians had little to protect themselves from such treacherous forces as neither the French military, nor their own leaders were trustworthy. Some indigenous chiefs actually assisted the Europeans in getting their human goods. In what must be one of the cruelest forms of Aboriginal collaboration, "chiefs sometimes made presents of [Indian] slaves to French officers in command of outposts."[12] Consequently, the French slavers were very successful and the colony's population of Indian slaves increased immensely. By Quebec's 1761 census, there were 7,600 Indian slaves in New France.

Slaves were regularly traded like cattle at the public markets in Montreal and Quebec. Indians were bought and sold like any other product. In 1772, Laurent Lefebvre bought a female slave in exchange for a pig and some peas. Like other private property, slaves were also passed on through inheritance. Records show that Charles de Longeuil left seven slaves to his two sons.[13] Of course, breeding was another method of obtaining slaves. The colony's laws stated that children born to a slave became the master's property. All of these children were fathered by slave masters, as property, and never as citizens. They remained slaves throughout their lives, unless, they succeeded in escaping.

The law of the colony stated that "Slaves could marry only with the permission of their master, . . . and their children became the property of the master."[14] Hence, Indians and mixed bloods entered into New France strictly as property, and not as citizens. Under these conditions it would have been quite impossible for other Indians to be freely assimilated into the colony. Such conditions would have made the control of Indian slaves an impossibility. The example of the Frenchman, Firmin Landry marrying the Sioux slave, Marie Caroline, who had five illegitimate children does not suggest racial blending. After marriage, the five children became the property of the husband. These children, as most offspring of slave women were mixed blood, thus Metis. Since Indian slavery extended over a period of almost 20 years, it is inevitable that a large Metis population would have been born in the colony, New France. However, it must be understood that they were born as slaves, and remained slaves throughout their lives. It was not until 1832 that slavery was abolished throughout the empire.

Who used the slaves? Indians were sought by a wide variety of people, ranging from business operators, such as millers, brewers, and ship builders, to the idle aristocracy. The seigneurs put slaves to work on their extensive farm properties. In 1759, 376 seigneurs owned approximately nine million acres of land on which the slaves were forced to clear land with crude and inefficient tools. Aboriginal slaves also planted and harvested crops, cared for the livestock, and generally did all of the heavy tasks, such as chopping wood and building fences. High-ranking government officials owned several Indian slaves for their personal use. Between 1703 and 1760, Governor de Vaudreuil owned eleven Indians while Governor de Cavagnial owned sixteen. A further twelve governors and intendants, including Bigot and Hocquart, in Three Rivers and Montreal owned Indian slaves. Documents also show that in 1743 the government owned twenty-eight slaves, whom were used for the onerous jobs, such as building roads, cleaning streets, and performing as hangmen.[15] However, none of this slavery would have been possible without the colony's immense military.

New France was essentially a military camp; its administration and organization was distinctly militaristic. At times, the army constituted as much as 35% of the colony's total population. The Governor General and local governors were usually military officers. When not busy attacking the English or Dutch, the French soldiers were terrorizing and capturing Indians. They often used Indian slaves to plunder and kill other Indians. The slaves had to attack their own brothers and sisters, or die from a European bullet. French soldiers, stationed in New France, were paid from the King's treasury. As a result, all economic sectors in the colony were able to make use of soldiers without any cost to them. Fur merchants, seigneurs, the Church, religious orders and slave owners made extensive use of troops in their slavery endeavors.

In terms of slavery, it is difficult to separate military slaves from the fur-collecting slaves. Because the military shared control and profits with the fur barons, slaves were used by both parties for forcibly collecting furs and Indians. The term 'fur trade' is misleading because in the early years of occupation, Europeans did not actually trade with the Indians. Except for the courier de bois, the French plundered and raided Indians, forcing them to 'contribute' furs. As the fur tribute flourished, so did Indian slavery. Fur merchants such as Tarrieu de Laperade, who owned twenty-one slaves, used them to construct a network of forts throughout the beaver-rich western territories. The fur merchants and military both used slaves to build and maintain the fur 'highways' and lines of communication on the land and water. In fact, Indian slaves did all the repulsive jobs, including cleaning the forts and scraping and preparing the pelts. Two prominent fur barons who owned slaves were Louis

LaCorne and his brother Luc who together owned forty slaves. Ironically, an Indian reserve in Saskatchewan is named after these white slavers and traders. How grotesque can colonization get?

Although Indian slaves were owned and controlled by the military and fur merchants, they frequently functioned together and were easily interchanged. Europeans never believed they had enough labour to make them as wealthy as they wanted. This led to further territorial expansion, genocide, and more bloodbaths. In 1688, Governor Talon sent a contingent of troops, seven colonists and two Sulpicion priests to take possession of the region surrounding Lakes Erie and Ontario. In addition, a party of white tyrants claimed lands further north toward Hudson Bay. The objective for such expeditions were always twofold: to obtain beaver pelts and to secure a reliable herd of Indian slaves.

Pierre Gaultier de La Verendrye, was the most highly recognized fur merchant of New France. He "boasted of keeping New France well-stocked with Indian slaves." *He claimed that* "one of the great benefits of his work was the slaves that it gives the country."[16] His mission to find the Western Sea was a ruse for his real operation, fur and slave trafficking. In 1731, La Verendrye, accompanied by his three sons and a crew of priests and soldiers, travelled inland toward the Western Sea. Using the pretext of exploration, he established a strong foothold across the interior and built several forts and portages as far west as the Red River. Typical of many French merchants, La Verendrye operated as a fur pirate and a slave kidnapper rather than as a merchant. He traded very few Europeans goods with Indians for their pelts. At St. Charles, he constructed a fort on the edge of the Lake of the Woods from where he ran a mafia-style slave trade. The Sioux, Assiniboine, and Fox were his main sources of captives. La Verendrye carefully chose the locations for building fur and slave-trading forts and was skilled at planning transportation routes for moving pelts and human cargo. He had 'highways' constructed for transporting the slaves from the prairies to Montreal. Many slaves were fastened together and travelled several hundred miles by walking and canoeing, stopping only at forts that La Verendrye had built for this specific purpose. The importance of his disguised operations is that they show what a significant part Indian slavery played in the French fur tribute system.

Although well served and protected by countless soldiers, most slave traders encountered hostile Indian resistance. It is this history of courageous struggles of resistance that makes our Indian and Metis heritage so great and glorious. Many died fighting for their freedom, and in the process killed their white enemies in the struggle. In one such battle, a son of La Verendrye and a group of white slavers under his command were killed by Sioux Indians. Today these victories are popularly labelled as Indian massacres. The distortion of linguistic imperialism has no limits. The Sioux heroes of this battle will, forever, remain unknown although they made a major contribution to opposing slavery. The subjugated and colonized are not recognized in history books. Monuments do not honour Indian bravery; instead in imperialism white Indian slave traders receive glorious recognition.

Slaves suffered regular cruel treatment and punishment. "In 1777 W.B. paid five shillings to the public executioner to whip Joe, a slave in the market square." "On the 22nd January 1757. . . the Panis slave of Monsr. de Saint Blain was found guilty of a criminal offense and condemned to the stocks on a market day in the public square."[17] The average life span of a slave was 18 years. Indian slaves suffered the most under Christianity and its institutions. The Catholic church, under the guise of holy and humanitarian intentions, was the most serious exploiter of Indian labour and flesh. All religious orders and all levels of the Church, from parish priests to bishops, were deeply involved in Indian slavery. For example, Monseigneur de Saint-Vallier, second bishop of Quebec, ruled the colonial diocese for forty-two years with several Indian slaves under his command. Monseigneurs Dosquet and de Pontbrian likewise owned Indian slaves; however, the bulk of them were in the missionaries' hands.

Christianity was the single most important criterion in claiming Western Europe as world's supreme civilization, in comparison to the remainder of the world. This was its justification for expansion into the Aboriginal nations throughout the world. It is obvious that the principles of Christianity were easily molded into a racist ideology that matched the economic and political needs of expanding European imperialism. It was the Church and its missionary orders which served to launch slavery. Western imperialism was a 'holy alliance' between European culture, Christianity and a colonial economy. The church and missionaries had no hesitations or scruples about destroying indigenous religions. Their creed, after all, was one of violent and coercive proselytization. The Christian church and its institutions was the arm of colonial destruction of indigenous culture and thought. With the delusionary rhetoric of love and peace, coupled with the false image of brotherhood and humanity, missionaries and church succeeded in the devastation of indigenous civilizations where guns could never have succeeded. This is where a serious analysis of the politics of colonization prove helpful in determining the consequences of colonialism. Not only was Indian slavery insidious and outrageous, but the role of the church and missionaries were even more contemptible and unforgivable.

The slave system and its brutality was created by Christians. The missionaries argued that indoctrination to Christianity was the only path to Western civilization, and to 'true humanitarian life.' In this manner, imperialism and slavery were given the quality of humanitarianism. Christianity contributed to the success of slavery by embracing it with morality. "'Christian ideology', *according to Ani,* has traditionally condoned and often mandated violent aggression and brutality on the part of the Europeans."[18] It was in most respects more barbarous than anything seen in the indigenous world. The Church's most vile practices were performed in western continents that pretended and paraded the greatest mockery of humanitarianism and true Christianity. Slaves were taught false Christian values that made them servile to their white masters. Their minds were stuffed with devotional hymns that developed submissive and docile attitudes while at the same time undermining their own authentic indigenous culture and spirituality. The features of Christian imperialism, "is that it strikes the death blow at a people's ability to resist aggression . . . and of destroying the ideological life of a cultural entity."[19] The violence of Christianity expressed itself not only in terms of wars and killings of indigenous peoples, but also through psychological terrorism.

Three male missionary orders: the Jesuits, Sulpicians, and Recollects, captured Indians for slavery and kept many for their own personal use. They obviously understood the immorality of slavery and made public gestures disapproving the practice, but it did not stop them from owning and trading slaves. The Jesuits used slaves at several of their fort parishes, especially in Detroit, Michilimackinac, Sault Saint Louis, Saint Francois-du-Lac, Quebec, and Montreal. A parish priest in Detroit, Louis Payet, owned five slaves.[20] The Jesuits at Michilimackinac owned four slaves aged seven, eleven, fifteen, and twenty years. In 1749, La Verendrye sold several slaves to the Jesuits. One of these slaves later gave birth to a mixed-blood daughter, who also became the Church's property. The missionaries in Saint Francois-du-Lac owned a Sioux woman slave, "a pretty enough thing with a soft and appealing voice . . . She attends to the errands and needs of the missionaries."[21] At Detroit, Leonard, a Recollect priest, owned three slaves, one of whom was pregnant. The Quebec seminary in 1763 kept thirty-one slaves at its Holy Family Mission. When its Vicar General returned to France, he sold twelve slaves to the seminary and gave two to the Recollects. In fact, slaves were such an important commodity that parishioners sometimes paid their tithes to the Recollect mission with Indian slaves. The church and its officials perceived slaves as mere objects, property that could be traded, donated or destroyed on a slave master's whim.

Female orders were equally guilty of slave trading, particularly the Grey Nuns who operated the Hotel Dieu, the General Hospital. The nuns received slaves in a variety of ways. Charles Joseph, a twenty-four-year-old Indian slave, was a gift from Governor General Beauharnois. Fur merchants, de Simblin and de Saint Saveur, also donated Indian slaves, mostly Sioux, to the Grey Nuns.

Marguerite D'Youville who founded the Grey Nuns Order in the early 1700s was a significant player in the trading and exploitation of Indians slaves throughout most of her life. Left a widow at the age of twenty nine, she took the vows to be a sister of the Grey Nun Order. In 1747 she was given charge of the General Hospital in Montreal. Within ten years the Grey Nuns had built up substantial holdings, including farms, an orchard, a mill, and a bakery. As the Grey Nun's empire expanded so did their supply of slaves. D'Youville was an aggressive and ambitious individual who was concerned more with power and wealth than doing 'good works' for the poor and aged. As administrator of the Sisters of Charity and the General Hospital, she "took in rich boarders to not only pay the costs of operation,"[22] but to make considerable profit. To accomplish this, she needed cheap labour. She was well acquainted with the importance of slave labour, having inherited several slaves upon her husband's death. In addition, she had the advantage of ready access to Indian salves through her uncle, Pierre de la Verendrye. At one time, Mother D'Youville had as many as 236 slaves in her employment.[23] She kept several slaves as her own personal servants. She had no twinge of conscience in exploiting and abusing human beings to further her ambitions. As a devout Catholic she knew it was immoral to be trading in human flesh. She forced Indian slaves to "work on her farms, and as orderlies at the hospital which she ran. Another four were set aside as 'personal attendants.' "[24] In being the niece of Piere de la Verendrye, she was always well stocked with slaves who attended to her personal needs. She also stood to profit from owning such valuable property. On one market day her list of goods for sale included "an Indian of about 10 or 11 years [and] a cow which twice calved."[25] Upon her death, the notary's inventory of her possessions included several slaves.

The irony of Mother D'Youville as a slaver and slave trader is that she was canonized as a saint by Pope John Paul in December, 1990. To become a saint, a person must be recognized as having lived an exceptionally holy life, and thus of being in heaven. The Pope and the Catholic Church seemingly have strange meanings for 'holy life' and sainthood. From an Indian slave's perspective, it is certain that Mother D'Youville would have been considered as an evil, cruel and dehumanized person. By all criteria, it seems incredible that Pope John Paul should have chosen Marguerite D'Youville to be canonized as a saint. At the time of her canonization in 1990, Msgr. Andre Cimichella of Quebec argued that "D'Youvilles' dealing in slaves is a tiny detail and has no bearing on her suitability for sainthood."[26] Would it have been a 'tiny detail' for Msgr. to have served his life in slavery to Indians? According to his mentality, Indian life was cheap; a throw away. The story of Mother D'Youville as a slaver of Indians is more than a mere anecdote in Canadian history. It explains a great deal about the economic and political nature of the so-called superior civilization that conquered the world of indigenous people. More importantly, it explodes the myths or the virtuous and blessed character of religious missionaries and Christianity. It shows that Christian churches and missionaries were an integral part of European imperialism in its most grotesque forms.

The church also imprisoned Indians in Christian settlements designed to convert Indians to a sedentary, agricultural life and prevent them from 'backsliding' into paganism. These prison-like reserves were built as modest replicas of the French colony. In 1637, nobleman Noel de Sillery had a fairly large reserve built near Quebec. It contained several houses, a church, windmill, oven, and brewery, a tranquil setting that contradicted the surrounding high stone walls. The inhabitants, mostly from the Sioux, Algonquin, and Montagnais nations, were virtually prisoners of the church. In many ways, they were treated just as poorly as the Indian slaves outside the compound.

The Jesuits were determined that this reserve, a pilot project for apartheidism, should succeed. The missionaries exercised total control over every individual within the settlement's walls. They "soon formed a community leading an intensely religious life under Christian Chiefs who imposed severely rigorous discipline."[27] In their zealous efforts to make an example of these Indians, the Jesuits resorted to extremely strict measures. The Indians were treated as children incapable of managing their own affairs and unable to leave the compound without a missionary agent's permission. Eventually, these prison-like rules were too oppressive even for the converted Indians who eventually shattered the reserve community and escaped into their natural free world.

Slavery continued after the British conquest in 1760. "The Negro and Panis slaves in the possession of the French or Canadians to whom they belong; shall be at liberty to keep them in their service in the colony."[28] Slavery of both Negroes and Indians was carried on by Anglo-Canadians in

Upper Canada (Ontario) as well as in New France. The first Governor of Canada after the British conquest owned slaves until 1794. "In the first 40 years of the British regime after 1760, slavery was also practiced by high officials, including Gov. James Murray, Lt. Governor H. Cramahe, 23 members of the Executive and Legislative Councils."[29] Slavery was not ended in Canada until August 1833 under the *British Act of Emancipation*.

Part Three

The Challenge to
Colonial Oppression

Chapter Six

Speaking Out To White Oppressors

When I returned to Saskatchewan in 1964, I could see that Indians and Metis were restless and ready to strike out against the hunger, oppression, and brutality created by colonization. More than twenty years had passed since I had left my ghetto, and I was now returning as a university professor. Yet, I had not forgotten the wretchedness, shame, and feelings of inferiority that dominated my halfbreed childhood. I still harboured deeply ingrained anger against colonial subjugation. It was only natural that I joined the fight against the system that tortured my early life. I did not have to think twice about taking up the battle against our oppressors. Our defiance was long overdue.

Now that I understood my heritage and had decolonized myself, it seemed amazing that halfbreeds had remained submissive for so many years. I appreciated why Aboriginal peoples wanted to hide from white society's mockery. We believed we were a defeated people. Our ancestors' liberation war at Batoche in 1885 was a humiliating defeat. Most of us in the St. Louis-Batoche area were descendants of Metis warriors who fought—and lost—against Ottawa's mercenaries. The imperial masters brutally suppressed our right to independence, and then duped us into believing that the Metis warriors were primitive rebels and sadistic savages. Metis, like other Aboriginal groups, were crippled by a communal sense of inferiority.

Another important factor contributing to our passivity was the lack of opportunity to assemble. Our oppressors had segregated Aboriginal peoples, isolating them in widely dispersed colonies. Most communities were not near establishment institutions or centres of production and transportation. Hence, communication was extremely limited. Under these circumstances, it was almost impossible for Indians and Metis to develop a sense of group interest and feelings independent from the white man's myths that labelled us inferior and backward. Furthermore, Aboriginals did not command the resources and facilities necessary for mobilizing a political movement. The instability of poverty, of living on the edge, discouraged mobilizing. However, beginning in the 1960s, Aboriginal peoples in Canada began to summon the courage to challenge colonialism and move ahead on their own terms.

By 1967, Canada's centennial year, Aboriginal peoples were increasingly raising their voices with renewed pride and determination. In their communities, at conferences and seminars across the country, they openly talked about their plight and organized to create change. Much of the militant political action, apart from that of the Mohawk Indians and a Kenora, Ontario group, was initially centered in Saskatchewan, where journalists covered the events and reported them to the entire nation.

As chairman of a national conference on Indian and northern education held at Saskatoon in April 1967, I opened the conference with a defiant speech. This was the first national conference in which all speakers were either Indian, Metis, or Inuit. The audience was predominantly white educators, teachers, government officials, nuns, priests, and others involved with educating Aboriginals. I began my opening remarks:

> As Native people we refuse to accept the popular misconception that we, Indians, Metis, and Eskimo are the problem. It is a white problem, but more precisely, it is a Canadian problem . . . The schooling system of the colonizer was built to colonize and inferiorize us. It has done a very good job, and continues to do so. It rapes our children of their humanity. It destroys their psychological being so critically that they are unable to fit into either the Native or white world.[1]

Following a short silence to allow my comments to sink into the minds of the white audience, I introduced the panel of speakers. The first speaker was a Cree woman from Saskatchewan, Mary Ann Lavallee, who had been involved in Indian education for a long time. She stunned the white audience with a surprisingly defiant speech. She stood on the platform facing a battery of microphones, television lights, and more than five hundred white delegates from across Canada. She spoke her mind freely:

> For far too long we have been puppets on a string who have danced to the manipulations of government officials. Indian residential schools' claim was to civilize the 'savage,' but what they did in reality was to inferiorize us. They silenced us. They tore out our tongues. But, the era of silence is over.[2]

After Lavallee sat down, Mary Carpenter made her way to the microphone. Sobbing, Carpenter damned the Northwest Territories school system for robbing Inuit children of their heritage. She cried, "They have emotionally raped us of the basic needs a human must have to function in our society. The schooling makes us feel our northern heritage is inferior; the essence of our family life is destroyed; and afterwards, we do not fit into our traditional way of living." Like the other Aboriginal delegates, Carpenter denounced Canada's colonizing institutions. The conference was one of the first major events where Natives spoke out publicly against the school system. Seizing the opportunity, they presented numerous proposals to improve Native education, but they also made a conscious effort to widen the conference's mandate to discuss political issues and colonialism, the fundamental sources of our suffering.

The next speaker was Irene Joseph, a Sioux Indian. She spoke of being dragged away from home by the Mounties when she was five to be put into a residential school. With great emotion, she spoke of the loneliness and the horrors of the school's 'shadow world.' She broke down and wept. She cried to the audience, "Why do you people not come to witness the hideous conditions of these schools?" The white audience did not understand why we spoke so personally and with so much hostility and anger in public. However, this behaviour was becoming common for many Aboriginal persons who were undergoing a political awakening. Colonized people usually express their political frustrations and abuses in personal terms, releasing anger and pain before discussing objectively the colonized institutions and how they must be changed.

Rod Bishop, a well-known Metis activist, spoke next. Bishop is a descendant of a militant halfbreed family, which assured his status within the halfbreed community. He understood and shared his people's problems, attitudes, and pain. A strong advocate of Native unity, he did not believe that Aboriginal liberation required integration or co-operation with white society. He walked proudly to the podium and addressed the audience, "This is the first time that the white man has allowed us to speak on an equal footing with him. We'll state the hard facts to the whole nation that has kept us hidden for so long. We won't be squelched any longer."[4]

As he promised, Bishop discussed the hard facts, whether the colonizers liked it or not; his boldness obviously shocked many of them. The Aboriginal speakers' open defiance must have offended those who still believed that Caucasians are God's chosen people and Aboriginals are everything savage, immoral, and stupid. Nevertheless, the speakers received slight, polite applause. The audience, tainted by snobbery and hypocrisy, was far too sophisticated to 'boo.' The Canadian Broadcasting Corporation and other media were broadcasting the conference live across the nation.

According to the agenda, the next speaker was Elijah Whitehawk, an Indian from the North, but he was missing from his seat on the platform.

Finally, the chairman addressed the audience in a troubled voice:

> I am sorry and shocked to tell you that Elijah Whitehawk, our next
> speaker, was badly beaten up on the street by a group of punks as he
> was walking to the hotel. He has been rushed to the emergency hos-
> pital. We have no report on his condition yet.[5]

The Natives were enraged. Mayor Sid Buckley quickly stepped in to save
face as best he could. Together with the Chief of Police he tried to assure
everyone that this 'terrible incident' would be dealt with immediately, that the
attackers would be brought to justice, and that Whitehawk would be given the
best of care. They said they were certain the attackers were not racists. The
conference resumed, but it was three weeks before Elijah was well enough to
leave the hospital.

Medric McDougall, a Metis, filled in for Elijah. He spoke to Canada's
Aboriginal peoples:

> It is time that the white people stopped blaming Indians and Metis for
> their poor educational record. It is the fault of the white man's sys-
> tem. As Native people, we refuse to accept the popular notion that it
> is an 'Indian or Metis problem.' We do not want to be integrated into
> a decaying white society. Why enter a house that is burning down?[6]

A rural proletariat, McDougall advocated class struggle and nationalism.
He believed Native peoples were victimized by racism and capitalism, and he
criticized the school system for practicing both evils.

As the conference progressed, it became clear that the Natives in atten-
dance were growing more confident and, therefore, more vocal. They
assumed the offensive and picked apart the issues causing their people's
agony. Even in discussion groups, Natives were not afraid to express their
anger to the white participants and challenge their every word. The conference represented another milestone in Native history; it marked a break with
the past and a revolutionary re-awakening.

On the second day of the conference, Kahn-tineta Horn, a Mohawk fash-
ion model and militant activist, was asked to speak. She, too, spoke vehe-
mently against colonialism:

> Christian religions destroy and stun the brains of the young Indians
> and confuse them for the rest of their lives. Indians trying to under-

stand religion are trying to cope with something they can't learn, which results in a devastation of self-confidence. If education is to survive, there must be a complete rejection of everything. Religion must be completely divorced from the education system.[7]

Horn's harsh words insulted the nuns, priests, and other religious zealots, but received applause from the Indians, Metis, and Inuit. They congratulated her for having the courage to speak so candidly about a topic that many of them felt very deeply about.

Under the media's scrutiny, the white attendees quietly and politely told reporters their concerns. For the most part, they tried to mask their biases. Professor Patterson patronizingly suggested that "conferences such as this should be encouraged . . . for many speakers it serves as an emotional cathar-sis, and that is good."[8] Another educator complained that the speakers "were being ungrateful for the many good things in education being done for them," and that "the conference was so totally one-sided."[9] The whites either didn't understand or they didn't care that Aboriginals have had to listen to biased, one-dimensional lies constructed by white colonizers for more than 200 years. When the tables were turned and Natives spoke freely, colonizers felt offended and threatened.

The conference created considerable controversy, generating statements that exposed the educators' racist leanings. One such example is Patricia Denhoff's article, which appeared in the *Teacher's Bulletin*, the official publi-cation of the Saskatchewan Teachers' Federation.

Once again hopes were raised, voices were heard and then the silence. That [Howard Adams] ripped out the vines of understanding and progress so carefully nurtured in the past few years by the resource people of the University of Saskatchewan, the government, the teach-ers and the church, meant little to the Native people . . . Saskatchewan citizens writhed in anger and humiliation at the ellubient rebel from St. Louis who branded them as Metis like himself. Theirs had been a hundred-year struggle away from their Metis ancestry.[10]

Denhoff's comments reveal racists beliefs that are common among white supremacists. She believed that the Metis of St. Louis had spent years strug-gling to distance themselves from their ancestry. That is, she was arguing that the Metis heritage was so shameful and hideous that our people were deter-mined to abandon it. Could a colonizer make a more outrageous and insulting statement? Denhoff represents the worst type of white, liberal colonizer. Whites like her fight passionately to hold Aboriginal peoples under semi-apartheid rule. They know no limits to oppressing others. After all, they have power, status, and wealth, all built upon Aboriginals' backs.

Besides controversy, the conference also produced a number of resolutions, all of which ended up gathering dust on some bureaucrat's shelf. Nevertheless, the conference highlighted the fact that the education system was grossly inadequate and a painful experience for Native children. It also allowed Natives to focus on their problems in a public forum, and it placed social issues in their proper context. The conference helped bolster Aboriginal pride throughout Canada. Native voices crushed, however briefly, the racist experiences that had silenced their cause for generations. Not long before, many of these same people would have probably never said a word in public.

The re-awakening of the Indians and Metis caused much public controversy as the media continued to cover our militant 'Speaking Out' assemblies. In some cases, such as in Duck Lake, the media actually helped our cause by 'advertising' events beforehand. The Duck Lake Pow-Wow, held June 10 and 11, was one of the largest Native celebrations of 1967. The idea for the event originated with the Indians and Metis who lived around Prince Albert, Saskatoon and Duck Lake. The weekend consisted of a five-hour talk-in featuring Native and white speakers, an evening pow-wow, and the unveiling of a monument honouring five Indians and Metis who were killed in the 1885 Duck Lake battle.

As chairman, I was the first speaker at the Duck Lake talk-in. I spoke about how Native peoples were still under colonial rule and that until we made governments cast off imperialism, we would always be treated as conquered people, and always forced to endure below-the-poverty-line living standards. Many of the reserves and Metis communities had no electricity, running water, or telephones. All authority rested with the colonizer. The principle that allowed these conditions to persist was the basic racist tenet that all men are not created equal. Colonizers wanted us to believe that whites were superior to Natives. I urged our people to organize themselves into a united political group. I was proud of my Metis heritage and said so, "It is time we said, 'To hell with what the white man thinks about us. We are Natives and damn proud of it.'"[11] I continued:

> Many Indian and Metis are not here today because they are ashamed of being associated with the Indians and low-class halfbreeds. It is time that we believed in ourselves—not as problems, not as savages, nor as drunkards and irresponsible people—but, instead sing out that we are proud to be Native and that together we'll do great things.[12]

Mary Ann Lavallee stepped up to the microphone and spoke firmly:

We are Canada's first citizens. We want you, the Canadian people to return our birthright of basic human rights. We demand equality of opportunity. We want the recognition of our individuality, our self-determination. We demand social justice. We ask for recognition and acceptance, not as a carbon copy of the white man, but as Indians who want to remain Indian and who want to keep his reserve system because his roots are there.[13]

She argued that Indians must maintain their distinct heritage. Other Native speakers stood up and spoke on several topics ranging from culture and education to economic development and police brutality. The white politicians and bureaucrats tried to defend their positions and policies. The Aboriginals had heard it all before.

The 'Speaking Out' was publicized by most major newspapers, radio and TV stations. In covering the weekend, CBC reported that "Canada's Indians and Metis know where their roots are, and they're prouder of them than they've been for years. They're more conscious of themselves and their condition than at any time since the Riel Rebellion."[14] CBC based two documentaries, *Warpath of Words* and *The Angry Young Chiefs*, on the event. Peter Gzowski summarized his report with the following words:

Here in our midst, and at the beginning of our second century as a nation, exists a separate—and, I'm afraid, not equal—people. They are a people who, in spite of our best efforts, have maintained a culture of their own.[15]

The Duck Lake event angered self-righteous Canadians throughout the nation. They were startled by the Native speakers' intense anger. They were displeased with the media attention we received. The weekend symbolized a remarkable departure from the supplicant speeches of many Indian chiefs, the Uncle Tomahawks. The new generation of Native spokespersons were advocating a change in the political system and a better life for Aboriginals. The old leaders and the Indian Affairs Department were irrelevant, as far as the new voices were concerned. Young Natives were demanding Aboriginal peoples, not the white man, to govern their reserves and communities. The Duck Lake event served as a call to action.

When discontent rises from the oppressed masses, the state often makes

empty promises and short-term programs in the hopes of placating their chal-
lengers. The state's success depends upon several factors, including the depth
of the oppressed's political consciousness, their leaders' commitment, and
whether the grass-roots movement remains grounded. If the leaders lose their
people's support, then the state can easily discredit them and dismantle the
entire movement. In 1967, however, that was not to be. The Aboriginals
speaking out and leading others to do so at that time were respected by the
general Native population. Nevertheless, 1967 was not the year for revolutionary upheaval. For true change to occur, the colonized must first experience a lengthy period of mobilization, and then fuel those passions and energy into political organization and class action for equality and social justice.
There must also be a national political atmosphere in which the colonized
masses are receptive to the idea of Aboriginal self-determination. In 1967, it
was still too early; our liberation movement was only beginning.

The government, on the other hand, didn't think it was too early to pro-
voke whites' fears. In a report it released in July 1967, the state claimed that
Indians and Metis "in middle-sized communities across the country are on the
verge of violent revolt against the injustices they suffer. Relationships
between Indians and non-Indians are severely strained and a precarious and
explosive situation exists."[16] The report further claimed that two
Saskatchewan communities, Prince Albert and Kamsack, were potential trou-
blemakers. Native leaders, saw this report for what it was—a scare tactic, an
excuse to introduce more police and troops to our communities.

After the massive 'Speaking Out' events of 1967, Indians and Metis grew
steadily more political and militant. More and more of our people were joining the movement. The Saskatchewan Native Action Committee (SNAC) represented Aboriginal youth who were aggressively demanding change.
SNAC's chairman explained that:

> the new organization had been formed because existing Native orga-
> nizations did not really represent the desires and needs of either the
> Indian or Metis people. The leaders of these official organizations
> have been brainwashed into accepting a second-class colonial status
> and have become Uncle Tomahawks. We know that we will never be
> accepted fully by the white man, so we want to build our own culture
> in our communities and reserves. We want our own schools, our own
> industries, and our own local governments with autonomy.[17]

Unlike the conservative leaders of the Federation of Saskatchewan

Indians (FSI), SNAC's leaders understood that the lively spirit and momentum of our movement must not only be sustained, but accelerated. SNAC decided to support running an Aboriginal candidate in the 1968 federal election. Several leading Aboriginal spokespersons were opposed to this action. They argued that because Indians had been excluded from voting until 1961, there was no reason why they should become involved now. Indians were disenfranchised and isolated from a system that never intended to include them in the first place. Our opponents said it was unlikely that we could get many Aboriginals interested in parliamentary politics. Although it was true that electoral politics never seemed to have had any relevance to our people's day-to-day struggle to survive, it was the opportune time to take advantage of national publicity and draw attention to the crucial issues affecting Canada's Natives. The decision to run a candidate did not represent a commitment to parliamentary politics as part of our liberation struggle, but it was seen as a timely way of expressing our concerns to white society. The lengthy campaign period and national publicity would help spread our message, and, of course, a revolutionary voice in the House of Commons would be helpful. We understood that political parties were intimately connected to the capitalist system that impoverished our people. For this reason, we believed that all parties, Conservatives, Liberals, and NDP, were incapable of making real changes. They could only make minor reforms that would never provide lasting benefits to Indians and Metis. Therefore, SNAC's candidate, Carole Lavallee of the Cowesses reserve, ran as an independent. Lavallee was well educated and articulate. She promised to represent her entire constituency, male and female, Native and white.

Lavallee ran in the Meadow Lake constituency because its population was 65% Aboriginal, of which only 8% voted in the last election.[18] Such a low voter turnout was not unusual nor was it surprising when one considered the fact that Indians were not given the right to vote until just seven years earlier. Many Aboriginals did not understand parliamentary politics. Some Indians believed they would go blind or lose their right hand if they voted. Indians were paralyzed by superstitions promoted by the colonizer for many years. Sexism was another problem; we knew many Indian men would find it difficult to vote for a woman. As for the whites, racism would affect their choice. Few, if any, would vote for an Indian, especially a woman.

Nevertheless, SNAC felt that it was an appropriate time to field a Native candidate who represented our liberation movement. A couple of Aboriginals had been elected to Parliament before, but as a Liberal or Conservative member. They had done nothing to advance their people's needs, nor had they promoted self-determination. In short, they were indistinguishable from white MPs. Our candidate's election platform broke with this tradition. Her campaign for Aboriginal people was based on two central issues: self-determination and autonomous control of our local industries and Native communities. She also promoted progressive policies covering major educational issues the state usually ignored. Lavallee spoke out about Aboriginals' impoverished colonized conditions. She asserted that Trudeau's promises for a 'Just Society' were only useless rhetoric. In fact, conditions had actually worsened during Trudeau's regime.

Lavallee had many supporters especially among the younger Native population, who were also willing to speak publicly against racism and colonization. But sometimes their passionate actions unwittingly embarrassed their organization and other Natives. SNAC had to be diplomatic because all campaigners were valuable, tireless contributors to the movement. Potential violent incidents occurred fairly frequently. The media occasionally blew incidents out of proportion, discrediting us and instilling unnecessary fear into whites. Unfortunately, the state used such incidents as an excuse for using force.

Rod Bishop, a Metis, worked as Lavallee's campaign manager. He was a popular grass-roots activist who knew Meadow Lake, could speak on its behalf, and had a lot to contribute to the campaign. But, just as the campaign was picking up, the RCMP seized him. Taken from his home, Bishop was placed on a plane and sent to fight forest fires several miles away. The government was sabotaging our movement and denying us our freedoms of election, free speech, and organization. We complained to the RCMP, the Department of Natural Resources, and finally to the Premier. Clearly, Bishop was kidnapped. He, alone was secretly flown away to a distant post, although there were many Metis men in the community who would have been willing to go. We demonstrated and held sit-ins, attracting national media attention. Our protests resulted in Bishop's sudden return. The authorities never explained their actions. There was no doubt that the Indian Affairs Branch and the FSI were working against Lavallee's campaign. Later, we learned that Indian Affairs had instructed chiefs in the constituency to denounce Lavallee. The state, through despotic Native leaders and chiefs, succeeded in pushing Indians into deeper submission and primitive politics.

In spite of the barriers the establishment put up, Lavallee was quite successful in the election. She won, 15% of the total votes—a percentage slightly higher than what most independent candidates achieve—of the 7,000 voters supported her. But her campaign's greater success was its role as a catalyst in raising political awareness among Indian and Metis people. After the election, Lavallee and many of her supporters carried on to fight for the Native liberation struggle.

By late 1968, meetings, workshops, and discussion groups were springing up in Native communities across Canada. Indian and Metis youth, embittered and restless, were strong advocates for more aggressive action and 'street politics.' These young people were elbowing the old, safe Native leaders aside. More and more, whites could not ignore this reality. A reporter for the Star Weekly picked up on this phenomenon and wrote that:

> there is nothing new in the facts of Native degradation; what is new is the Native determination to change these facts, a determination reflected in an astonishing variety of ways across the country. Red Power is being wielded when Natives [begin] to assess frankly the chances of violence. Dr. Howard Adams told me, "I deplore the thought of violence, but I'm rapidly changing my mind on the possibility of it. A year ago, I would have said never, not in Canada. But, today there is a strong likelihood."[20]

To assess the potential for violence at that time, all you had to do was to imagine yourself in an Indian's or Metis' position, and ask yourself how you would react. Rod Bishop, among other activists, remembered teachers bursting into school yards to tell Native children and adults to stop speaking Cree. And they remembered obeying the white teachers' orders. Burning racial slurs were hurled at Indians and Metis. Bitterness was perhaps one of the most significant bonds linking Canada's Natives. Bitterness made us impatient with even the most helpful whites. We did not want them speaking for us any longer. At conferences, Natives were finally asking pushy and patronizing white liberals to shut up. We insisted on keeping the Red Power movement, our liberation struggle, from being hugged to death by white liberals, who wanted to do all the speaking and lead the counter-establishment movement. Indians and Metis had at long last found their voices, and they were not about to have them drowned out by pseudo-supporters. With such open determination on our side, governments began paying attention and listening to our demands.

In June 1969, Senator David Croll established a committee to address Metis poverty. Metis leaders representing organizations from the three prairie provinces were invited to Ottawa to present formal papers and discuss the issues. The Aboriginal leaders told the senate committee of uniformly distressing circumstances in Metis communities throughout the prairies. The senators were painted "a grim picture of abject poverty compounded by white racism," and were told that "conditions among the Metis in the northern regions of the prairies have deteriorated to the point where civil disorders are a real threat. Metis are awakening to the discrimination they face and are becoming angry about it."[21] The president of Manitoba's Metis Foundation stated, "If our demands are not met, I'm afraid this country is going to be torn apart like the country to the south of us."[22] June Stifle, representing the Alberta Metis Association, stated that "the government authorities are condescending toward our people, and their programs are in fact destroying our people."[23] The leaders also accused the Catholic Church of acting like a despot and contributing to our people's suffering. Most of the Metis leaders insisted that the priests were becoming worse, probably because they felt threatened by our renewed sense of independence.

The senators were told that the Northern communities were probably among the worlds most underdeveloped regions. Several senators admitted that they had been unaware of the seriousness of the situation. Senator Roebuck suggested that it might be a good solution to move the Metis further south. I replied that such a move would have disastrous consequences; that alone would spur our people into open revolution. The Albertan and Saskatchewan spokespersons strongly argued against integration, but the Manitoba leaders wanted to see the Metis join Canada's mainstream society. To our dismay, they presented a conservative brief calling for assimilation and a grant so their organization could carry out a poverty study.

When the discussion turned to education, we were questioned about our children's high drop-out rates. Apparently, the senators had not read the documentation on the 1967 conference on Native education. Once again, we had to spell out the specific problems. We told the committee that the public school system is of little—if any—value to Metis children. The schools are designed for urban, middle-class colonizers, not the colonized. All the teachers are white and the curricula and texts degrade and cripple the Aboriginal psyche. We argued that Aboriginals should control their schools and their communities. We wanted Aboriginal decision-making powers.

If not sympathetic, most newspapers at least gave our voices a large audience. *The Toronto Telegram's* June 26th headline read: "We're 'Slaves' of Just Society, Says Metis." The article correctly quoted the Metis leaders describing how Aboriginals were oppressed and products of colonization. The media, whether it criticized us or not, recognized and reported the fact that Natives were developing a political counter-consciousness, an understanding that, as an underclass, we had little or nothing to lose.

During the formative years of the liberation movement, Native people across Canada were beginning to question old values and institutions. Our people were recognizing for the first time in a very long time that they needed to reclaim their history and economy. We began by re-assessing how colonization dehumanized us. Suddenly, we were no longer ashamed of being Aboriginal. We were fostering our own terminology and ethos, which strengthened our sense of community. The struggle to decolonize ourselves gave our people's lives meaning, but we still had far to go, and it was clear that we would have to become increasingly political and revolutionary if we were going to succeed. As deeply colonized people we were inferiorized, timid and submissive, but, we were also filled with pain and anger. We began our struggle against oppression with a roar that was heard across the nation. Shortly, the masses of Aboriginal people from coast to coast were on the march. The struggles of the 1960s had begun.

Chapter Seven

Metis/Indian Struggles Of The 1960s

All Native peoples across Canada, from Vancouver to New Brunswick, were restless. They were fed up with oppression, racism and injustice. They were fed up with being pushed around and they were ready to start pushing back. All across the land Indians and Metis were talking back to agents of Indian Affairs and Metis Council Administration. "Some Indians and Metis," wrote Stewart of the *Star Weekly*. "the timid, the elderly, the responsible—call this new aggressiveness 'self-determination'; others, bolder, younger and more determined call it Red Power."[1] Tony Antoine, an Okanagan Indian and Red Power advocate argued that "Violence is part of our society; if it has to come, it has to." In Manitoba, Metis leader, George Munroe claimed that "Sympathy is for the weak; I have never seen in history where sympathy alleviated poverty. If Natives want something, they are going to have to take it." And a Saugeen Indian spokesman in Toronto, Duke Redbird claimed that "There are terrible things happening every day to Indians in Canada . . . there are many communities like powder kegs ready to blow up." These young Native leaders represented more than a minority of the Indian and Metis population. "In recent travels among the Indians and Metis," Stewart reported, "in cities and villages and reserves, I found the strong talk of the militants far more common than the whispers of the conservatives."[2] In the 1960s there was a parallel between Red Power in Canada and Black Power in the U.S.

When a racial minority people are oppressed for a lengthy period, despised on racial grounds, they will inevitably decide to fight back. "Hundreds of Native people marched from Victory Square to the courthouse on Georgia St. last Saturday (March 2, 1992). The demonstrators carried placards denouncing the RCMP and demanding justice in the name of the late Fred Quilt,"[3] a Chilcotin B.C. Indian, allegedly murdered by the RCMP, while driving home on his reserve. The demonstrators gathered around the courthouse steps to hear speakers from across the nation demand a full public inquiry and due process of the law for the alleged RCMP killers. A Metis speaker pointed out that Fred Quilt's death was only one of the great many examples of the oppression and brutality inflicted upon Aboriginal peoples of Canada. He urged the Native people to band together and put an end to the kind of police state that Native people are forced to live under. Clarence

Dennis, a local Indian organizer ended the day's demonstration with the admonition that "this was only the beginning of a long battle." Besides the full block of city police lined up across the street from the courthouse, with jack-boots, billy clubs and helmets, "Two well known city intelligence agents roamed conspicuously throughout the demonstration, as they used video and camera to record information for their files on Vancouver subversives."[4] The Indian and Metis struggle had reached not only national attention, but also international. The New York Times reported that "Canada, a traditionally Anglo-Saxon society simply ignored its Indian people as long as they stayed on the reservations and in small hunting and trapping settlements in the North. But they can be ignored no longer."[5]

Self righteous Canadians were looking across the border and saying to themselves that it can't happen here. But, what was happening in the U.S. was also happening in Canada. Indians and Metis were turning militant and radical, and proclaiming that they had nothing to lose. In Duncan, British Columbia, the Shuswap Indians, under the prominent leadership of George Manuel held a mass meeting, in which the main speaker was a Red Power advocate. On the other side of the continent, the MicMac Indians of New Brunswick under the leadership of Chief Nicholas held a huge gathering where militant, radical Natives were the major spokespersons. During a heavy snowstorm in late October, 300 Indians and Metis marched on the Manitoba Legislative Buildings in Winnipeg to condemn Premier Ed Schreyer for failing to meet Aboriginals' requests.[6] However, the strongest and most highly visible protests came from the Mohawk Indians of the Kahnawake reserve in 1969. They had many legitimate complaints against Ottawa. One important issue in which the people rallied around was the Federal Government's earlier seizure and use of Kahnawake reserve land for a main highway. Under the capable leadership of Mike Mitchell and Kah-tin-eta Horn, the Indians held the most powerful and effective highway blockade ever held to that date. *Time Magazine* wrote in May 1967 that "There is impressive evidence that for the first time, Canada's Indians have begun to think of themselves as a single ethnic group . . . an Indian civil rights movement is gathering."[7]

In spite of the widespread protests and confrontational demonstrators, the history of Indian, Metis and Inuit liberation movement during the 1960s and '70s remains hidden from the public. Although there has been an explosion of publications, written by both Aboriginals and whites, on the Metis and Indians in the last twenty years, none includes a discussion of the Native peoples' struggles during that important period. The ruling establishment has hidden this history in order to silence our people and deny us a sense of power and heritage. By obscuring this political struggle the colonizer conceals our colonized state and marginalizes our heroic efforts to achieve liberation. It is this type of censorship that allows the colonizer, and the academics, to dominate and propagate a biased view of the Indian and Metis colonial situation. Any history relating to Aboriginal political struggles comes from those who rule the colony. In the 1960s, establishment writers bragged of Prime Minister Trudeau's generous policies and programs for the poor and disadvantaged. They reported extensively on Trudeau's Just Society, and even claimed that Indian/Metis activism arose due to the 'generous' benefits we were supposedly receiving. It implied that our people's consciousness was stirred into political action by the government's justice and generosity. We were, apparently, not intelligent enough to mobilize ourselves and probably too lazy to activate ourselves for struggle. However, from the bottom up, this situation appeared very differently. The relationship between Aboriginals and the state is particularly aggravating when the latter fails to fulfill its promises.

When our battle for justice and liberation began in the early 1960s, Metis and Indian leaders, were unsure what it would involve, what direction it would take or how it would eventually end. The only thing we knew with any certainty was that our people were no longer willing to tolerate exploitation and oppression in the colonies, ghettos, and reserves. We were demanding political rights and better living conditions. We needed sufficient food or, as we put it, we wanted to put 'bannock and lard' on our tables. Our cold, leaking shacks needed to be fixed. We demanded welfare cheques that didn't leave us begging at the end of each month, but, more than that, we needed to be free from the colonizer's imprisoning welfare system. As indigenous peoples of Canada, we were determined to rid ourselves of colonial oppression in every possible manner.

Although Metis and Indians had occasionally resorted to local demonstrations and confrontations in the past, they lacked systematic organization, and strong collaborator-free leadership. Because of the lack of strong leadership in the beginning of the movement, there was a certain friction within most Aboriginal organizations and their leadership. Some were no sooner elected, when their position was challenged. Since I was intimately involved with Aboriginal organizations and liberation struggles in Saskatchewan, I have greater knowledge about them than those of other provinces. Consequently, I will focus on Saskatchewan organizations and political confrontations. However, Indian and Metis organizations throughout the nation are quite identical to those of Saskatchewan, that is with regard to the nature of leadership, policies, procedures, collaboration and corruption. All are organized on the same bureaucratic system, and massively funded by the Federal and Provincial governments. The one exception in Saskatchewan is that the Aboriginal liberation struggle—not the organization—was originally more militant, and politically radical than those in other provinces, with the exception of the Mohawks.

In Saskatchewan, the Federation of Saskatchewan Indians represented status Indians, while the Metis Society, led by Joe Amyotte, a mainstream Metis, served the province's southern regions. Amyotte sunk the organization into the mainstream psyche; he supported integration and government domination. In the north, Malcolm Norris and Jim Brady, devout socialists, led the Metis Association. These men had steered the organization for years, nourishing and politicizing Aboriginal issues. Rod Bishop a Metis from Green Lake and I shared their views and joined them to turn Native dissension into a national democratic movement emphasizing the politics of self-determination. As activists and radical leaders, we opposed traditional tribal chiefs and Metis collaborators who had betrayed the movement. Likewise, we opposed the growing class of Native elites allying with our enemies—government bureaucrats, white politicians, and other members of the corporate elite.

Dissent grows among the oppressed when state suppression is reinforced. Radical Native leaders advocated socialism; after all, capitalism was the system on which we were robbed of our lands, resources, and rights. Activists like Brady and Norris educated our people about how the state prevented Natives from adopting or forming alternative ideologies, such as collectivism or socialism. They explained that the state masked this reality by keeping the colonized masses politically ignorant and illiterate; that is, incapable of reading the political and economic signs outside our isolated ghettos. To survive, the white rulers must uphold the imperialist ideology, which dominated mainstream political parties, the media, religion, schools, business and even the cult of patriotism. In this way, the state smothered Aboriginal peoples culture and traditional ways of thinking, and then forced us to adopt a false consciousness.

Because colonized people have been socialized into a state of dependency, they tended to leave important matters to their leaders. To combat this phenomenon, we held study sessions and organized community gatherings to discuss critical issues about decolonization in simple terms. We had to tap into our people's most intense and personal emotions if we were going to encourage them to actively fight in decolonization struggles. Leaders spoke of our struggle in the context of world imperialism in the Third World. It helped to feel that we were part of a global revolution against oppression. In the 1960s colonized people throughout the world were reclaiming their culture. In speaking out, we were not telling the colonizer to give us a share of their powers—we were demanding the right to govern ourselves. We were fighting to change certain structures of the colonial government and break down the ideological, psychological, and economic walls that had caged us in the bowels of imperialism. We did not want to submit to the racist status quo and its bourgeois values. We wanted to revive our culture and indigenous lifestyle, and we wanted it on our own terms. We rejected entirely eurocentric historians' and anthropologists' distorted interpretations of our economy and culture. To us, these eurocentric academics were mere apologists for the colonizer's oppression and its corrupt imperialist state.

If the ruling power gave us freedom, they could take it back whenever they wanted. To truly obtain freedom one has to own it, and our people could only own their freedom if they fought and seized it. Local people must be involved if they wanted local changes; they must become part of the solution. Local people should participate at all levels from strategy planning to mass demonstrations. Also, it is important to begin the battle where there was considerable home support. By concentrating on local issues, we engaged in confrontations we felt we were sure to win. Neighbourhood activists acted as leaders and got a taste of victory. Regardless of the prize's small size, success buoyed and motivated our people to continue. We embraced the concepts of Aboriginal nationalism and the necessity for confrontation. We knew that liberation would require a struggle against the government and if necessary, certain force might have to be used.

In the 1960s, our people arose with confidence and a counter consciousness—ideas against the ruling class—and we were prepared for aggressive confrontation. We began picketing and holding sit-ins and street demonstrations. Naturally, our actions were directed against brutal colonizers for their discriminatory behaviour. Our goal was to expose and then discredit racist policies, such as those practiced by the Baldwin Hotel in Saskatoon. In August 1972, forty Indians and Metis were refused service one evening at the hotel. As the local paper reported, "The situation began when waiters of the beverage room refused to serve anyone of Indian origin."[8] Although we were ignored, we did not cause a disturbance. We eventually decided to move to the service bar as a group to demand an explanation, but by that time the manager had called the police. The bar was immediately surrounded by several policemen, but we were not intimidated. A few of us made passionate speeches condemning the manager and the police. They were treating us like trash. The tension was rising and many people in our group were on the verge of smashing the bar in anger and frustration. We left at that point because the incident, no matter how damaging to our pride, did not warrant a major confrontation. The Baldwin's policy to deny Indians and Metis beer would never be condemned by the majority of whites. The public was incapable of understanding the racism underlying the hotel's actions and would not sympathize with us on this particular issue. We returned to the Friendship Centre,—two blocks away, where we formed a committee to organize a demonstration to be held in front of the hotel the next day. These actions were part of learning to manage confrontations. It also taught us that racism is part of the Canadian nation.

A large group, including white supporters, turned out for the demonstration. Once we began picketing outside, the hotel stopped serving the white drunks they had already been pampering to most of the day. The customers were told that it was the Indians and Metis' fault, thereby encouraging them to attack us while we were demonstrating peacefully. They came out and taunted us, hurled profanities, and called the Native women 'squaws' and 'whores.' The police were also there, waiting with their paddy wagons, but not to protect us. In a white supremacist state, Aboriginals who challenge the white master's system are never safe. We concluded the demonstration without incident. Afterward, a complaint was laid under the *Fair Accommodation Practices Act* against Mr. Beavis, the hotel manager, but, as expected, the white supremacy rulers and its institutions stuck together. Roy Romanow, then Attorney General, the judge and city police would not prosecute Mr. Beavis. Nevertheless, the incident was a valuable lesson to the civil rights fighters. It highlighted the interlinking network of the dominant colonizer class and the imperial judiciary. It fuelled our determination to expose Canada's racist and oppressive society.

When seriously oppressed and discriminated against Aboriginals became impatient and threatening. They demand forthright answers immediately—not ten years from now. Indians and Metis, particularly young Native activists, were tired of being exploited and suppressed. Their only saviour was to repulse this false ideology and counter the government's strategies of control. Unlike unions, Aboriginal disruptions and mass defiance were often spontaneous and immediately disruptive, and, therefore, all the more effective. Although spontaneous, they were well organized. The state bureaucrats would seldom predict our next move, and our tactics confused the police's usual procedures for gathering facts and names, and the government's method of tracking us.

Similar concrete issues that caused much of Aboriginal peoples colonial suffering became the focus of our attacks. Almost every Indian and Metis had experienced the twisted and racist labyrinth of Canada's present colonial policies. Natives had spent hours upon hours sitting in crowded, shabby waiting rooms, listening to arrogant case workers asking them repetitive questions. Aboriginals were regularly humiliated and denied services. We knew who the colonizers were and to what degree they suppressed us. Therefore, when the issue emerged, we knew where to strike. It was very important that as dissenting Natives we directly attacked central government institutions like Indian Affairs and welfare offices. Not only were bureaucrats less able to use punitive measures, the mere appearance of disruption threatened rigid bureaucratic alignments. The state, always fearful that conflicts will widen, is highly sensitive to social disturbances. Indian and Metis youths actually baffled state officials, who could not function outside their strict, policy-driven world. Bureaucrats, unable to deal with defiant youths, always responded by asking to speak with Aboriginal 'representatives.' In other words, they wanted to deal with the collaborators; Aboriginals with middle-class values and a facility to communicate in the colonizer's language. Imperial tactics continue to operate in Canada. Our unorthodox approach and aggressive actions intimidated bureaucrats and politicians. As Native activists, we benefitted from playing on the colonizers' deep-seated fears and internalized racial stereotypes.

The fact that we were forced to create public disruptions at the risk of imprisonment highlights the few alternatives we had for seeking justice. Canada's system for controlling its Natives is still very oppressive. Open confrontation seemed to be the only available channel to achieving freedom from suppression. Mass conflict is important if the oppressed want to make their problems visible and challenging to the ruling class. In many cases, it is the only way to open the white settlers' eyes to the truth of Canada's colonization, because for most people, Aboriginal experiences were portrayed to them in the form of historical myths and stereotypes. Disrupting services that provide for major public and state institutions is one of the most effective ways of commanding the ruling class's attention. Disruption is one of the colonized's strongest tools; it confuses petty white authorities, excites the media, and, at the very least, attracts the public's attention. This was Aboriginal history in the making. But, despite the extensive national media coverage we received, academics and mainstream writers have hidden these Aboriginal struggles from publication. The Canadian establishment's determination to hide the politics of Aboriginal resistance to colonization has, and continues to be, translated into an indirect method of thought control and deceptive scholarly work.

Contrary to popular belief, state repression is the norm in 'liberal democracies' such as Canada's. If the dominant class wants to keep its privileged status, it must have an authoritarian society. Suppressive laws and policies are used to control the colonized and potential disruption. During times of social change, however, authorities readily turn to extreme and violent measures. They regularly deploy police and military in the name of 'law and order.' For example, in 1970, Trudeau's administration felt free to implement the police state's *War Measures Act*, against the people of Quebec. Very few Canadians complained of this despotic rule. In a sense, it is quasi-fascist action. Most people accept the use of state violence against internal threats to Ottawa's ruling order. This acceptance is natural behaviour because of the socialization to the state's ideology. Historians write books to justify this oppression and camouflage the violence of the corporate state. Dissenting groups are often blamed for bringing their troubles onto themselves, especially when activists become militant. Not surprisingly, it was relatively easy for the government to solicit sympathetic support from the conservative population for its suppressive actions against Native activists. Canadians' hostility toward Aboriginal peoples always lies slightly below the surface, ready to flare at any time. It happened in 1870 and 1885, and it happened again during the 1960s and '70s. The state's quasi-apartheid practices are never far away. Likewise, the state's system of violence seemingly acts automatically.

Ron Thompson, a white social worker in North Battleford who supported the Metis/Indian struggle, was forcibly taken to the local police station without cause and brutalized in June 1968. The officers refused to say whether he was being charged with anything, or why he was being held. Thompson later told us that when he attempted to leave, "The policeman threw me back to the floor, jumped on my back, put a hold on my neck, and said, I'll break your neck."[9] He received considerable injury before he was finally released. The incident was clearly an example of state-sanctioned violence, and was meant to be a warning to Aboriginal activists. The police knew that Thompson would tell us everything. They were hoping that they could intimidate Aboriginal activists into submission through Thompson. If they would treat a white man like that, what would they do to an Indian or halfbreed? We were later informed that the police were not supposed to brutalize Indians and Metis, when the media was present. Apparently, this was an unofficial imperialist policy by Ottawa. It is understandable that as Natives we fear the state police.

Thompson sought legal action against the police. After studying the case, his lawyer concluded, "Although we think technically you have a case against the police involved, we do not recommend that you take any civil action against them."[10] Next, Thompson complained to the Attorney General. He replied, "I have had the matter investigated and am satisfied that the chief of police and members of his department did not act unreasonably in the circumstances."[11] Many other similar incidents occurred during the period of Aboriginal resistance, and the victims' complaints were always ignored or denied. The legal system was used to control or intimidate political activists and Aboriginal leaders in a ruthless manner often as devastating and violent as the conqueror's guns. We had learned a new lesson. The entire police and legal systems of the corporate ruling class are intimately interlinked to serve their class purposes.

Broken campaign promises continued to fuel Aboriginal discontent. In 1969, Saskatchewan's Premier, Ross Thatcher, raised Metis and Indian expectations with extravagant, well-publicized promises, including a pledge to establish a new Indian and Metis Department that would employ many Natives and have a starting budget of several million dollars. His failure to deliver, perhaps more than anything else at the time, encouraged more Natives to break with the past and mobilize against colonization. On the federal level, the government was trying to dampen Aboriginal anger and confine discontent within the structures of parliamentary politics. However, as usual, the state had no intention of altering the imperial balance of power. Trudeau's government continued uttering empty rhetoric, but was totally inactive on actual reforms for Aboriginal social justice. Instead of implementing programs that would finally put an end to our chronic colonial suffering, the state stalled by assigning task forces to 'study the problem' and 'find out what the Natives want.' This was nothing new. Indians, Metis and Inuit were already suffocating under volumes of reports that never produced concrete changes. Since 1966, there have been 900 Royal Commissions and other government studies on Aboriginal peoples, which amounts to at least 34 studies per year.[12] Apparently, these studies justify the government's oppression of Indians, Metis, and Inuit, because most of our people are no better off economically today than they were in 1966. These studies are for international publicity to show Canada's mythical image. We retaliated with more demonstrations and defiant actions. The average Canadian citizen saw our actions as threatening and believed us to be 'restless savages.'

Our Native nationalist movement gradually heightened in intensity.

Young Natives became increasingly bold and aggressive. After years of submission, our people were feeling power and a sense of control. The state, which had become accustomed to Native passivity, responded with even greater repressive measures, coercing activists and bribing elites. When not harassing leaders, the RCMP and other authority officials intimidated the general Native population in an attempt to weaken and neutralize our supporters. A new prison was hurriedly built in La Loche, a large and desperately poor Metis community in Northern Saskatchewan. Indian and Metis fishermen, on their way home with their daily catch, were often surprised by an RCMP pontoon plane landing beside their boats. With brutal arrogance the officers ruthlessly searched the boats looking for anything that could, even if only in the most remote sense, be considered an infraction. The local priests also joined the state's cause, and tried to regain control of their Native flock by refusing sacrament and confession to Indians and Metis who took part in the Native movement. In response to our new found strength, the colonizers exercised their power, but also displayed fear. White officials, especially those situated in isolated Aboriginal communities, felt threatened. Six-foot-high wire fences with padlocked gates were installed around the local teachers. One would have thought that this was South Africa. In many ways, it was.

Matters took a turn for the worst when the state decided to stop our protests with mysterious violence; seven Indian and Metis activists met suspicious, possibly violent deaths. Despite our lengthy and careful searches, the bodies were never found. Then in February 1969, a Metis family in a northern community was axed to death. Was this an act of terror against our people? We became very anxious and truly fearful about our leaders' futures. Native groups began watching for any strange or suspicious behaviour, especially where the white Local Community Authority (LCA) was concerned. Comprised of provincial authorities who administered the Metis villages, it was well known that LCA members carried guns. The mysterious deaths of our people blanketed many Natives with a sense of fear and terror that was inclined to paralyze liberation activities.

About the same time, Jim Brady and Tom Hacklett, both Native activists, went out to their usual trap line and never returned. To this day, we don't know what happened to them; however, there is reason to believe that these men met violent deaths at the hands of 'hit-men.' They were very familiar with the geographical area, had ample supplies, and were in excellent health. As activists, the two were visible targets for racists agents. Moreover, the establishment authorities remained suspiciously silent and made little effort to find them. Their inaction forced us to draw frightening conclusions.

As conflicts increased and more Native activists disappeared, the media, especially the Canadian Broadcasting Corporation (CBC), became more interested—ugly confrontations make good copy. It gave relatively accurate accounts of the incidents, and discussed the issues in their proper political context. Such frankness on TV national news drew criticism. The white power structure attacked. Newspapers like Saskatoon's *Star Phoenix* issued reports about CBC, detailing how "Eric Krieck, overseer of the Local Community Authority issued a statement critical of CBC reports covering last week's (February 14, 1969) multiple slaying. The authority feels the situation there had been grossly distorted."[13] These charges were nonsense. CBC's description of Northern Saskatchewan as the 'Mississippi of Canada' was indeed appropriate. In Canada, the government has a long history of distorting and concealing its brutality of the Indians and Metis people.

During the summer months, I drove my Volkswagon hundreds of miles to visit many Metis communities. At that time, the Metis Society did not receive any government funding. Hence, the government had no control over the organization or my actions. It was no secret that I advocated liberation politics. More importantly, the majority of the Metis were likewise militant, ready to challenge their white oppressors and change the colonial structure into an Aboriginal type of self-government. They were living in ghettos much like the one I had left twenty years earlier. Most of the brothers and sisters were living in log shacks connected by crude trails. When I visited their homes, I could see that they had little food and were hungry. Just by walking about their communities, I could sense the Metis' deep hostility toward the colonizers, the white administrators, RCMP, Hudson Bay managers, school teachers, and, above all, the priests. These colonizers had dominated our people for years, treating them as children. But now, Metis' attitudes were changing, and I was anxious to ensure that we organized into a powerful political liberation force to battle apartheidism and colonization.

Local struggles played leading roles in demystifying the government's colonial strategies of racism, oppression, and impoverishment during the confrontations that arose during the 1960s and 1970s. As Aboriginal leaders, we tried to establish methodical practices of disruptions against the establishment, but by 1969 many confrontations were emerging spontaneously in Indian reserves and Metis colonies. The Metis Society had to devote immediate attention to these protests—such as the racist-class struggle that emerged suddenly in Cochin Provincial Park in the summer of 1969.

Indian and Metis workers at the park were being subjected to racist/class practices; they were denied the right to collective bargaining, and were subjected to unfair wages and unsatisfactory working conditions primarily because they were Aboriginals. The Saskatchewan provincial government, refused to allow these workers to join the union, so the Natives were kept at an annual wage of approximately $1,500.00[14] This was somewhat equivalent to Third World wages. The park's Aboriginal workers complained about their working conditions to the provincial Indian and Metis Department in Regina. Native workers were often hired to do the casual, dirty, and temporary jobs that white workers would not do. The Natives' poor wages were a race-class issue in that the government authorities paid higher wages to the white employees, who did the same work and were no better qualified. On August 11th, the Aboriginal workers held a meeting to discuss the matter in full and to decide on a course of action. Approximately sixty people attended, indicating the seriousness of the problem.

The Park Department claimed that it had hired 191 Indians and Metis workers in the past five summers, and that it hired 23 Natives in the summer of 1969. The Indian and Metis park workers, however, claimed that only a few Natives were employed in the summer of 1969, and the same occurred in the previous summers. The government was obviously using inflated figures or an unprincipled counting scheme, one that included Indians and Metis who were hired for a couple of days or weeks only to be laid off and then rehired on a similar basis. The Park Department counted each of these 'hiring' as a new employee. It fired some Aboriginal workers and replaced them with white workers, and continued to hire Aboriginals only as a casual workers, thereby keeping them from joining the union. These government practices amounted to semi-apartheid methods.

The issues surrounding Cochin Park were raised at the government Indian and Metis Task Force, but the authorities failed to do anything to improve the Native's situation. Instead, government officials did the opposite; entrenching their position against Metis/Indians and allowing the problem to deteriorate. The state's Native task force was revealed to be another empty vehicle it was using to make the public think it was dealing effectively with Natives. This is a government tactic used to divide whites from Natives. Undoubtedly, the government bureaucrats denied Indian and Metis workers at the Cochin Park the opportunity and right to make a success of their jobs and lives. Government officials responded to the Natives' demands with insulting and racists actions. The state wanted to crush and deny Natives' aspirations and industry, when they only wanted decent jobs, and fair wages. But, this has not been a possibility in the history of the Canadian nation.

After the August meeting of Indian and Metis workers, we agreed that the workers would go on strike the next day, and that a large group of Aboriginal supporters would block all the entrances to the park. Because the workers were the struggle's key figures, it was essential that they took part in all the action. After all, they had initiated it and it was in their interest that they continue the battle and not betray it. Betrayal arises from a vulnerability of the colonized, and from the oppressor's effort to divide the Aboriginals in their struggle. As chairman, I concluded the meeting by saying that the workers may be visited by government midnight riders who may offer them wonderful, highly paid jobs located elsewhere.[15] The workers laughed at this possibility.

The next morning, back in my Saskatoon office, I received a phone call from a Metis colleague in Cochin who told me that the Aboriginal park workers were mysteriously missing. Later that day we learned that a government agent visited the home of each Native worker and persuaded each one to abandon the park struggle. He promised them that he would take them to 'marvellous jobs.' As if the news was not painful enough, we learned that one of the Metis Society collaborator members accompanied the state agent. The collaborator presented himself as an Aboriginal brother and exerted whatever pressure was needed to abduct the workers and smuggle them to an unknown location. These workers were not heard from again. We questioned the traitorous brother, but he remained loyal to the government's mafia. The Native leaders and supporters true to the liberation cause learned a new lesson from this incident. It was now clear that the Canadian state was active in bartering human flesh; the so-called democratic governments of Canada also used ruthless tactics to silence its opponents, maintain colonialism, and oppress Aboriginals.

The Cochin case showed that the class struggle of the Indians and Metis did not lie outside of the mainstream national historical development. This incident was part of the Canadian class struggle that was happening in the neocolonial period. The park workers, although rural proletariat had a weak class consciousness because of ethnic/race nationalism. Racism/ethnicity is useful to the imperialist state when racial minority workers challenge the state. The colonizer, however, is able to manipulate and exploit the oppressed as they do not have a clearly developed class consciousness. It is an aspect of capitalist society, which serves to obscure class interests of Native and white workers, thereby reinforcing the existing colonial structures. The provincial government played on racial/ethnic identity by recruiting a Metis con man to emphasize a phony racial brotherhood and job interest. The sense of class consciousness of the park workers was not strong enough to make them feel their loyalty to other park workers and to the Aboriginal people who supported them in a class struggle for better wages, improved working conditions and the right of collective bargaining. Furthermore, the kidnapping action by the government of the key workers ripped out the heart of the liberation struggle, thereby reinforcing the existing imperialist structures. Racism is always effectively exploited by colonized rulers to oppress the racial minority workers.

For many decades white commentators and academics had written as though Metis and Indian society was a different and a separate area, to which ordinary, economic and political practices did not apply. This situation had changed by the late 1960's. Most Indian and Metis workers were rural proletariat. This class consists of people who work in farm labour, ranching, fishing, logging and hunting. They are primary producers who are compelled by circumstances to work seasonally or part-time in subsistence production. They are the lowest paid and most oppressed group of the working class. It is argued that "Most of the rural proletariat are forced to adjust to a permanent state of unemployment and humiliation, eking out a miserable existence on the margins of society."[16] They are people who cannot find jobs because of their race, gender or residence in an economically depressed area, such as reserves. These were the people who constituted the mass of Aboriginal activists in the 1960s. According to Veltmeyer, "The high level of oppression of these classes gives them a strong motive for revolutionary battles."[17] This principle seemed to be true for Indian and Metis activists in our Native nationalist movement.

The white society had excluded racial minority workers from the better and higher paying jobs. As a result, distrust was generated between the two groups. This racial condition prevented class solidarity. Such action deflects anger towards each working class, rather than against the corporate employers. White workers in attempting to preserve their advantages oppress racial minority workers. These suppressive tactics express themselves in the form of arrogance and caricaturing minority workers as racially inferior. Also, scapegoating takes place, whereby white workers' frustrations are thrust upon Indian and Metis workers. These conditions were taking place in the Cochin Park work place where they served to stabilize, rather than break-down the social structures of privilege and advantage within the total worker situation. Through these tactics racist ideology served to sink Indian and Metis workers even deeper. They were stereotyped and entrenched to work in menial, low level jobs as compared to the white workers clean and privileged jobs.

The rural proletariat, argues Veltmeyer, are the most difficult to organize in a struggle to improve their working conditions. This proved to be the case at the Cochin Park struggle. This was due primarily to the fact that their places of work are removed from centres of working class population and production. Also, they did not have a broad working class support, therefore, they did not get help from other workers. Their low wages did not allow them to build up a financial reserve needed for strike or protest action. There are many difficult problems in organizing the underclass, largely because they are migrant workers. As a result many drift around looking for jobs, eking out a bare subsistence. Whenever a mass was needed for political confrontation, many were working in the beet fields in southern Alberta, or fighting fires in the far north. However, today, many workers are forced into urban areas to find the lowest level of menial jobs that pay the least. The rural proletariat consisted of 1 1/2 million workers in 1981.[18] However, in the current recession the unemployment rate would be considerably higher. Many Metis communities claim that the jobless rate is closer to 85%. Kelly Lake, British Columbia, a typical Metis community states that "Most people survive on welfare, unemployment insurance or a pension and that the unemployment rate is 90%."[19] How different is this from Soweto during the Aparthied regime?

During the Native national movement in the 1960s the focus was on ethnicity, race and nationalism. Although the movement was vaguely rooted in class consciousness, it remained very much in the background. However, since the 1970s a class structure has developed within the Aboriginal societies. The major base of Indian, Metis and Inuit society today is the petite bourgeois class which continues to stress race and ethnicity. Its members dominate the tribal councils, Metis village councils, all provincial and national Indian and Metis organizations, and representative positions to mainstream bureaucracy. This class was brought into existence by the state during the period of neo-colonialism. Its basic interest lies in preserving the colonial social and economic structures. These people become alienated from tribal and village roots and Aboriginal consciousness. Their goals and future lie in the mainstream of imperial society. They serve the oppressor in positions such as police, soldier, civil servants and the intelligentsia. They are committed to white middle class society because of their background, their western education and the enjoyment of positions of privilege. "They are the life of their colonial masters, and are determined to preserve the status and power inherited from them."[20]

Starvation was the most serious confrontation between the Saskatchewan Metis and the governments during the winter of 1970. A provincial government inquiry revealed that almost "900 families in all were in danger of starving."[21] The Member of Parliament from Meadow Lake constituency raised the issue in the House of Commons and immediately attracted national and international media coverage. Trudeau's government was stung and bitterly humiliated by world attention. Indian and Metis people were well aware of the fact that the government had made extravagant promises to improve their living conditions, although often based on welfare. Welfare wardship is a system whereby the state holds all authority and decision-making powers over Aboriginal peoples. They may increase payments, but never enough to provide Aboriginals with true social justice. Welfare cheques imposed a structural dependency; it was the governments' key method of 'keeping the Native people in their place.' During the bitter winter of 1970, our people were not about to stand for this any longer.

To fight for basic human rights and economic equality, the Metis organization set up welfare grievance committees. Committee members volunteered to accompany Metis to welfare offices to challenge racist bureaucrats. In many cases, they were helping fellow activists who had been cut off because of their political activities. This strategy worked on two levels: first, it frequently succeeded in renewing the Metis' payments, and, second, heated exchanges with suppressive government employees heightened the Metis' political consciousness. The experience fortified the volunteers' determination to fight for decolonization. Not surprisingly, welfare committees became an integral 'institution' in several Metis communities.

The media continued to publicize stories on starving Metis. The coverage struck at the heart of the government's self-righteous claim that it was so generous and kind to its simple, primitive peoples. The world was finally seeing a different picture:

A two-year old Metis girl from La Loche had only a chunk of bread covered with lard for breakfast yesterday. For lunch she had a tiny piece of moose meat. There was much the same for dinner. There are many times, like this week, when they go hungry. There are other children like Victoria in this outpost of 1600.[22]

Hunger and starvation were very personal and intimate issues, from which the Metis could not hide at that time. And now, neither could the government. Three high-ranking, federal officials from the Trudeau federal government were flown to Metis settlements with their private propaganda operations. Their task was to distort and repress the truth. These arrogant agents ruthlessly invaded Metis's homes and privacy to question them and take pictures of them, all of which seriously humiliated our people. Claiming to be experts, they denied that Metis were starving and accused the Metis organization leaders of lying. They wanted to crush the publicity exposing the Trudeau government's phony human rights program and kindness to its Aboriginals. Tragically, they succeeded—volumes of media reports exonerating the federal government of any wrongdoing were subsequently released. These reports discredited the Metis leaders who were struggling for the survival of Metis families. These are the historical apologies and myths that journalists and academics include in their professional texts. The cruelty of the Canadian state!

But, the state's 'victory', however successful on the surface, actually showed its weakness. The false sense of humanity and justice that the establishment had so carefully cultivated was shattered; it would not be as easy to convince our people again that this was the best of all possible worlds. In fact, the government helped promote our political movement by further angering and radicalizing our people. Aboriginals were determined to live better and with dignity. Moreover, white people came to our aid. In February 1970, the Saskatchewan Farmers' Union, under the direction of their president Roy Atkinson, donated surplus wheat and requested a permit from the Wheat Board to grind the wheat for us. The Liberal Minister of Agriculture, however er denied the Farmers' Union the permit. The state was trying to prevent us from gaining strength. The confrontation heated up. Many farmers decided to grind the wheat in domestic mills and then they trucked the flour to the hungry Metis. Here was a case where Metis and whites united in an authentic, political mass movement. Our actions, dubbed the Flour Power Operation, lifted the Native movement to its highest level yet. For one thing, it strengthened our alliance with white groups. The most important, however, was that the intensity and intimacy of this conflict instilled the Metis people with a revitalized and increased counter-consciousness as no other confrontation had done, and gave them a new realization of the inhumanity of the Canadian state.

A colonized consciousness had perverted our belief systems since the first days of colonial control and was responsible for our material and intellectual poverty. Under rigid colonialism, we had acquired a warped sense of values that were inconsistent with our economic situation and Aboriginality. For example, we were led to believe that jobs would be available when we were ready; this was a cruel hoax. The colonizer's ideology had also led some of our people to ape their oppressor. These dupes glorified the Europeans' cultural patterns and distorted their perceptions of Aboriginal life—of inferior-ization, powerlessness, and cultural devastation. This perpetuated a colonized consciousness that blocked liberation aspirations. Brothers and sisters were discouraged to think for themselves; and political education or independent learning of any kind was considered to be dangerous and subversive. We had been trained to obey and follow colonizer forces that socialized us to accept the colonizer to make all the decisions for our colonies.

The state, however, was losing its ability to enforce docility. Although some Aboriginals in the early struggle may have been hesitant to protest, even ashamed and frightened to be seen on picket lines or at demonstrations, these attitudes gradually changed. We became confident. By its very nature, activism rejects feelings of inferiority and fears of being too weak and igno-rant to confront the oppressor. Holding mass demonstrations decolonized us and developed a counter-consciousness. We questioned and developed the skills and power to discard our sense of helplessness. We saw and understood more clearly than ever before how wretched we were living and why this was so. More importantly, we made headway on our turf; that is, in our colonies and reserves, and on the streets, not in the colonizer's parliament, courtrooms, and conferences, and we were more successful than we had originally dared to hope.

During the 1960s and '70s, Metis and Indians in Canada challenged the politics of colonization, class and racism. Our movement was based on rev-olutionary decolonization and political awakening. Today, several of us con-tinue the battle and strive for liberation. Our victories of the 1960s and '70s inspired Indians and Metis to a heightened counter-consciousness and moti-vated them to struggle toward self-determination. Unfortunately, we did not recognize at the time the totalitarian power of the state and how it could manipulate the entire apparatus of the government, which would transform the radical period of the 1960s into a reactionary and increased oppressive society: neocolonialism. Since neocolonialism is a complex concept, I have devoted a chapter to an explanation of it.

Chapter Eight

Criticism Of Metis Historiography

Until recently, eurocentric history has dominated much of the world. It has shaped most people's view of world history and, particularly, the history of Indians and Metis. These mythical interpretations of Native history have been chiselled into the minds of the oppressed masses. However, over the last few generations there has been a slow movement, most notably in Africa, to introduce Aboriginal perspectives into the historical material. The greatest obstacle to defeating eurocentricism and improving Aboriginal intellectualism is the fact that colonized people are denied their true history. Until the 1970s, Indians and Metis had been excluded from the mainstream of intellectual thought. In the 1970s, a few Aboriginal writers in Canada began to decolonize history and tried to present a more relevant Native perspective. Until then, Indian and Metis history was held in the white supremacy vice. The struggle to break the encrustations of static colonial history has been extremely difficult. White supremacist academics and quasi-apartheid institutions have heavily vested interests in maintaining and controlling Indian and Metis people and their intellectual thought. One of the first steps in decolonizing imperial history is to critically analyze the dominant eurocentric interpretations and ideologies of establishment historians.

The Metis emerged in North America as a distinct racial group of people. Although we are part European, we were never part of the Euro-ethnocentric society; and most of us can never be an integral part of it. Historically, we were definitely segregated from white society and isolated into our distinct Aboriginal community. For us, it is a world divided in half, in which the Metis are the 'evil, savage half', and the whites are the 'pious, civilized half.' There is no in-between, or cross-over. It is definitely two separate worlds. In one is the colonizer: the dominant, superior Euro-Canadians. In the other is the colonized: the subordinate, inferior Aboriginals. I lived much of my life, not knowing the reasons why the Metis were quarantined from mainstream Canada. I believed that we were the subordinate half because of our race, class, intelligence, history and culture. I believed it uncritically, because I had been socialized by the dominant ideology of Western liberalism. I had not been taught the true history of European imperialism. It was not explained that the nations of Western Europe had invaded and conquered almost every indigenous nation in the world. In so doing, they crushed and devastated all Aboriginal civilizations. With gun and sword they captured or slaughtered most of the Native people. Within a short time, these European invaders established imperial/colonization structures and institutions, whereby they dominated the indigenous colonial nations.

European plunderers succeeded in shattering most indigenous nations due to their military superiority, greed and obsession to expand. Their self image told them they were to conquer all they imagined, and to spread their control over all they saw. They had a self proclaimed mandate to save the world, because they had superior qualities and knowledge. An intense racial, cultural and religious superiority commanded European ideology. It held that Europeans had not only the right, but the obligation to 'think and act,' and make decisions for people of the indigenous worlds. This allowed them to commit any atrocities, when and where necessary. Imperialists believed they could impose 'liberty' on all mankind. To them, 'liberty' meant European patterns, customs and values. There were no other cultures of equal level of civilization as far as Europeans were concerned. Consequently there could be no such thing as integration or assimilation. European imperialism, therefore was strictly a unilateral force of colonization. According to the white colonizers, Aboriginal populations were suited only for universal domination. For this reason, there is no possibility for equal cultural integration. It had to be total and complete assimilation into European society. This ideology which has prevailed throughout the centuries of imperialism is still dominant in white Canadian mentality today. It is imposed into the minds of citizens. This is reflected intensively in all writings and publications that are produced in the nation. This colonization bias is most prevalent and profuse in the intellectual writings of academics, particularly historians and anthropologists.

After 500 years of imperialism, the Manichean/colonization society is too deeply and permanently entrenched to even permit any change or adjustment in Canadian society that would allow for a true and meaningful participation of Metis, Inuit and Indians. This is not a possibility anymore. Academics, professional writers, teachers, public media and state ideology have effectively shaped the quasi-apartheid system, which seals our cultural destiny as a colonized/subordinate nation. The most dominant and persistent theme throughout the centuries has been the savagery/civilization one. All writers have been guilty of this thesis, but some more than others. George Stanley, the 'authoritative' historian on the Metis, wrote in 1936, "The European, conscious of his material superiority is only too contemptuous of the savage, intolerant of his helplessness, . . . The savage, centuries behind in mental and economic development, cannot readily adapt himself to meet the new conditions."[1] As a promoter of quasi-apartheidism in Canada, Stanley has been the most eloquent and influential. Succeeding historians on the Metis have literally copied Stanley's racist biases. Despite his severe white supremacy prejudices and historical myths, they are "very prevalent and deeply rooted world views that have been imposed on Metis history and on the characterization of Metis."[2] Stanley bases his interpretation and description of the Metis of the Social Darwinian theory. To him, the halfbreeds were biologically less intelligent, physiologically inferior, and culturally and politically lower. He writes, "A primitive people, the half-breeds were bound to give way before the march of a more progressive people. It was the recognition of this fact and the gradual realization of their inability to adjust themselves to the new order."[3]

George Stanley is hailed by white supremacist academics as the 'high priest' of Metis history. *The Birth of Western Canada*, published in 1934, is a pseudo-Bible to those who write about the Metis. Yet, this book is one of the more racist and mythical histories of Aboriginal people in Canada. The book's central thesis is the clash between primitive and civilized peoples. It is a kind of Hollywood version of the Indian battle between the 'scalping savages' and the innocent white settlers. Typical racist and stereotype terminology are used as standard language.

To malign the Metis, Stanley consistently resorts to using racist slogans like, 'they trafficked in furs.' He also depicts Aboriginals as savages bent on destruction: "The Indians, . . . having brought with them only a sufficient number of squaws to do camp drudgery—a significant indication as to their hostile intent. . . ." And again as: "two hundred savages all armed and in war paint . . . raided several abandoned farms."[4] After five hundred years, such racist myths still pose as standard historical authority. In Canada, classroom students are taught that "when Indians attacked a white village and won, the result was a massacre. If whites attacked an Indian village and won, it was described as a victory." Exaggerations, and distortions and myths form the backbone of the establishment's belief systems. "Today, most Canadians continue to associate 'savage and heinous' behaviour with Canadian Natives." As a result, white academics continue to destroy Aboriginal society and legitimize a European-settler, white supremist system.

Stanley's superficial knowledge of Metis people is shown when he states that ". . . the half-breeds, too, were unable to withstand the impact of the new civilization . . . [they] viewed that their primitive society would be trampled upon by the march of an intolerant and superior civilization."[5] Stanley's perspective as a colonizer academic is shown by labeling Metis as 'problems.' In his eyes, the problem may have been, as he claims, that Metis did not want to be civilized. He suggests that they were still living at a kind of stone-age level. ". . . the Metis were unable to preserve either their primitive economy or their racial identity, and forced back by the advancing frontier of settlement."

Thomas Flanagan is another professor who has written in a style similar to Stanley's form of eurocentricism and colonizing division of society. Flanagan is an Anglo-American historian working at the University of Calgary and for the Reform Party of Canada. His book, *Riel and the Rebellion: 1885 Reconsidered*, would have probably gone unnoticed if the media and certain institutions had not been producing calculated criticisms of the Metis when his book was published. Flanagan and his writings, however, cannot be dismissed as mere annoyances. Rather, his racist interpretations of Aboriginal history serve a specific political agenda.

One reviewer of *Riel and the Rebellion* claims, "For pure nastiness and revengefulness it is unmatched in recent literature . . . it is a shameful and wasted effort that people would be well advised to avoid."[6] In other words, Flanagan's book is devoted to promoting cultural genocide of the Metis and to dispossessing them of land claims and Aboriginal title. To accomplish these goals, Flanagan states that his book "will serve its purpose if it raises the level of discussion above slogans and catch-words by showing the true issues."[7] Such lofty ambitions are soon dispelled when, in the book's first paragraph, he exclaims with a perverted slogan: "A few other Indian bands rose in an uncoordinated spasm of murder and pillage."[8] Flanagan, makes use of sloganeering and pejorative language when he refers to Indians as rampaging on "The credulous Metis had been led by a madman."[9]

Flanagan, like Stanley, implies that Aboriginals are incapable of rational thought or acting on their own deliberations. Despite his promises, Flanagan cannot and does not rise above simplistic jargon and racist depictions of Aboriginals. This is particularly true where Aboriginal leaders are concerned. For instance, Flanagan consistently ridicules Riel: "But, the Rebellion itself was the product of Riel's insanity."[10] Like the majority of Canadian history texts, *Riel and the Rebellion* is a diatribe of racist slurs and verbosity. We already have too many eurocentric books of this kind stuffing Canada's library shelves.

A critical review of *Riel and the Rebellion*, which appeared in the *Alberta Historical Review*, accurately evaluates Flanagan's book. The reviewer argues that the book's tone when vilifying Riel is so vicious and unfair that the book is close to a diatribe.

He reveals only too clearly where his bias lies. And the zeal with which he pursues that bias leads him to contradict his own evidence, ignore evidence well established by other historians and indulge in ridicule of the Metis people and their leader.[11]

Flanagan's book clearly lacks scholarship and reflects his zealous crusade to ridicule the Metis people and Riel. He deals primarily with trivia of the Riel Rebellion, and thus fails to develop any depth of analysis. His language borders on emotional jargon. His writing is the kind of eurocentric history that dutifully serves the apartheid practice. He distorts historical reality and, as such, is effective in perpetuating the colonization of Indians and Metis. Flanagan's works promotes race/ colonization division in Canada. They serve the manichean/apartheid principle.

The immensity (more than 1,000 pages) of Marcel Giraud's book *The Metis in the Canadian West*, gives the impression of a significant social history of the Metis people of western Canada. His writing, however, is seriously distorted by racist notions steeped in eugenic theories. The basic premises of eugenics are the superior intellect of the white race and miscegenation— the mixing of races—produces mentally inferior people incapable of adapting to the superior ways of the white race. Giraud wrote during the time of the Nazi occupation of Europe, when eugenics was in its heyday. "The race theories of the 1920s and 1930s can [also] be heard echoing in the Northwest of Canada."[12] It is, therefore, understandable, but not excusable, that he viewed the Metis as he did. To 'support' his eugenics-based thesis, Giraud puts forward 'proof' such as: "The mental make-up of the Metis was a feast or famine existence . . . their mentality was shaped by their nomadic existence."[13] The fact that the Metis did not adopt the imperialist 'white settlement' pattern by European colonizers was used to explain the Metis' 'downfall' and depressed economic situation.

Giraud's writing reveals his eurocentric bias against the Metis and the racist stereotypes he held. For example, he describes the Metis as "children who had savage temperaments, were indolent, loved to boast, drink, dance, tease and talk, engaged in other puerile amusements, were unconcerned with improving their circumstances."[14] Giraud claims to prove that the Metis are inferior because he says they do not sustain themselves in an 'obviously superior' agricultural economy. Even the upper-class Metis, says Giraud, are subject to primitive impulses: "the Metis of the West dwelt outside of the nucleus of civilization; the life they led was dictated by their natural and archaic tastes."[15] The Metis' impoverished conditions are said to be the result of their attitudes and behaviour which was bound to re-emerge in their [Indian] descendants."

Distortion of Metis history is furthered in Giraud's book by his use of research data from the imperial records of the Roman Catholic Church and the Hudson Bay Company. And as a result, a strong Catholic bias is basic to The Metis in the Canadian West. Unfortunately for the Metis, academics, especially historians, have regarded Giraud's book as a masterpiece of socio-logical analysis. This fictitious piece of eurocentric writing fits comfortably with the stereotypes of Metis people that Canadians hold as truth. Such a highly racist publication based on a pseudo-scientific theory has served to intensify colonialism and reinforce apartheidism, even deeper in Canada. The racially divided society is strengthened by the exceedingly white supremacy works of Giraud.

Above all, eurocentric historians show their true colours by consistently belittling Aboriginal history: "Canada's North-West Rebellion of 1885 was a trifling affair."[16] Yet, more books have been written on the Riel Rebellions than on any other topic of Canadian history. Dismissing the 1885 resistance as a 'trifling affair,' reveals the white's lack of sensitivity for Native people. For the Metis and Indians, the 1885 resistance was hardly a trifling affair; it was a revolution against Anglo-Canadian imperialism. The battle at Batoche resulted in the loss of their homes, land, and autonomy. Metis leaders were either jailed or killed, and their people were reduced to the misery of deeper subjugation. At the end of this 'trifling affair' twenty-one Indians and Metis were killed in action; nine were murdered by the hangman; forty-four were sentenced to prison terms of twenty years. Even most eurocentric historians admit that the imperial state fielded approximately 8,000 men at a cost of $5 million. Seizing Aboriginal land was clearly important to the imperialist government.

The dominant history of the Western World as depicted by eurocentric historians is formed and imbued with the belief that the Euro-American world-view is the only or best world-view. Of course, all historical research and theories entail some basic assumptions about the world and human nature, but eurocentric history is founded on the assumption that human reality for the colonized is imperialism and racism. What is not appreciated is that capitalism is the comprehensive reality. Eurocentric history glorifies the Western Anglo-Saxon Protestant (WASP) minority. Other histories and cultures are considered to be and treated as caricatures. Whatever is beneficial or profitable for the WASP corporate minority is assumed to be beneficial and truthful for all other people in the world.

The assumptions on which eurocentric history is based upon are not empirically derived, "but they nevertheless pervade our perceptions of the world and how we theorize about it."[17] Mainstream academics have avoided critically examining the basic assumptions of eurocentric history in relation to the history of Aboriginal civilizations. This avoidance is due in part to the fact that Aboriginal intellectuals have been colonized. The other reason is that white supremacist historians don't want to undermine their profession by admitting that they do not engage in a strictly empirical discipline and that their work is tainted by racism. As illogical, deceptive, and erroneous as eurocentric history may be, for these reasons it has been accepted as fact throughout much of the Western World.

The grim result of distorted histories written by eurocentric academics is that Metis, Indians, and Inuits are denied a true and honest account of their past and culture. Eurocentricism uses the notorious vacuum theory—the theory which claims that the colonized have absolutely no history previous to the arrival of the 'Saviour' whiteman. This results in the erasure of Aboriginal people from Canadian history. It is the notion that Native people had absolutely no civilized culture, or history before contact with Europeans. Although that is not possible, scientifically, it is of no consequence to eurocentric writers. This imperial practice weakens our intellectual and social capability to challenge the oppression and colonization resulting from such distortion about history and culture. It serves to obliterate or distort our perceptions of reality as colonized people. Through the use of the 'vacuum' theory, eurocentric history denies Native peoples participation in creative meaningful involvement in cultural and intellectual development. In this process, it became easy for white supremacists to distort our culture and psychology, and cripple of our societies.

From our experiences of oppression, and from the oral history of the elders we have, nevertheless, developed a specific sense of our past even though our culture has been devastated by imperialism. The colonizer imposes his history and culture on us, and thereby ensures domination. "The colonizer must destroy and paralyze the culture of the oppressed" writes Shafer, "for as long as these oppressed people have a cultural life, foreign domination cannot be sure of its perpetuation."[18] It is for this reason that Metis culture has been grafted to either Anglo or Franco culture. As a result, the Indian side of Metis culture was thrust into the background for several generations. This existence of ambivalence of Metis culture—between Indian and European—causes confusion, ambiguity and conflict over heritage and culture. In this manner, it serves to immobilize many Metis for cultural, intellectual and artistic creations.

As oppressed people we have had no decision-making of our economy, political order, community organization. More importantly, we did not have any say where we would live. Our ancestors were driven out of the Red River area, Batoche and even the road allowances. They were shipped like cattle to northern Saskatchewan and to Alberta Metis colonies. Often scrambling to save our lives—we cannot possibly write our history or literature.

In the colonial society there is always a certain number of indigenous intellectuals who are subservient to the imperial master. To these elites, the Native masses have only small minds; thus, incapable of any serious or analysis of their indigenous heritage and historical struggles. As agents for cultural imperialism, these elite collaborators perpetuate the decadent and racist values of Western society. According to Fanon, they have a permanent wish for identification with the colonizer. In fact, they want to be the oppressor; hence, they have learned well from their imperial master. They copy close interpretations of the racist historians. In this capacity, such intellectuals serve to legitimize the distortions and myths of imperial history and literature. In such volumes, Metis future is filled with pessimism and doom, which serves effectively to prevent any liberation struggle. To apply the term Metis retreat—in their own Aboriginal land—conveys a beggarly and powerless notion on behalf of Native people. Instead of criticizing the imperialist culture, the discriminatory political system, and colonizing education, theses academics passionately embrace the total imperialist system. Obviously, these Aboriginal academics are not involved in writing for the oppressed masses in the struggle for liberation.

On the other hand the greatest break-through in Aboriginal scholarship is the theories of Ron Bourgeault in the political and economic thought of Indian and Metis history. He has made a monumental innovation to Native intellectual thought that has impact in many disciplines. Bourgeault has developed the theory that European domination, both politically and economically created an unique international structure—ie. Indian fur trade—which prevented the possibility of independent development by the indigenous people of Canada. It was a distinctive form of dependent development that was subject to the dictates of the powerful Western imperial nations and corporations. The lack of autonomy in terms of economic and political power placed Indians and Metis in a dependent and subjugated relationship to European nations. Bourgeault's theories represent a great advance over the traditional establishment notions on the history of Aboriginal people and fur trade. He has shown that the Indian nation and the mercantile fur trade could not be studied in isolation from the historical context of imperialism and cultural domination. He has unearthed and examined the 'non-existent' history of Indian/Metis struggle and its radical tradition, which leads to recognition and understanding of its past in order that it may continue to develop and inform present and future struggles. Bourgeault has provided us with a new interpretation which is truly representative of an indigenous perspective. Although Bourgeault's writings have not yet reached the popular mainstream society, they have already become influential in the Aboriginal academic community. There is no doubt that his theories and writings will bring an entire new development of intellectual thought to Indian and Metis scholarships. It is not surprising that it had to be an Aboriginal scholar (Metis) to create a new theoretical break-through in Native intellectual thought.

By excluding the role of economic factors and the capitalist drive for seizing Aboriginal territory and resources in Western Canada, eurocentric historians have stressed the cultural and physiological primitives of the Metis to explain their subjugation and oppression. The fact that Metis are colonized and subordinated in Canadian society is due not only to economic factors and early imperial structures of semi-apartheidism, but to the continuous writings of white supremacy historians. They have saturated the ideological hegemony with notions of the 'savage/civilized' society.

To prevent a total loss and destruction of Aboriginal cultures, a few Native writers began struggling against cultural imperialism in the early 1970s. This was a call for decolonization. Inuit, Metis and Indian intellectuals began to shed light on the glory and hope of Native history and culture. They brought to the surface, a rich body of indigenous literature and authentic history, which only the day before, seemed impossible. Confronted with pressure from the colonized, the Canadian Government seeks ways to accommodate our challenges, without having to give away any of its power. A technique that governments and universities use is for Natives to use the existing institutions and structures that allow us in on the condition that we function without altering our colonization. That is, as Natives, we must continue to use the imperial formations, such as schools, curriculum, counselling, social work, etc. The entire system of intellectual colonization, which includes the academic, literary and artistic regions may not be consciously orchestrated, but the methods and processes are very systematically and effectively exercised.

Chapter Nine

Metis History From Native Reality

The history of Aboriginal people in Canada is the history of their struggles against colonial oppression and economic exploitation by Euro-Canadian imperialism. To understand the history, it is necessary to understand the political economy of the fur trade system and the politics of colonization with regards to race, class, and oppression. Indian communal society was transformed into an economic class of labourers by European fur trading companies, particularly the Hudsons Bay Company. Although imperialism has changed over the 400 years, the Aboriginal under class of casual, unskilled, manual labourers has remained relatively the same. Since fur trade dominated the economy of Canada through the 17th and 18th centuries, Indians were required as fur gatherers. In order to assure this labour, European merchants had to gain control of Indian societies. This was done by destroying Indian civilization, and then constructing a dependent tribal village society. Indians were then coerced into quasi-slavery as collectors of furs for European merchants without being paid any wages or benefits, whatsoever. It was the most scurrilous form of exploitation imaginable. As a result, Indians no longer produced goods for the collective use of their community. Instead they formed the basis for the type of colonial relations that developed in Canada. Since Europeans were incapable of providing for themselves, Indian workers were responsible for providing food for the posts, such as meat, grains and vegetables.

In the transformation of their society, Indians had to produce furs for exchange, rather than for their own internal use. Manufactured goods were introduced in such a way as to intentionally create a dependency on foreign goods and tools. At the same time, Indians were forced into the idea of private property. Trade was based on an individual basis; that is, trap lines led to private ownership. Trading was directed toward individual units in trapping, which led to the notion of private land areas for the production of furs.

The historical emergence of the Metis population development differed from Indians, which has never been fully explored and clarified. There is more than a single source of their origin. The French Metis, are one subgroup of the mixed-bloods who, including the English halfbreed, once composed two distinct societies. These societies were unique, inter-racial mixtures of

Indians and Europeans that could trace their beginnings to the fur trade. However, few records were kept by Europeans despite the fact that Metis formed the largest racial/cultural group in New France and the Red River region in the 17th and 18th centuries. The lack of authentic historical information on our ancestors is one of several eurocentric tactics designed to keep Aboriginal people politically and intellectually uninformed. The little documentation that is available on the Metis has been carefully sculptured to serve the colonizer's past and current goals. Consequently, the early history of Canadian mixed-bloods has to be constructed from facts primarily about the external economy and the socio-political characteristics of French and the British imperialism during that period.

The Coureur de Bois

One source of French Metis roots was through the serfs or indentured servants of New France's land owners—seigneurs. Although illiterate, the serfs were not blind to the lucrative opportunities of North America's fur industry. They, too, became interested in wealth, beginning with their escape from the seigneurs' fields to the woodlands. There they resided with Indians and became popularly known as the coureur de bois. "As many as 15,000 took to the woods in this [Indian] manner."[1] Largely because of their success in fur trapping, they were declared lawbreakers. In 1696 the Governor of New France passed a law forbidding all Frenchmen from travelling into Indian territory "and absolutely suppressed all licenses and permissions to trade with the Indians."[2] As a result, the coureur de bois sold their fur catches to the Dutch and English merchants located in other parts of the country. Furthermore, they established permanent residences with Indian women in indigenous villages.

If the French did not want the coureur de bois' beaver pelts, there were plenty of others who did. Even the French Governor soon realized that ostracizing the coureur de bois had backfired. Within one year, he granted amnesty to all previously outlawed French trappers. The purpose for this change was based solely on economics. Because the coureur de bois had distinguished themselves as the fur trading source in Indian territory, special efforts were made to discourage them from selling their furs to the English. However, neither friendly persuasion nor a show of military strength at trading posts succeeded in swaying the coureur de bois from their trading practices. In fact, the Governor's tactics drove the trappers farther into their adopted Indian collectives.

Trapping kept the coureur de bois in the woodlands where they often formed stable family relationships. These Frenchmen immersed themselves in Indian society. They "learned the Indian languages, adopted the lifestyle of the Natives, travelled like them and with them, and entered into temporary and sometimes permanent unions with their women."[3] At the same time, they imparted their language, religion, and social and economic values to their children. The mothers' Indian culture may well have superseded the fathers' European influences, but the consistent, albeit sporadic, contact with the French ensured that succeeding generations inherited a French heritage. As a result, a large Metis population was established throughout the French territory in North America. In 1870 there were thirty thousand Metis in the West.[4] It must be kept in mind, however, that the Metis were outcasts on the periphery of a totalitarian French colony. Their land and resources were regularly invaded and usurped. They lived in constant terror of the mercenary troops of New France. These threatening conditions gradually drew the Metis population closer together, bonded by a common identity and sense of purpose. As independent commodity producers, they were a semi-petite bourgeois class.

French Mercantilist

The French mercantile fur traders and their supporting entourage formed another distinct group of colonists who shaped the Metis lineage. Simultaneously with the coureur de bois, French traders and merchants, anxious to stay ahead of their competitors, advanced deeper into the woodlands during the 17th and 18th centuries to establish trading posts in indigenous villages and solidify their trading relationships with Indian trappers.[5] These traders with their French labourers and military troops travelled freely and intermingled with Indian women throughout the colony.

Unlike the coureur de bois, these Frenchmen did not establish permanent residences with Indians and were absent for extended periods of time. This class represented the worst of the colonizers. Nevertheless, some fostered ties with their Metis children. With great profits at stake, wayward fathers, as well as a steady stream of new French traders, continued to return to the indigenous villages. Due to the rich beaver pelt, French culture remained an essential part of the Metis' social make-up. In addition to their French names and knowledge of the French language, the Metis people's partial assimilation of some European values and customs distinguished them from both Indians and Europeans. They were never an integral part of the society of New France.

The vast Metis population was known among the French as 'brois-brule' or burnt wood because of their darker skin colour. The term was a derogatory slur, symptomatic of the systematic abuse inflicted on the Metis people. Whether they could trace their French roots to a coureur de bois, an outcast of French society, or a wealthy French merchant, racism doggedly stigmatized them. Restricted at all levels, they were forced into subordinate socioeconomic class that reflected their unique mixed heritage. This population of Metis would become the underclass or subproleteriat in the fur trade industry.

Another source of origin of the Metis, that is well concealed, is from Indian slavery in New France during the 17th and 18th centuries. Although it is well hidden, it is possible to discover enough evidence to show that Indian slavery not only existed, but that it played a major role in developing New France from the late 1600s to the early 1800s.[6] It is difficult to determine exactly when Indian slavery began in New France, but it is clear that it was precipitated by the colony's shortage of cheap labour. By Quebec's 1761 census, Indians constituted 80% of the colony's slave population. Negroes constituted the other 20%. Moreover, the 7,600 Indian slaves in New France accounted for 10% of the colony's total population.[7] La Verendrye was one of the greatest slave traders and "boasted of keeping New France well stocked with Indian salves."[8] Fur merchants used them to construct a network of forts throughout the beaver-rich western territories. Fur merchants and military used slaves to build and maintain the fur 'highways' and lines of communication on the land and water. In fact, Indian slaves performed a myriad of tasks, including maintaining the forts, cleaning and preparing the pelts, and occasionally acting as interpreters. Mother d'Youville, a Grey Nun of Montreal, who was canonized by the Pope in 1992 was one of the major slave owners and traders in New France. Being the niece of Piere de la Verendrye, she was always well stocked with slaves.[9]

Of course, breeding was a method of obtaining slaves. The colony's laws stated that children born to a slave became the master's property. Although,many of these children were fathered by the masters or other French men, they entered the colony as property, never as citizens, and remained slaves throughout their lives. It is very difficult to trace the movement and eventual settlement of the descendants of these Metis slaves. In spite of this difficulty, genealogical records show that my mother, a French Metis from Red River is a descendant of slave families, named Lavallee and Lepine. Indian slavery was not outlawed until 1831, therefore, there exists a large population in the surrounding regions of Quebec. However, over time, many of them have probably migrated to other areas of Canada and the United States. The historical question remains: how will this large group of Metis people be traced?

When and how did the French Metis migrate to the Red River area? One of their major routes was through the Northwest Trading Company. The headquarters of this Company was in Montreal, therefore the majority of its workers were French Metis from the Quebec region. Its trapping and trading route to the Northwest Territories followed a similar path and pattern to that of the Hudson's Bay Company. Hence, the French Metis and English half-breed crisscrossed in their travels and work. Gradually the workforce of each company consisted of both French Metis and English halfbreed. Many Metis families simply migrated to the Red River area seeking employment. It had become the headquarters of the fur industry because the Northwest Company had established a sub-headquarters there. Since the Metis were involved in the fur business, it was natural for them to follow the main centres of fur operations. The migration of French Metis to Red River was quite gradual in the beginning. There were none there in 1750. At that date the Hudson Bay Company had a serious shortage of labourers; and promoted the policy of reproducing a mixed blood population as a work force.[10] However, by 1821, at the time of the Union of the two companies there was a substantial population of French Metis living in the Red River centre. The Metis spoke French, were Catholic and had a French based culture, in contrast to the English halfbreed who spoke English, were Protestant and had a British based culture. Also, in the larger Red River district, each group lived in their separate sub-communities. However, these cultural factors were overridden by the class structure. Both groups were part of the same relations of production in the fur industry. In addition, the race/ethnic factor of colonialism subjugated them as the underclass workers and with the same racial stereotypes. In the resistance struggles against Euro-Canadian imperialism that began in the 1840s Metis and halfbreed aligned themselves by class division, rather than by ethnicity and culture. A common imperial oppressor brought the two mixed blood groups together as a colonized class structure within the colonial system. Distinctions among them were based on class, rather than on language, religion and cultural customs.

As the fur trade grew, so did the need for labour. European trading companies required cheap labour that could be discarded when not needed. Usually, this type of labour was supplied by European workers. However, in the latter 1700s there was a shortage of such labour due to wars in Europe. The Hudson Bay company concluded that a cheap labour pool had to be reproduced within Ruperts Land. As a result, the Company decided to relax the policies with regard to relationship of white workers and Indian women.

European workers were now allowed to take Indian women as 'wives.' The Company saw the potential benefits of mixed-blood children who would become a source of cheap wage labourers. This pool of workers would be separate from Indian semi-slaves who gathered furs. Although they would be employed in the same capacity as European workers, they would not have the same status, nor the same rate of pay.[11] English halfbreeds would therefore become a special pool of cheap labour based on race and class.

English halfbreeds were the offspring of English or Scottish employees of the Hudson Bay Company. The majority were fathered by the company's labourers and semi-skilled workers. A directive was written by The Bay's Governor in London in which he explained that "a very useful class of servants might be raised from among the Halfbreed sons...to be apprenticed for a term of 7 to 10 years . . . Some might be brought up as tradesmen, others occasionally hunting furs . . . they would form a valuable body of attached servants."[12] Boys at 14 years were apprenticed to work for extremely low wages. Halfbreeds formed a labour pool that was considerably cheaper and more accessible than European workers. Two classes of halfbreed workers arose from the Bay's directive: an underclass of labourers and a small elite group of petite bourgeois. The class division depended partly on the fathers' positions. Labourers passed on their low status to their sons.

By the early 1800s, French Metis and English halfbreeds, as a class-structured society were well on their way to developing a strong sense of independence and self-determination. As early as 1816, a group of English halfbreeds, led by Cuthbert Grant, attacked and destroyed a small regiment of the Bay's soldiers under Governor Semple. Grant was representative of the new petite bourgeois class that was emerging among the halfbreeds. Educated in England, he was the son of a high ranking Hudson's Bay official and Indian mother. The battle was a definite statement of halfbreed resistance against the Bay and it forced the Company to realize that it had to begin recognizing halfbreeds as a national political unit. Their resistance also sent a convincing message to the imperialists in Ottawa and London that halfbreeds were a force willing and able to defend their right to the Northwest Territories. The victory also gave the oppressed halfbreeds a greater sense of confidence and national pride. The seemingly indestructible Company was suddenly reduced to a level equal to that of the halfbreed, who had become sufficiently powerful to enforce a greater balance of economic and political power in their region.

Another serious instance of Native resistance against British colonial rule took place in the late 1830s. The Indian Liberation Army, heavily supported by halfbreeds attempted to eliminate British rule from Ruperts Land, and replace it with Native control. Its main failure was that it did not have adequate support from the Aboriginal labouring force. Eventually the leadership was co-opted into junior positions in the Company.[13] From 1830 onward, halfbreeds began to develop a counter consciousness and recognize that the source of their powerlessness and exploitation was the Hudson Bay Company. This halfbreed national consciousness was accelerated by the combination of race and class power and from the Bay's refusal to share political rule.

Between 1830 and 1870 there were distinct and separate periods of unrest in Red River, marked by an agitation on the part of the halfbreed inhabitants of the colony. They objected to the lack of consultation, and not being given any form of representative government with which to make their views known. The mixed-bloods' grievances were both specific and general. Their new consciousness was the product of their class struggles against oppression and their need to establish a distinct national identity. The colonizer now became increasingly oppressive and brutal. "Officers of the Company at Fort Garry armed with muskets and bayonets broke open a halfbreed cabin and confiscated all the furs that it contained."[14] This type of action, however, only accelerated counter-activity. A decisive turning point in the liberation struggle was their freeing of G. Sayer, a halfbreed fur trader, who was arrested and tried for 'trafficking in furs' by the Hudson Bay Company in 1849. Sayer's case was dismissed because of "the hostile manifestations of the Metis, three hundred of whom . . . were armed with rifles and buffalo guns."[15] This was a great victory that further elevated the mixed bloods' class unity and served as one more reason to celebrate the cause of national liberation. The labouring class and buffalo hunters joined with the small business class to form a formidable liberation force.

During the 1840s the class interests of halfbreed were being formed more precisely. Voyageurs were probably the most highly organized and militant. One of their major demands was a 'rest on Sunday.' "Many a strike and mutiny occurred over this issue, as well as issues such as wages and working conditions."[16] A mutiny of voyageurs was mobilized at Portage la Loche, Saskatchewan. They supported the armed insurrection at Red River in 1849 against the Hudson Bay Company in its attempt to stop free trade. The political alliance between the subproletariat and petite bourgeois was a strong force for struggle against the authority and repression of the Bay.

Whenever fur operations were slow, halfbreed workers were laid off. When unemployed, they would resort to fur trapping—the same work as the Indians. This would be strictly temporary, as the Metis were wage earners and found it difficult to work for no wages. This factor separated the mixed bloods from Indians as a class and society. Also needed was a mixed blood elite that could work together with the Company under colonial rule. The creation of this petite bourgeois class began in the 1760s. They were given junior positions as clerks in the Company. Some of the mixed blood male children were sent to England for education. This class was no longer to be considered Indian, but, neither were they English. They were mixed bloods who were later called halfbreed. Thus, by 1800 a definitive class structure had been developed within the Native society in Ruperts Land.

A few worked as middlemen in trading with Indians. Halfbreed middlemen acted as buffers between Europeans and Indians. Europeans exploited the halfbreed's awkward position to protect their own vested interests. To survive, they had to obtain fur pelts from Indians at the lowest possible price and trade them for manufactured goods at substantially higher prices. Undoubtedly, this would have engendered some Indian hostility. In order to trade successfully, halfbreeds required tact, diplomacy, a keen sense of business, and a solid knowledge of the value of furs and manufactured goods. In other words, halfbreeds conducted sophisticated economic transactions with Europeans and Indians, successfully balancing the two extreme interests of the fur industry. Nevertheless, they were considered to be dispensable. Halfbreeds were denied any form of security and were, at the very least, vulnerable to the whims of the fur trade companies.

Mixed Bloods consisted of four classes. After 1821—the union of the Hudson Bay and Northwest Companies—the Bay centralized and entrenched all its operations at Red River. Because of the decline in fur trade, most posts were closed and labour that was considered unnecessary was dismissed. Many mixed bloods who were engaged in wage labour jobs, buffalo hunting and fur gathering were brought to Red River. Part of the reason for placing this working mass in a concentrated area was to maintain control over them. Buffalo hunting had become a systematic, disciplined operation which came to function within capitalism. Local farmers produced food for the remaining internal posts and for pemmican. Many halfbreeds were working in seasonal transportation, either with Red River carts or boats. As well, many engaged in general, unskilled labouring jobs around the central post.

It was difficult to make a living in the Red River region where subsistence farming on twenty acres of land was a troublesome existence at the best of times. Most did not have the luxury of ploughs or harrows; grain and hay were harvested with the sickle and scythe. Their limited livestock of sheep and hogs was used strictly for home consumption. The halfbreed practiced a peasant type of farming patterned after the river lot seigniorial system in New France. Each family had a share of the fertile soil for crops, with space to spare for hay and pasture, and access to the water for transportation and fishing. From Winnipeg to the Rockies, the Metis practiced this farming pattern. They shared some common land among themselves.

A halfbreed business class became established by contracting certain jobs, which were too costly for the Hudsons Bay to manage, such as milling. In commercial enterprises the only market for most of these businesses was the Bay. It was from this class, only, that halfbreeds were appointed to the colonial Assiniboia Council. During the 1840s, halfbreeds expanded their trading business with the United States. This, however encountered resistance from Bay authorities. Tariffs were imposed on all goods entering Ruperts Land. British colonial rulers made every effort to prevent the development of the Halfbreed business class. They were afraid that the growth of this Metis class would lead to aspirations of political control of the Northwest Territories. True enough, it was this class that came into conflict with the Bay's and Euro-Canadian imperial rulers. The halfbreed struggle for freedom and independence was expressed in the demand for free trade and development of democratic government and institutions. However, as impotent advisors in the Assiniboia Council, the Metis were politically powerless and had very limited access to forms of democracy that was allowed to the Red River settlement.

During the resistance struggles in the mid 1800s, halfbreed classes realized that they had a common enemy: the imperial industrial class in Ottawa and the Bay. The people drew closer together, fostering a race and class consciousness and nationalism, regardless of cultural and economic differences. Halfbreeds were fighting for the same goal; liberation and freedom from Euro-Canadian colonization. The general mixed-blood population realized that they needed a united struggle on a national level. The true alignment between the English and French halfbreed was drawn on class/colonization, rather than cultural lines. Although the small group of halfbreed petite bourgeois tended to move towards the white mainstream, in so far as the whites permitted them, the underclass mass remained as a unified group fighting for their land and Aboriginal rights. They claimed a historical and sovereign right to specific geographic boundaries in the Northwest Territories.

Political power in the fur trade was gradually taken over by the industrial ruling class, i.e. the Canadian Pacific Railway. The Bay had become merely an agent for the changes in imperial interests. The new colonial masters created a revised political state in Ottawa to deal with the internal class formation and division of labour as a way to advance their industrial interests and at the same time maintain oppression over the halfbreed population. Industrialism required more land and raw materials to feed and support its infrastructure. In particular, it required a vast railroad system that would rob the halfbreeds of their economic security; grazing land, farming settlements, fishing, hunting and commercial enterprises.

Industrial capitalism never did penetrate into the far Northwest Territories. Mercantilism maintained a hold on fur trade so long as it operated within the interests of industrialism. British imperialism maintained a dominant economic and political system throughout the Dominion. As a result, the far North became seriously underdeveloped. It was intentionally kept within the confines of a fur trading economy, thereby making it increasingly more backward than ever. The northern economy stagnated and remained a traditional, subsistence fur trapping, fishing and hunting economy. Internal changes were never made towards an industrial society which served to create a critically underdeveloped society. This region was prevented from becoming part of the industrial economy and labour force because of its lack of resources and being isolated as an economically depressed area. As a result, halfbreeds and Indians of the north became separated and somewhat different from the southern Aboriginal society due to their economic and class structure.

The Euro-Canadian colonizers of Ottawa had no intention of dealing honestly and fairly with the halfbreed people of Red River. As early as 1860 they had decided that Ruperts Land would be annexed to form a confederated British North America.[17] Halfbreed people were unanimously opposed to this move, but in different ways. Their opposition became aligned according to class within the Metis nation. The small business class, such as James Ross, an English halfbreed wanted to unite with Upper Canada in order to gain access to industrial wealth of that area. This class recognized its interests as compatible with Anglo-Canadians in Toronto. This would give this land owning class access to agricultural markets for their grain. As the anti-colonial struggle developed, Ross and his class aligned themselves with white and halfbreed land owning farmers. However, by the mid 1860s a radical democratic force developed against colonialism under the leadership of Riel and other progressive thinkers. This political force was comprised of people from all classes: the lower level of the business class, the subproletariat, and the underclass, such as buffalo hunters. They had no doubt that Euro-Canadian colonialism was extremely oppressive and that exploitation would continue if there was no fundamental change in the political and economic system in Red

River. They clearly understood that a responsible democracy and the creation of a nation with decision-making power by Metis people had to take place. Without these fundamental changes, halfbreed people would remain powerless and landless. They fully realized that the annexation of Ruperts Land to Canada would perpetuate colonial rule, and provide no guarantees for liberation or equality. The only way for halfbreeds to achieve liberation was to separate from the imperial regime at Ottawa and declare their independence. The provisional government which the halfbreed established was truly democratic and in the interests of all people in Red River. This national liberation struggle for self-determination had been going on for thirty years. Liberation could be achieved only by a revolutionary struggle and by development of a democratic nation composed of the oppressed people. This, of course, excluded the Hudsons Bay Company, Anglo imperialists and Orangemen.

The Anglo-Canadian class, however, was interested in expanding its national and economic interest. These colonizers were determined to annex Ruperts Land to a confederation, as a territory, and not as a province. Imperialism, as part of its natural development demands a white settlement in the colony. In Canada, most of this white settlement was to be in the plains region for agricultural production. Such settlement would provide a market for manufactured goods of eastern industrialists. White European colonial settlers would inevitably displace the indigenous people of the country, who would be relocated to marginal, isolated regions in the form of internal colonies and ghettos. For the Indians, they would be imprisoned in reserves; a form of apartheidism used in other British colonies, such as Australia, New Zealand and South Africa.

The invasion of the fanatical racist Orangemen as white settlers brought increased turmoil into Red River. Although they had no mass following, the Ottawa regime encouraged and supported them. Their harassment and brutality against the halfbreed population created serious racial conflict. Many were hired as government surveyors of land in Red River, which deliberately fostered hostility against the halfbreed.[18] They were opportunists, plunderers and thugs who wanted to cash-in on quick fortunes from land seizure and sales.

The political and economic institutions of Assiniboia began to crumble after the restructuring of the Hudsons Bay Company in 1862. The halfbreed working class became increasingly agitated due to the reduced wages, unemployment and poor working conditions. Strikes increased among Native voyageurs. Boat brigades engaged in shut-downs in the 1860s. As a result, brutal oppression was used on the people of Red River in the 1850s and '60s when imperial troops occupied the area. This military occupation was more than a mere threat; it was severe colonial repression. At the same time, however, the Hudsons Bay Company made attempts to co-opt the halfbreed business class. It made political concessions toward representative government in the Assiniboia Council. This typical 'half measures' proffered by the colonizer to the oppressed is a tactic of stalling national liberation. While Red River was under political seige, Riel managed to keep most of the political supporters in line with the radical democratic program. Because the independence movement was a political and economic threat to the Canadian nation-state formation, it was defined as a 'rebellion' by imperialist designers and scribes.

The revolution of 1870 was not a strategy rebellion by a few individual halfbreeds. It was a national liberation struggle supported by all classes in Red River. The foundation of the struggle was provided by the political alliances of the working classes with the small business class. It was a struggle for national liberation from colonial oppression by most people of Red River, and not a cult rebellion. Let it be very clear about this interpretation. Ottawa exploited the ethnic/race issue as much as possible to divide the people. This is normal practice for the colonizer and imperialism. Witness the multitude of tribal/ethnic wars in ex-colonies throughout the Third World today.

Land grants in Red River were allocated according to one's class position within the fur trade industry.[19] Retired white officers with their Native families were given the largest land grants. The father, however, was required to subdivide this land among his halfbreed children. This procedure of land grants created a small petite bourgeois class of land owners. Halfbreed labourers, on the other hand received small twenty-five acre plots of land. These families eked out a subsistence livelihood from the small farm, typical of peasant subsistence. They supplemented this by working for large neighbouring farmers in the busy seasons. They became the common peasant class of both English halfbreed and French Metis that continued in existence throughout much of the prairie provinces until the 1950s. The reason for giving only small allotments to the labouring class was to keep them at a low level so they would have to supplement their farm income as cheap wage workers. For this reason, wage labour of the halfbreed society never completely developed as a true proletariat class. The Metis underclass of buffalo hunters were not given any land whatsoever. They were allowed to settle as squatters. After the revolution of 1870 many of this halfbreed class became the 'Road Allowance Squatters.'

After imperial commander Wolseley's troops conquered Manitoba the industrial/military regime marched steadily westward to complete its invasion and conquest of all Aboriginal land and resources. To consolidate its rule, Ottawa was forced to launch a series of 'low-level' wars against Indians and Metis of the Northwest Territories between 1870 and 1885 to complete Anglo supremacy and the dominance of industrial capitalism. This plundering was necessary for its political and economic ascendancy, and the increased exploitation of the countrys' land and resources. Indians and Metis were not just to be conquered, subjugated, and separated; they were to be made dependent on their commanders for every aspect of their livelihood. Our ancestors were reduced to beggars and prisoners. The struggle for land which had lasted for three hundred years had now drawn to a close. The Euro-Canadian imperialists and white settlers capture most of the Indian/Metis territories. In 1876 when the *Indian Act* was passed, Ottawa established Canadian apartheidism. The transformation of the western interior from Aboriginal communalism to private ownership was through a massive military invasion and a tidal flow of Indian/Metis blood. "This turbulent decade, 1875-85, ended in violence and, in betrayal of the Indian people."[20] With the arrival of thousands of white settlers to the west, the so-called 'empty' Indian land was purchased as private property from the conqueror, the Federal Government. Within ten years, one half of Indian land on the prairie area was sold to white homesteaders, or given to the Canadian Pacific Railway.[21]

The racial structure of Canadian society arose from severe exploitation of Indians and Metis, in terms of their land and labour backed by judicial and military power. Racial and colonial laws are the means by which potentially violent class relations are contained and masked. For example, the 'Pass' law created in 1885 prohibited Indians from leaving their reserves without a written pass from the Indian agent. It prevented Indians from working and participating in the development of the territories of the Northwest. The close lines between class, race and colonization developed in Canada according to mercantile/industrial exploitation. Cheap labour was the basis of it, beginning and lasting all through the lengthy fur trade period. The structure of racism and the form of racial violence in Canada was dictated by two facts: the conquest of Indian territory and the exploitation of Aboriginal labour in the pursuit of wealth from fur pelts. A racist social structure is inherent in all colonial situations. "In a racist-capitalist power structure, exploitation and race oppression are inextricably linked."[22] The subjugation of Indians and Metis was due to the dominance of capitalism and its institutions.

In the agricultural west a class structure developed. There existed, of course, a race/colonization category. A rural/urban white petite bourgeoise were at the top. This class included those who possessed enough capital for a business and those who were able to cultivate the land which they owned. A few Metis farmers were part of this group. Next, was the class of small farmers that cultivated at a subsistence level, and were often forced to sell their labour as seasonal workers to large white farmers. This large class was classified as peasants.[23] Peasant, in this sense refers to families which reside on land, whereby they have to pay a share or mortgage to maintain possession of the land. In the case of the Metis, they were never given scrip or possession of land in Saskatchewan and Alberta, but were allowed to reside on plots of land on condition that they made annual payments to a colonial landlord, usually a Land Holding Company. This was the typical peasant farming of the huge population of halfbreed throughout the Batoche-St. Louis-McDowall region in Saskatchewan, where I grew up. Finally, there were the agricultural labourers, the rural proletariat. This class was composed largely of Indian and Metis seasonal workers and some European immigrants.

Native colonies were always under totalitarian control of the white federal government.[24] The Metis lacked economic and social means to develop independently. They could never become economically self-sufficient or autonomous. Being incapable of economic independence internal colonies were structured as cheap labour pools. When the settler economy is agricultural, as it was in Canada, then internal colonies are scattered throughout farming regions. Without political power and insufficient land to provide an independent existence, Indians and Metis had no choice but to become dependent. Reserves and Metis settlements were reproduced for cheap labour. In addition, these areas could be used as dumping grounds for the human waste discarded by the fur trade and railway industry. This is the harsh unspoken politics of colonization.

In considering the conquest and administration of the Northwest region, the industrial class in Ottawa had to have the Metis/Indian population foremost in their mind. As ninety-five per cent of the population in the Northwest Territories, in 1875, was Aboriginal.[25] The federal government's main concern was to bring this massive Indian/Metis population under subjugation of its regime. The treaty land system was devised as a method of dispossessing Indians of their territories, and at the same time imprisoning them onto reserves. Between August 1871 and September 1877, seven treaties were completed with Indian nations that covered most of the land in Manitoba, Saskatchewan and Alberta. In other words, within a six year period after the conquest of Red River, the Anglo Canadian industrialist class had appropriated the huge central territory of Canada. This was achieved through fraudulent treaties and military conquests. Canadian governments did not deal honestly or democratically with Indians and Metis, but instead employed violence and deception. Many Indian nations struggled against seizure of their land, and confinement to desolate reserve enclaves. Such that, "There were many isolated Indian resistance battles during the period of relocation to reserves."[26] "In their meetings with discontented Indians, white man's injustices were discovered. Many angry Indian leaders spoke out."[27] Although most Indians had agreed to Treaties and accepted confinement to compounds, they harboured considerable bitterness and dissatisfaction. For this reason the Northwest Territories was a powderkeg during the period between 1870 and 1885. It is understandable that Ottawa found it necessary to establish a permanent state police force, the Royal North West Mounted Police, for occupation of the Northwest Territories in 1873. In addition Ottawa's military forces for the Northwest expanded enormously. "Its military expenditures jumped from one million to five million dollars . . . in other words this part of the federal budget increased by 400%."[28]

In the meantime, the white business class in the Northwest urban areas faced difficulties arising from Ottawa's policies. Besides paying high prices for manufactured goods in Ontario, they were charged excessively high transportation rates. It was difficult to pass these costs on to the buyers. As a result, their profits were meagre, and they found it difficult to stay in business. They demanded responsible government for the Northwest Territories, lower tariff rates, an end to the monopoly of the C.P.R., and that a railway be constructed to the Hudson Bay.

People of all classes talked of secession from Canada and annexation to the United States. As a business class, Metis and whites struggled as a single force, opposing Governor Dewdney's corrupt and despotic rule. In this case, class overrode race and ethnic concerns. The politics of colonization became so heated that Macdonald found it essential to co-opt the white business class, in 1884 whereby he made many concessions to their demands. The Metis bourgeois also removed themselves from the revolutionary struggle. The large farmers, likewise were dissatisfied. They were forced to pay expensive prices for the necessary farm machinery. In return, they received low prices for their grain and agriculture products. Many were forced to live on credit, and were charged high interest rates. "The Western farmers hated the high Canadian tariff. It forced up the cost of machinery while the price of their wheat was left unprotected on a world market."[29] They were furious at Prime Minister John A. Macdonald for suddenly moving the location of the transcontinental railroad 300 kilometers southward. How would they ever get their produce to the market?"[30] The peasant farmers suffered the greatest. They were unable to sell the few products they produced. Consequently, they were forced to live at a subsistence level in which they could eke out of their small plot of land, since there were exceedingly few jobs. "The more radical farmers realized this and when they formed a farmers' union they approached Will Jackson to become the first secretary. "By the summer of 1884 Jackson argued that the white settlers must widen their movement to include the Metis and the Indians."[30]

Since Metis consisted of 24% of the population in the Northwest and the majority were of the peasant class, it was natural that they would be foremost in the revolution. They had the least to lose. There was, however, a lack of class consciousness and cohesion within it to sustain a revolutionary force. The English, Protestant halfbreeds who were geographically located between Prince Albert and St. Louis, which is to the north of the French Metis of Batoche did not actively support the revolution. Likewise, the Metis under-class of hunters and trappers of the far north did not become involved at all in the struggle. Many reserve Indians constituted the majority of warriors in the 1885 struggle. Indian warriors who captured the reserve headquarters at Frog Lake, Fort Pitt, and North Battleford were representative of the colonized. However, having being confined to a tribal enclave, for sometime they had not developed a class consciousness. Furthermore, it lacked enlightened leader-ship and organization by individuals who had well developed class under-standing, and a high political awareness of the colonial situation. In 1885 the single most important reason for the failure of the revolution was the under-developed awareness of class formation and forces. Revolutionary leaders, such as Gabriel Dumont, were able to provide the military knowledge, as well as the guerrilla war strategy, but there was a lack of an Aboriginal underclass class support sufficient for a victory against the military might of Ottawa and London. The revolutionary forces consisted of a limited group of Metis peas-ants and Indians who had broken free of reserve imprisonment. After Macdonald separated the white business class and settlers from the struggle through economic and political concessions, he had effectively removed them from the active revolution. The failure of the white and Metis petite bour-geois, as well as most of the English halfbreed peasantry, to support the French Metis allowed the imperialist military to eventually defeat the Aboriginal revolutionary forces.

Immediately following Middleton's victory, the Canadian and British mercenaries desecrated the Metis settlements and reduced the Aboriginal peoples to homeless wanderers. Their rich land and resources were seized by the industrial colonizers. Those Natives who escaped genocide, execution and imprisonment became prisoners by poverty, racism and oppression. Our struggle for national liberation was abruptly and viciously quashed. In the history of most oppressed nations, the national revolution represents a peak of achievement. It is the period when its people are most united, most involved, and most active in their fight for liberation. Certain persons usually emerge as the revolution's principal leaders and sometimes even as heroes. However, in some cases the Aboriginal leader may be falsely chosen by imperialist manipulators.

We are told by white historians that although we lost both the 1870 and 1885 wars of national liberation, our leader and hero was Louis Riel. It is true that Riel's roots were with the Metis masses and that he gave superior leadership and made the greatest sacrifice for our people. However, is he truly our hero? We did not win our freedom, or sovereignty. In fact, our people were worse off after his execution. More importantly, there is no evidence to prove that Riel was a revolutionary during the 1885 liberation struggles. Riel acted as a pacifist and negotiator. He did not mobilize the Metis people in Batoche for revolutionary war. In both the 1870 and 1885 struggles, Riel was strictly involved in constitutional negotiations for a provisional government. He took no part in the guerrilla fighting and even commanded Gabriel Dumont to stop killing our enemies, the police and soldiers. Furthermore, Riel willingly surrendered to General Middleton, leaving the Metis people to scramble for their personal survival. If Riel had not been at Batoche, the Metis and Indians may have had a much better chance of winning their liberation battle, and may have maintained control of their territory and established a nation.

As Metis historians, it is important that we analyze and resolve the contradiction between Riel, our supposed hero, and the revolutions. Riel's life and leadership is one of the most overstudied topics, researched by imperial white historians. Our national liberation wars have always been overshadowed by an excessive emphasis on Riel. They are studies strictly of cult rebellions. We must get beyond this distorted trivia. The colonizer has magnified Riel's role to obscurity of all other factors. Other leaders may be the true heroes of our liberation battles. Did Ambroise Lepine not play an equally important role as Riel in 1870 in Manitoba? The colonizer often contrives false images and myths about indigenous leaders. The events surrounding Riel's trial and execution should be placed in their proper historical context. Ottawa had its own colonizing agenda and political reason for the judicial murder of Riel.

Today, colonizers still use the personal history of Riel to fulfill their racist agenda. The statues of Riel, the posthumous pardon, and the new title as one of the founding fathers of confederation are all designed to serve our oppressors guilt. Riel's preeminence is largely the result of promotion propagated by imperialist rulers and their media. Government-sanctioned hero worship is designed to confuse our people. In this manner, it makes them vulnerable to reactionary and colonizing beliefs, and obscuring the real issue; class struggle.

Chapter Ten

Challenge to Colonized Culture

When European invaders conquered Indigenous nations, they did not destroy completely the Indigenous cultural and political institutions. First European imperialists established their culture and values, while at the same time negating and mocking those of the Indians. The imperialist needs the cultural destruction of the Aboriginal society in order to command a place in the system of colonialism. Therefore, he constructs the culture of the colonized and shapes it according to his distorted view of Native people. Imperialist structures and institutions are forced upon the colonial society and its population. As a result a caricature colonial culture is developed. Eventually the Natives adjust to the colonial situation, and accept the stereotyped cultural traits of the colonized. Through this process the imperialist develops a system of severe cultural oppression.

Smashing indigenous culture has been imperialism's most effective weapon in conquering Aboriginal populations. Aboriginal cultural institutions were restructured, as well as their mode of behaviour and way of thinking. Upon conquest, the imperialist destroyed this cultural warehouse and broke the link of Aboriginal identification to which the people belonged. This cultural destruction hastened denigration and mocking of indigenous culture and its values. The colonizer loudly proclaimed Indians were immoral, wicked and debauched. Conquered indigenous societies were characterized as the most negative and grotesque cultures that Christian Europeans had seen: barbarians, cannibals, head-hunters, pagans, etc. The colonizer did not permit any positive aspects of indigenous cultures to prevail, as this might serve as a grain of confidence or power that would eventually challenge the authoritarianism of imperialism. As far as the colonizers were concerned there was nothing positive or admirable in Aboriginal societies.

European imperialists did not completely destroy indigenous cultural and political institutions; only what they determined to be a threat to imperialism. Certain institutions were restructured to serve the functions and benefits of imperialism. Traditional Indian governments were weakened, and chiefs and council members were co-opted. In the case of British imperialism, deliberate changes were made to the political culture that would allow the British to govern through 'indirect rule'; meaning through collaborator chiefs and councils. This method prevented the development of a class structure and consciousness within the indigenous workers. European imperialists drained the power and functions of the Elders and tribal government, but kept them as symbols for manipulating Natives into submission and subservience. Through these restructured formations, Indian people were forced to conform to a caricature of indigenous government. This practice was carried on for hundreds of years, and has resulted in a serious problem of determining today what is authentic Indian culture, and what is phony.

Since imperial strategies and institutions completely dominate Aboriginal society, there is no interaction or reciprocal exchange of cultural characteristics. It is strictly a one-way action from European white supremacy culture to the subordinated Native culture. This is what imperialism means. It does not contribute any positive or beneficial elements to the indigenous society.

In colonization there are two distinct societies: the colonizer and the colonized. Fanon claims that it is "A world divided into compartments, a motionless Manicheistic world. The Native is being hemmed in; apartheid is simply one form of the division . . . The first thing which the Native learns is to stay in his place, and not to go beyond certain limits".[1] On the other side is the colonizer with his barracks, military, police, law and order.

It is a divided world, that of the Native and the colonizer, that of darkness and light, of vice and virtue. It is a world of opposition between the well fed and the hungry, the rich and the poor, the haves and the have nots. Since this is strictly a one way society where everything moves from the top to the bottom, it is impossible for the subjugated Aboriginal society to have any force, or even influence on the dominant white society. For this reason it is impossible for the Aboriginal society to be racist because the structures and institutions of racism are determined and controlled exclusively by the white dominant society.

In a colonial society Aboriginal people are defined by biological and inherent characteristics that are all negative in definition, and which apply to all members of the Aboriginal population. Hence, all Indian, Metis and Inuit people experience the same racial stereotypes, regardless of class. Physical appearance does make some difference; however, if it is known that a person has a 'drop of Indian blood' then he/she is automatically an Aboriginal person, and treated accordingly. Racism is produced through institutional discrimination such as schools, churches, bureaucracy, parliament, etc. It is an economic structure of exploitation and exclusion, and not a product of biological or innate differences.

Racism can thus be seen as a cause of the development of a 'shame and inferiority complex' in regards to Indian and Metis peoples culture. As a result the whitemans culture begins to become glorified. Due to this notion, Aboriginal peoples come to believe that the only way in which they can 'rehabilitate' themselves is through the oppressor's culture; by adopting his social values, morality and language. By accepting these character traits, we inferiorize ourselves, and thus we function within this colonized framework. By doing so, we legitimize the stereotyping of our culture and personality. Furthermore, we complete the self-fulfilling prophecy by behaving in accordance to many of the stereotypes. However, in order to maintain this caricature culture, oppression must be regularly reproduced. Constantly ringing in our ears are shouts of damnation, such as 'you are useless good for nothing, stupid bastards' etc. We are conditioned to believe that the oppressor is accurate and justifiable. When we internalize these stereotypes, we paralyze ourselves of all cultural creative productivity.

In Canada, capitalism is the base of society, and thus shapes the social ethic, customs, culture and economy of our society. Culture can thus be seen as a product of the economic base of society. According to Syzmanski "Workers relationship to the means of production shapes their whole social and cultural experiences."[2] The term relations of production, means the relationship among people in the process of making a product or good. For instance, workers at factories are concerned about wages and unions, whereas the owner is concerned about profit. These relationships grow into a culture, consciousness and participation of a particular class structure. Consequently workers will have a consciousness and culture that is consistent to their working class level. However, since the production of culture is created through the interaction of the relations of production, workers are exposed partly to those values and culture of the ruling class, which is the prevailing culture of the state. Within this theory, people are basically socialized into a culture according to their class. However, I maintain that in addition to class, Indian, Metis, and Inuit peoples are socialized into a culture that includes not only class, but, also race/ethnicity and colonization.

In the white dominant society, class structure can be more easily determined and recognized than in most Aboriginal colonies and reserves. In the latter, class structure is much more difficult to determine because of the interaction of tribal customs, as well as the remnants of traditional Indian spirituality and communal societies. Within the working class structure, Metis, Indian, and Inuit peoples represent a subordinated group with a different cultural environment because they have different social relations to the productive forces. For instance, Natives are often given menial, casual jobs, and seldom belong to unions. Within internal Aboriginal colonies, class structure and working conditions can be manipulated both internally and externally by imperialist forces. Hence, class structure and culture can be formed and restructured somewhat by the colonizer's personal control, and not exclusively by the social relations of production. Within Veltmeyer's class category, Indians and Metis workers would be classified as Rural Subproletariat.[3] They are the lowest paid and most oppressed section of the working class, commonly referred to as 'low class.'

The concept 'low class' is used to classify a group of workers who do unskilled, menial work within a class society. It is, however, a purely subjective fabrication; not an objective structure and is a classification peculiar to a bourgeois society. The definition of 'low class' distinguishes the nature and type of work according to an imaginary social scale such as unskilled and dirty jobs. Since most Indians and Metis work in these type of jobs, they are classified as low class. Workers in this classification are stigmatized and stereotyped in a negative way. Low class is allowed to exist because of the culture and ethos of capitalism. In order for a capitalistic society to preserve its social values of mobility, success and achievement, the society must have a ladder of social class; otherwise, a hierarchy of social classes could not exist. Consequently, upper, middle and low class would be meaningless. Since the Establishment determines the nature and controls the national culture it also determines the category of workers and the type of culture for that class. Aboriginal people, being powerless, colonized and discriminated against, are as a matter of course designated as 'low class' workers. This classification has no relationship to intelligence, skill, or personality. Rather it has a great deal to do with ethnic, race and oppression. For example, colonized, Aboriginal peoples are driven to self-denigration within their communities. These are cultural patterns of racial colonized groups, and not necessarily of a particular economic class. These patterns are due to the peculiar history and the restructured culture of Native peoples. In empirical terms, 'low class' workers are of the subproleteriat class and their culture corresponds to that class.

To claim that a culture of the subproleteriat is an inferior culture is a distortion and misrepresentation. The fact that the majority of Aboriginal people are economically poor, does not mean that they are culturally poor. To make such an assumption that white middle class is the standard of measure for 'good quality' culture, suggests that all lesser levels of culture are expected to aspire to the level of the supposedly superior and higher middle class culture. This makes bourgeois mainstream culture a prominent social value which dominates the ideology of capitalism. Those of us, who are labelled as subproleteriat are seen as vulgar, crude and unwashed, because white middle and upper classes command it. Therefore, because I do not enjoy or appreciate opera and symphony music, I am classified as being coarse, rude and unpolished. As a unique society, Indians and Metis have never been allowed to participate and share fully as cultural equals in the dominant mainstream society. There is a paradox, however. While Indian and Metis peoples have been largely excluded form white middle class culture, at the same time, they have been socialized to some extent to the cultural and ideological hegemony of the nation. This causes a certain frustration and hostility among Aboriginal peoples, which is largely due to the contradiction between the ideal and the reality of capitalistic culture. Those persons who deny the reality of Aboriginal culture argue that Indians and Metis think and live very much like white middle class Canadians. Fundamentally this is incorrect.

Historically, we have not emulated white European Canadian society. In the 250 years of the fur trade, Indians were forced into a segregated fur gathering class and kept completely isolated from the white imperialist merchants. Indians were forbidden to live close to European trading posts. Both, the British and French maintained a strict caste system with regards to Aboriginal workers. Although Metis had a blood link to Europeans, the mixed blood population was an outcast from the white conquerors. After the fur trade, Indians were imprisoned in rural compounds on isolated regions in an apartheid system. Metis were forced into similar colonies, rural ghettos and road allowances maintained under vagrancy laws dictated by white bureaucratic oppressors.

The segregation of Aboriginal peoples from white mainstream society was a deliberate strategy employed by the state. This separation tended to reinforce stereotypical images of indigenous peoples who were cast aside as being dirty, lazy, vulgar, and unsuitable to live amongst so-called civilized and clean white society. These images become internalized and Native peoples developed a shame and inferiority complex about their culture. As a result we function within this colonized framework of culture and thus legitimize the stereotyping of our culture and personality. However, since the Native national movement of the 1960s, the Native young people have become outspoken about the hypocrisy, and are inclined towards rejection of mainstream culture. This movement has caused them to align more closely and intimately to their true indigenous culture, which serves to enrich, revitalize and expand within the appropriate subproleteriat class structure. It has resulted in an upsurge in the direction of humanism and collectivism.

The 1960s nationalist movement created a new cultural awakening among the Aboriginal people throughout Canada. It caused them to redefine themselves from their colonized position. Aboriginal communities began to recognize the need to assert their own definitions, to reclaim their history and culture. They began to create their own sense of nationhood. The movement forced a reassessment of racial stereotypes which had dehumanized us for centuries. There arose a terminology and ethos particular to our culture that gave us a new sense of pride and confidence. We referred to ourselves as brothers and sisters which emerged from the realization that we have a common blood bond among us. It became important for us to know our true heritage and culture.

One of the most important developments during the decade of the 1960s was the evolvement of a new cultural consciousness. This was the first step towards the recognition that as Aboriginal people we are a separate ethnic/racial group, and that we were challenging the comfortable white middle class society. We were questioning, but also contesting the old values and institutions of colonization. We were searching for new and different forms of political and cultural structures to solve economic problems. At the same time we were careful to broaden the base of political participation to include the masses of underclass Aboriginal people, and to include them in the decision making processes.

When Aboriginal peoples first started to speak out during the 1960's they spoke with a certain anger and hostility. They expressed their deep discontent of the white middle class culture and language. We spoke in definite unrefined terms which were stereotypical of our colonized/underclass culture. Our angry and direct language was a sharp contrast to that of the traditional chiefs and Metis leaders who had played the puppet role and who had used accommodative, submissive language. It was the first time that the imperialist ruler had been challenged by Indians and Metis in the last 100 years. Our language expressed frustration, empowerment, and violence. Our liberation spirit had become strong and powerful. It was linked to a national political ideology that inspired Indian and Metis activists. Instead of trying to cloak our subproleteriat class, it became a source of strength and pride.

When colonized people challenge the colonial system, as Indian and Metis people did in the 1960s then a change takes place in the colonial/class culture and language, the underclass colonized culture becomes a positive and forceful factor towards liberation. The oppressed Aboriginal population were anxious to identify themselves with rude and anti-middle class concepts, such as 'warrior, trapper, breed, bannock-eaters, etc.' These were expressions of counter-consciousness and counter-culture. It was the language that main-stream whites and academics called rhetoric and sloganeering. Colonized language was threatening and offensive to them.

An ethnic/race culture, such as the Indian/Metis culture, becomes viable and proud when it is activated in conjunction with a progressive political working class consciousness. At the same time, the typical negative stereo-types, such as 'low class' or 'culture of poverty' decline or disappear. Lewis claims that this has occurred among the Cuban poor. [4] During my stay in Cuba, I found that there is no 'low class' workers and no 'culture of poverty.' All workers are employed in dignity and paid a wage that provides comfort-able living conditions. Hence, no welfare system. My experience supports the premise that an ethnic/racial group will not be effected by negative stereo-types in a socialist society. However, in Canada, as capitalism is the base of our society the stigma of 'low class' culture is extremely powerful in inferi-orizing and intimidating that section of the population, which includes the majority of Indian and Metis people. This is painful because of the fact that the Native people in Canada have been stripped of certain aspects of their tra-ditional, authentic culture and their institutions.

Linguistic Imperialism

In our cultural renaissance there are certain concepts and movements which we should understand and give attention to. The first of these is lin-guistic imperialism. Language is more specifically, a linguistic code that communicates and indoctrinates all individuals to a particular set of values and culture. How individuals are socialized into society depends largely on the ethnic/race group and social class to which they belong. However, in the case of internal colonies these factors will be co-mingled with racism and col-onization. People from different ethnic/race and class vary in their linguistic code and in their use and knowledge of speech. For example, individuals from white middle class speak more articulately and with more varied vocab-ulary than individuals in the colonized underclass. However, the language differences between white middle class and Aboriginal underclass is not in the quality of language; eg., the degree of excellence; but in its use; eg. how well it serves the people of that class or group. The nature and level of lan-guage comes from the occupational and race/colonial experiences. For instance, the language of Indian/Metis workers in subproleteriat jobs use a style and level of language that is culturally common for them in terms of their communication within their colonial, and occupational community. On

127

the other hand, white middle level bureaucrats and teachers use more sophisticated style and level of language which is 'proper' and effective for their social class.

An important value of middle class culture is correct 'Standard English.' The failure to speak such language has long been a definite mark of low status and class. As a result, considerable emphasis is put on the importance of white Standard English. There is an assumption that it is the only proper language for effective communication and thought. It has a definite social status in the Anglo-Euro-American society, but at the same time carries a certain hypocrisy. This type of English is held as being superior to any other language or speech pattern. Searle argues that the "English language has been a monumental force, institution of oppression and rabid exploitation throughout 400 years of imperialist history."[5] There is no doubt that it has scorned and mocked indigenous languages throughout the world. English has served to humiliate and subjugate the masses of many Aboriginal nations as well as to impose the notion that language and speech patterns of Indian and Metis peoples are inferior.

Language can be seen as content specific. This means that it is specific to that ethnic/race class. The differences are not only the spoken language but also the cultural content. Concepts and perceptions are reinforced by stimuli and responses from that particular cultural environment. The symbols and concepts that are embedded in that particular language shapes the style of speech for that group of people. Therefore, Indians and Metis express thought and concepts that are unique to their language. Information and communication can be readily perceived and understood if it is within the linguistic code of that particular ethnic/class. Therefore the denial of our Aboriginal languages denies us confidence and the articulation of full creative expression. A culture cannot develop without a language; thus the stamping-out of Aboriginal languages has halted the development of Indian culture. In other words, the loss of Aboriginal languages was the loss of much indigenous culture and history. Also, language that conveys negative views of the colonized can cause serious damage to the culture. Distorted notions, such as the following can be very destructive: ". . . the weaker, more primitive tribal life simply collapsed and fell apart as it met a more advanced civilization."[6]

From this information we can understand that the situation within a colonial society is that the function of the colonizer's language is to promote political and cultural domination over Native people. For Indians and Metis this has been English and French, as they are imperialist languages. Although most of us speak the colonizer's language, it does not mean that we embrace all of its culture or ideology. English is seen as necessary for communication and social efficiency among Aboriginal people throughout most of Canada. It is the language which the ruling class understands, and therefore can be used as the language to express our protest and liberation.

During the Native nationalist struggles of the 1960s the English language was used to highlight concepts and notions of racism, inequality, oppression, and apartheidism. In the struggle it was important to bring to the mainstream's attention and reality those abuses and inequalities within Canadian society. Terminology which expressed these realities of suppression and injustices was important and effective as liberation language and served to bring to the public's attention the realization of the Nation's apartheidism.

In the struggles of the 1960s the Indian and Metis militants used certain words with scorn and contempt, such as 'racist pigs, white honkeys, Uncle Tomahawks' and so on. Naturally, the white middle class and the media condemned them as vulgar sloganeering and rhetoric. At that time this was sufficient to inform us that such abrupt language was effective in a counter-consciousness struggle. It is not until the Aboriginal underclass is able to publicly and unanimously voice their concerns using the colonizers own weapons (to Native peoples benefit), such as language, that the reality of the colonized situation can be rectified. As long as the Native colony remains silent, then no threat is posed against the ruling class culture, and at the same time very little achievements are made in the Native culture.

Literature/Arts as Empowerment

The Aboriginal cultural protest of the 1960s and 70s was not only a counter-cultural expression, but a 'return to the source.' It was a revival or a renaissance of Indian, Metis and Inuit culture and nationalism. In the decolonization process, it is the Aboriginal of the underclass that make the first significant contributions. In a colonized culture where written creative literature is sparse, autobiographies, and poetry are the first in national rejuvenation. This is so, because the first expression is to release the pain and suffering of our lives before we can proceed to the next level of more deliberate and rational thought and writing. Indian and Metis traditional culture became the context of the new publications. Self-identity and pride of indigenous society became expressions in the new manuscripts and publications. Some Aboriginal writers and artists succeeded in expressing a specific cultural heritage by selecting appropriate Indian and Metis themes in their style of writing. The story, *Halfbreed* by Maria Campbell is a deeply moving semi-autobiography committed to traditional values of the Native society. Campbell combined description and comment very effectively with analysis and personal commentary. *Slash* by Jeannette Armstrong portrays the self-contained work of Aboriginal society and the conflict of the intruding white man's world. In addition, she makes a considerable analysis in the personal experiences of the colonial situation. Lee Maracle in *Bobbie Lee: Indian Rebel* brings to life the grim realities of the struggle of Indian and Metis workers, and how they survive in the brutal white supremist system. Lee's simple and direct words convey the powerful feelings experienced by rank and file Aboriginal people. These artists and others played a major role in launching the cultural renaissance; as well they also enriched Aboriginal literature. The majority of Indian and Metis writers are not necessarily highly educated, and that may be a good thing, as Native writing has tended to be more candid and less academic in style.

Unfortunately, in white Canadian society, Aboriginal literature has to exist largely according to the white mans' stereotype and in caricature form if it is to be successful on the market. To new renaissance Aboriginal artists and authors this is repugnant. We are determined to produce new and revitalized cultural creations that are authentic, and not fictitious. To go against our beliefs would not only be a fabrication but a mockery to our culture. Often, white liberals are quite anxious to usurp our creations, as well as to embrace them as successes of the imperialist bourgeois nation.

An example of this practice occurred at the University of Saskatchewan, Saskatoon, in July 1993. Tomson Highway, a prominent Cree playwright was giving a talk at the University, and a memo regarding the speaker was distributed. The memo read as follows: "He reads Dostoevsky, plays Chopin on the piano and sprinkles his conversation with references to classical Greek drama."[7] This is a mockery to Indian and Metis people. All references to Highway's success and greatness are to white European notables. It defines our Aboriginal creations through white imperial cultural heroes. Most white Canadians cannot seem to understand that Indian/Metis creations must be products that are consistent with our ethnic/race and class. Aboriginal culture is not an appendage of white supremacy bourgeois culture. Of course, as colonial artists, some are vulnerable to the flattery and patronage of the colonizer.

For Aboriginal artists it is difficult to straddle two cultures and classes without being hypocrites as well as frauds to our indigenous culture and class. It is precisely this paradoxical practice of either being mainstream or being true to Aboriginal culture that is so critical to the formation and revitalization of our Indian/Metis culture that forces our artists and authors into difficult decisions and creations.

Aboriginal literature and creative arts need to be expanded and elevated in their unique indigenous nature. Under such conditions, it is necessary to indigenize the English language as a medium of Aboriginal artistic and intellectual inventiveness. Indian and Metis authors must avoid portraying Aboriginal people in popular mainstream stereotypes. Enthusiastic reception by white middle class public is not necessarily a measure of literary or artistic success for Aboriginal literary artists. Popularity likely means that the Aboriginal story or creation harmonizes with the archaic racial stereotypes of eurocentric society. If it is not in accordance to these typical stereotypes, most white readers are likely to disbelieve or discredit the creative work.

The present position in the Aboriginal nation is a renaissance of self-conscious artists, authors, poets, actresses, film producers and intellectuals who hold strong national/class themes. It emerged from the nationalist movement of the 1960s and has become a successful reality within the last few years. The Indian/Metis consciousness and culture-building movement of today is stronger and more significant than ever in our history. It is crucial that we work in unison as an Aboriginal nation, and not in terms of tribal units and middle class pretenders. It is inevitable that our productions reveal colonization, oppression, racism and subproleteriat class; however, they will also reveal decolonization, Aboriginal traditions, spirituality, freedom and liberation.

Cultural Nationalism

Another cultural viewpoint in the Aboriginal renaissance that needs critical examination by Indian and Metis authors, artists and intellectuals is cultural nationalism. The core notion of cultural nationalism is that a subordinated underclass is dominated by a more powerful European group within a total political order. It means being a member of a particular racial/ethnic group that is culturally different and unique from the dominant white group. The subordinated group is an indigenous nation that has developed a counter consciousness with the aim of moving from subordination to independence. Cultural nationalism can also be defined as Aboriginal nationalism, because it constitutes Indian, Metis and Inuit groups. Aboriginal nationalism can be seen as the demise of imperialism and all the ugliness of the Euro-Canadian Christian society. It is the rejection of white supremacy and the values that represent oppression racism, passionate individualism, consumerism and the torture of racial/ethnic groups, as experienced by the Innu at Davis Inlet.

The aim of Aboriginal nationalism, is to restore, revive and preserve Aboriginal history and traditional culture. It means that Native people look inward to their own private world of indigenous customs, rituals, symbols and language. In cultural nationalism there is a reconstruction of authentic Aboriginal history and heritage, and at the same time, a rejection of the stereotypical images of white supremacy. Efforts are made to correct the ugly distortions of the culture and to construct a new positive vision. By confronting white domination, Aboriginal nationalism does more than draw together sentiments and attitudes that go into a collective. It also embodies them into a heightened form that moves toward a positive national culture. This serves to give identity to the racial underclass group and strengthens its internal cohesion.

Cultural nationalism generates from a desire to reverse an intolerable situation, and to challenge the legitimacy of the dominant system. It is a desire for freedom from both domination and contempt. Cultural quality and the unique characteristics of the Aboriginal nation is the main focus of Aboriginal nationalism. For Indian and Metis peoples, nationalism develops out of experiences as fur trappers, voyageurs, buffalo hunters, isolation in racial colonies, and most importantly from the struggles against imperialism, suppression and colonization.

Since the Canadian Aboriginal renaissance of the 1970s cultural nationalism has become the norm. It has resulted in an explosion of Aboriginal creations in the fields of literature, art, theatre, video productions, etc. There has been a shift from the old style of arts and crafts to new creative expressions, aesthetically and artistically, without sacrificing the traditional essence. At the same time it is a statement of self-affirmation of pride of heritage and of identity. It is not unusual today to find Indians and Metis who were previously denying their Aboriginal identity, to now proclaim their Indian ancestry. Generally we as Aboriginal peoples are not seeking integration into mainstream society; instead, we are praising our Aboriginal nationalism. We know that integration can only be superficial, casual and trivial.

Without a radical ideological base, however, cultural nationalism can be an oppressive, colonizing force. As a result, cultural nationalism can be an elusive and risky force in a liberation struggle. It is easy for the colonizer to manipulate the Native people who are politically and culturally weak and vulnerable. The colonizer can change cultural nationalism from being a strong feeling of Aboriginal nationalism to cultural imperialism. It then becomes a force in self-suppression—an opium of the masses. Native people who adhere to cultural imperialism accept a situation of submissiveness and obedience. Often the result is a pseudo-Indian nationalism which looks back to the traditional Indian customs, ritualism and false spirituality that is destructive and oppressive. As Metis and Indian artists we need to be on continuous alert to prevent cultural nationalism from becoming cultural imperialism.

Cultural Imperialism

Cultural imperialism is one of the most oppressive forms of colonization. It is a form of policy and activity by the colonizer to subjugate Indian and Metis peoples ever deeper into colonization. It manipulates our people into distorted and deceptive cultural activities that serve to obscure political awareness and action. The lack of counter-consciousness for political transformation keeps indigenous culture in a state of fakery and mockery. Cultural imperialism is the re-tribalization of Native culture to the stone age level. Such a backward step is cultural genocide. It is an act of returning to pre-conquest rituals and beliefs that have been emptied of power and have become meaningless. These are 'primitive' cultural creations by the colonizer, and are not appropriate for current Indian and Metis cultural references. Through centuries of imperialism, indigenous customs and institutions have become ossified. Today, they are a mockery of our contemporary culture.

Cultural imperialism is characterized by Natives' weakened cultural identity. The state takes advantage of this situation by promoting contrived Aboriginal traditionalism. Cultural imperialism usually is a reactionary form of nationalism emphasizing outdated and archaic rituals. The state promotes it because it hinders Natives' development of progressive political ideas. Government officials recognize the significance of cultural imperialism as a control mechanism. They generously fund archaic Aboriginal ceremonies and activities, thereby reinforcing an ossified and caricatural culture. Aboriginal culture is now packaged and paraded before white spectators throughout Europe. The tourism agency, TourQuest of Regina, has packaged a group of Indian dancers "who will perform wearing traditional feather headdress and beaded costumes" on a holiday package tour for overseas companies.[8] Canadian governments impede Natives' development of a political consciousness, thereby keeping them vulnerable to manipulation. Rather than uniting on the basis of national liberation Metis and Indians are led backward to greater oppression. They think that government-sponsored Native performances are signs of their growing freedom, but nothing could be further from the truth. Cultural imperialism is a retreat from the necessary class and political struggle—it is a form of political and cultural oppression.

Many Indian ceremonies and pow-wows have become cultural imperialist performances. At the same time they are commercial performances that entertain the white public who hold typical racist views. The Indian show at the Calgary Stampede is a display of caricature traditions and culture. Much of Indian spirituality has also become an aspect of cultural imperialism. It is deeply entrenched in the Indian Ecumenical Festival held at Stoney reserve, Alberta every summer. This is a huge ceremony that is generously supported by the Bureau of Indian Affairs and several of the established churches. The fact that these ceremonies are funded by the government and established churches clearly indicates that they are a function of cultural imperialism. The Glenbow Museum in Calgary and the Batoche Museum are beacons of this concept. The Shell Oil Company, which is the main support for the Glenbow Museum is the major oil company 'operated' in the apartheid regime in South Africa. Not only are these institutions mockeries of Aboriginal culture, but they are powerful diversions from counter-consciousness and political liberation.

Cultural Imperialism also functions within the Metis society. The most prominent activity is the 'Back to Batoche' celebration held annually in Saskatchewan. The fact that a Metis performance is held at the location of our ancestors' defeat in the liberation struggle of 1885 is a retreat to subjugation and colonization. Batoche is the site of the white oppressor's triumph over the Metis and their revolution for freedom. While it gives a cultural appearance of a Mardis Gras, it is a trek and a replay of our Waterloo. No political discussions or activities are allowed. This event is controlled by the sixty-thousand dollars granted from the Federal Government to the Metis National Council which administers the celebration. The ultimate insult to our ancestors who died fighting for our freedom is the parade of the RCMP— the murderers of our dead heroes. How culturally and historically ignorant can we become? The government mocks us more every year.

These types of performances give the illusion to Indians and Metis that they are celebrating emancipation and cultural renaissance. In reality, they are celebrating the glorification of the white oppressor and his murderous victory over our ancestors and nation. Indian and Metis leaders obviously do not recognize the profound oppression of cultural imperialism, but the colonizers do. It is a caricature form of Native culture which the colonized have internalized as their authentic culture. Thus it becomes political oppression of the worst type. These Aboriginal people behave and perform in functions that are consistent with forms and practices of 'primitive' society. These Natives feel that this type of tribal culture automatically brings them freedom and liberation from their oppressors.

Of course, having Metis and Indians explore their identity and culture is not necessarily dangerous nor negative, providing self-awareness includes a political consciousness. Cultural imperialism often does not. It is a false form of nationalism stressing legends and myths the state uses to direct Natives' attention away from revolutionary nationalism. Cultural imperialism rejects issues of class struggle and, therefore, leads Aboriginals to accept domination uncritically and submissively. A genuine, liberating nationalism must include and promote revolutionary and working class and socialist ideologies; these are essential and perhaps the greatest weapons Natives need to win their struggle for self-determination. Nationalism in its subjective, ideological, and even spiritual forms should provide Aboriginals with a sense of solidarity and pride that moves them forward, not backward. A sense of identity rests with understanding a common history and heritage, as well as the community's collective place in the mainstream society.

A counter reaction to cultural imperialism is revolutionary nationalism, which serves as a basic ideology for freedom and self-determination. It is a nationalism that is progressive; politically and culturally. Revolutionary nationalism is a force for the transformation of the socio-economic system. It is a motivation for changing the structure and institutions of capitalism to a new society of freedom, equality and justice. It is more than a reform of the existing racist, colonizing institutions. It is more than multiculturalism and sensitizing white supremist Canadians to their racism. It is a complete change of the colonial structure of capitalism and domination of pseudo-apartheidism in Canadian culture and bureaucracy.

Culture of The Aboriginal Petty Bourgeoisie

The Aboriginal petty bourgeoisie has become an increasingly significant force over the last twenty years. Today, they are one of the major forces in the Indian /Metis nations—thanks to the promotion and support of the Federal and Provincial neo-colonial governments. As a class, it consists of a large group of various Aboriginal middle class types. The most visible is the comprador leaders of Indian and Metis national organizations, such as the Assembly of First Nations, the Metis National Council and the former Native Council of Canada. The numerous individual hangers on to these organizations are part of that petty bourgeoisie clan. The next largest group would be the professionals and intellectuals, namely teachers, lawyers, social workers, academics and accountants. Governments have sponsored programs in these areas so extensively over the last twenty years that the public market for Aboriginal teachers, lawyers, etc. has been flooded.

The third large group of petty bourgeoisie are small business operators, administrators, program directors, etc. Although the majority of these Indian and Metis trainees continue on government grants or welfare, they are, nevertheless, now part of the petty bourgeoisie pattern. Driven by the need to establish a sense of personal identity, this middle class is caught between the romantic Hollywood Indian and the mythical traditional 'primitive.' They have a fanatical desire to achieve mastery of the colonizer's cultural practices and language.

The moral and intellectual corruption of the Aboriginal bourgeoisie is brought about as a result of the barbarizing character of western civilization. The behavioral and personality changes they have undergone are purely superficial and deceptive. "It is simply a shift from one style of life to another, not a fundamental transformation from one life to another."[9] The freedom they have gained is simply the privilege of eating at the master's table, assuming his attitudes and adopting his behaviour. The Native petty bourgeoisie have long been pampered by the European oppressors. Yet, they accept servitude and contempt, because they have fear of death of their class. Such death means a loss of their funding, pay-check, social and material status.

The Indian/Metis bourgeoisie are without an Aboriginal value system. They do exactly the same as their white oppressors. They speak the same bureaucratic language, think the same notions, value the same objects, and have the same taste. LeRoi Jones argues that the internalization of a white middle class system will always militate for white decisions about the way middle class society should be.[10] Since the Indian/Metis bourgeoisie live largely in the white middle class structure of make-believe, the masks which they wear to play their sham life-style, social roles and attitudes conceal the feeling of inferiority, frustration and hypocrisy that haunt their inner lives. Although they loudly proclaim their Indian heritage, they desperately attempt to escape from the real identity with the Aboriginal subproleteriat. However, they are only fooling themselves. They cannot escape the mark of racism and colonization culture.

In attempting to evade identification with the Indian/Metis subproleteriat they have developed a self-hatred that reveals itself in their disparaging of the cultural and language characteristics of 'lower-class' Aboriginal population. Their feelings of inferiority and insecurity are shown in their pathological struggle for status among their own people and for recognition in the white society. Their escape into a society of make-believe leaves them with feeling of non-fulfillment and fakery. As a result, they constantly flee into new pretensions.

These Aboriginal petty bourgeoisie try to shield themselves against racial discrimination, and the contempt of the white as they pretend at assimilation. However, despite efforts to insulate themselves and the children against the semi-apartheid society, they cannot evade racism and colonization. The majority of Aboriginal bourgeoisie would deny that they reject their Indianness, and the desire to be white, since this would be a confession of their inferiority and hypocrisy. Instead, they constantly boast of their pride in their identification and heritage of Indian or Metis. Their feeling of inferiority is revealed in their fear of competition with whites.

It is for this reason that they struggle, fanatically to establish and maintain Indian and Metis organizations and institutions that are segregated exclusively for Aboriginal people. Organizations such as the Assembly of First Nations, Metis National Council and the former Native Council of Canada work furiously to obtain massive government grants that will maintain their continuance. Likewise, the multitude of government programs that promote small business entrepreneurship and economic development for Aboriginal individuals are areas that the Indian /Metis bourgeoisie preserve as their exclusive domain. Any new employees hired from the Aboriginal subproletariat are required to adopt the petty bourgeoisie culture, language and ideology. If they do not, they are not only fired, but also ostracized.

Indian/Metis bourgeoisie are the most vocal in demanding the right to compete on equal terms with whites; yet, they will discriminate against white workers in their Native organizations, institutions and programs. They prefer the security afforded on the monopoly on their exclusive occupations within their segregated Aboriginal organizations and programs. This particular class is notorious for their inefficiency and corruption in the management of their organizations and institutions.

Because of the fear of competition from whites it probably accounts for the reason they fear first rate performance within their own ranks. When an Indian or Metis is highly trained and competent, and insists upon reasonably good work, this class will accuse him of trying to be a white man. As President of the Metis Society of Saskatchewan in the early 1970s, I experienced this situation. In education, I held a University degree, and as leader of the organization I pressured for efficiency, accountability and avoidance of corruption. Within a short time, I was accused by the Metis bourgeoisie of being a white man, and using his policies and procedures. The Executive and Board members insisted on haphazard and unaccountable methods, although the Society was being supported and financed by the Trudeau government. This Native bourgeoisie has continued to dominate the Native communities. Today they slavishly follow the customs and standards of the white middle class bureaucratic society.

The self-hatred of Aboriginal bourgeoisie is shown in their keen competition for status and recognition that exists among themselves. It stems partly from the lack of self-esteem and inferiorization as colonized people. For the bourgeoisie, it also results from the frustrations which they encounter in attempting to obtain recognition from the white society. There is constant criticizing, and belittling of individual Metis and Indians who achieve recognition or status above them, and whose ideology is contrary to their views. This seems to be an obvious practice with some exclusively Aboriginal owned and operated publication businesses. They prefer to foster the eurocentricism and racism of white authors and academics rather than Indians and Metis.

It seems that it is often difficult for Aboriginal bourgeoisie to cooperate in any field of Native endeavor. This failure, according to Frazier, is because in every (Native) he encounters his own self-contempt. It is as if he said, "You are only a (Native) like myself; so why should you be in a position above me."[11] This is indeed a mark of the culture of colonization, and a critical problem in national and class unity. The Indian or Metis who elevates him/herself above the underclass masses apparently feels that he/she has created an image of prestige, which will result in envy from the 'lower class.' He has created a world of make-believe to protect himself from the harsh cultural and economic realities of society. This mythical 'success, fame, wealth, achievement,' which is bestowed on individual Indians and Metis by the establishment and media is a hoax. The Canadian media has given extensive patronizing and applause to the national leaders of the Assembly of First Nations and the Native Council of Canada. This is noted in a cover story by the *Saturday Night Magazine*:

That evening in the Winnipeg Convention Centre, Ovide Mercredi is a good speaker. The words come in deliberate, measured bars, each note inflected upward and punctuated by a formal pause. If whites were allowed to vote, he says, I'd win. It was apparent that he straddled the white and Native worlds easily, his closet, a melange of expensive suits, tribal dress, and western shirts. He grew up speaking Cree and was trained in white law.[12]

These Aboriginal bourgeoisie often neglect issues which are of concern to the members of the subproleteriat Aboriginal communities whom they are supposed to be representing. Instead, they devote their time and energy to issues such as the Constitution. These leaders have lost identification and communication with those Indian and Metis peoples in the rural colonies and urban ghettos. These leaders are inclined to believe that their 'wealth and prestige' will gain them acceptance into white mainstream society. The greatest delusion of all, however, is power. It is one of the main factors of colonization culture. As a result, we are inclined to focus excessively on gaining some semblance of power. The only positions of power for Indian and Metis individuals is within the Aboriginal nation. The top leadership positions in the national Native organizations are the prizes of power. Although these positions are only token, Aboriginal leaders delude themselves into thinking that they are in the circle of power of Canadian society. The constitutional talks of the late 1980s, the First Ministers Conference on Aboriginal Constitutional Matters, were a 'field day' for the petty bourgeoisie leaders because they were called into negotiations with the top ministers to give advice. These meetings gave the Aboriginal bourgeois leaders a temporary moment to bask in the sun of power, only to realize later that these talks were nothing more than a political dance around the table.

Part Four

Maintaining Colonization Under Neocolonialism

Chapter Eleven

Constitutional Colonialism

"Canada's Aboriginal people are front and centre in the debate over the Constitution . . . [T]heir demands for constitutional recognition, self-government and land claims played a major role."[1] So read one Canadian newspaper during the recent constitutional fiasco that led to the birth and death of the Charlottetown Accord. Why did this turn-about for Aboriginal people take place? Throughout Canada's history, Aboriginal people have never been given any consideration—other than to exploit them—in constitutional negotiations. *The British North America Act of 1867* does not contain a single clause about the legal rights of Indians, Metis, and Inuit. In recent years, however, rich resources—most notably oil, but also gas, uranium and water—have been found on Aboriginal people's land. A change in the ruling class to transnational corporations has created an even greater demand for such raw materials. But because of a different attitude toward Aboriginal people at the level of international human rights, the colonizer could no longer use 17th-century tactics of plunder and violence to get what he wanted. So, the colonizer had to use a more subtle strategy to gain inroads to the coveted prizes by maintaining a pretense of negotiating constitutional issues with Aboriginals. Also, the Conservative government under the former Prime Minister Mulroney was having serious problems with Quebec and its threat to separate. By highlighting Aboriginal issues in constitutional negotiations, the federal government pushed the Quebec issue to the background. All of these reasons, however, do not to take away from the fact that Aboriginal people had become politically sophisticated and aggressive since their liberation struggles of the 1960s.

Constitutional colonialism is European encroachment upon Aboriginal sovereignty and territory. It extends back in history to when European powers first interfered with the internal affairs of indigenous societies, and gradually established a system to dispossess and suppress Aboriginals. The goals of 'civilizing' and 'christianizing' were pushed as excuses to undermine the power and legal authority of indigenous states. Using alliances with neighbouring tribes to attack Native collectives, the British and French gradually weakened the economic and military strength of powerful nations, such as the Iroquois. The colonizer used documents like the *Royal Proclamation of 1763* to further encroach upon Native governments, to weaken them, seize Aboriginal land and resources, and to proclaim absolute control over the indigenous people. They were forced into several unequal and unjust treaties, accords, and pacts. Some of the more outrageous of these colonial treaties were those the British Euro-Canadians made with the Indians during the late 1800s.

Constitutional colonialism is always a protracted, hostile affair between the European plunderers and the indigenous societies. The conquest of one nation by another is never a quick or pleasant event. European conquest of North America took almost 250 years, and involved a series of brutal wars and genocide. Although the indigenous peoples fought fiercely and won several battles, in the end they were conquered and subjugated to colonial oppression. Constitutional colonialism eventually completes this process by seizing control of all Aboriginal land, resources, and rights. Constitutional colonialism follows the practices of plunder and greed, which are the basic principles of most constitutions.

The new colonizer state rules that Aboriginals "have to be kept in a condition of tutelage and treated as wards of children of the state."[2] British colonialism everywhere adhered to the Cecil Rhodes doctrine: "The Native is to be treated as a child and denied the franchise. We must adopt the system of despotism."[3] Tracing the development of the Canadian Constitution within this context, it is difficult to understand why the *Royal Proclamation of 1763* is held up as the Aboriginal people's Magna Carta. Why some establishment historians and Aboriginal elites hold this document in such high regard is a puzzle.

How could the *Royal Proclamation*—or even why should it—show preference to the Indians? This statute was drawn up by British imperialists after bitter and fierce wars with several Indian nations under Chief Pontiac. North America was under the authoritarian rule of the British military regime. Britain gave herself exclusive claim to Indian territory, preventing Indians from selling their own land, which they occupied. Indians could only 'sell' the land to Britain. But why should Britain buy what she already possessed by conquest. Did Attila the Hun pay for Rome? In effect, the *Royal Proclamation of 1763* declared British ownership of Indian territory. Indians were given the right to hunt on this territory, but they were stripped of all their rights to possession and control of their land. The Proclamation simply made a specific area of land into an Indian reserve in a manner that later became the standard for all Canadian Indian reserves.

And yet today, this type of constitutional colonialism has captivated the imagination of Aboriginal politicians who believe the Proclamation to be some sort of Magna Carta. Aboriginal leaders have deceived themselves into believing that the colonizer's constitution actually provides Aboriginals with certain rights and claims. With manipulative documents like the *Royal Proclamation*, the colonizer has been able to convince Indians that they have historical rights and should participate in constitutional negotiations—it's only a matter of negotiation. The Canadian federal government has been playing constitutional games with Aboriginal people by making such deceptive promises. A Royal Commission on Aboriginal people claims that "This arrangement [*Royal Proclamation*] is the historical basis of the enduring constitutional relationship between Aboriginal nations and the Crown, and provides the source of the Crown's fiduciary duties to those nations."[4] Such misleading propaganda misinforms Aboriginals and serves to maintain Aboriginal oppression. In this way, the state maintains constitutional oppression of Aboriginals.

Constitutional colonialism in its imperial formation also purposefully develops a bureaucracy and judicial system of oppression. This was clearly proven in the 1991 Gitskan Wet'suwet'en land claims case in British Columbia. After many months of court hearings in which the Indians and their fleet of lawyers presented their arguments, Judge McEarchan concluded that "the Aboriginal rights of the Natives were lawfully extinguished by the Crown in the colonial period."[5] He further said that "the Proclamation of 1763 has never had any application or operation in British Columbia"[6] McEarchan, however, noted that Indians had user rights "confined to berry picking, hunting, trapping and other 'Aboriginal' pursuits."[7] McEarchan's decision denied the Indians title to the land they claimed. It was a shock to Indians across Canada. However, if one fully appreciates the nature of imperial constitutions, one would see that the McEarchan decision is consistent with the private property principles of the ruling class—the basis of all imperial constitutions.

Aboriginal people, as well as white citizens, do not seem to realize that a constitution is a document made by imperialist conquerors and used to manage all individuals of the nation to their advantage. The development of constitutions in most imperial states has followed a similar pattern as the state advances from a colony to independence. In the early period of colonialism, it is imperial rulers of the mother nation who create constitutional documents. In Canada, it was the British industrial class, more specifically, the Canadian Pacific Railway Company, who drafted such documents. Their purpose was to get control of the colony's property and resources. The foremost issue in the minds of those drafting constitutional documents was to obtain control of land, raw materials, and markets.

The second condition common to producing constitutional documents is the exclusion of the masses from participating in the decision-making process. The majority of people have no say in drafting a constitution and, therefore, have no say in the allocation of resources. A constitution is constructed so that the public is kept ignorant or confused about the facts. Such was the case with the drafting of the Charlottetown Accord to amend Canada's Constitution. The public was given little opportunity of time to know and absorb the Accord's provisions. The manner in which the U.S. Constitution was established is another good example of how widespread ignorance surrounds constitution-making process. The U.S. document was "made by a small and active group of men immediately interested through their personal possessions. It was originated and carried through principally by four groups of personality interests . . . money, manufacturers, trade and shipping."[8] Only one-sixth of the adult male population voted on the ratification of the U.S. Constitution.[9] Needless to say, the Aboriginal population had no voice in the development or ratification of that document.

The third condition on which a constitution is based is the private property rights of the dominant class. Private property, which in Canada was all originally Indian land that was militarily seized from them, and placed beyond the reach and benefit of the nation's common people. In constructing constitutions, special efforts are made to guarantee that the constitution does not give the masses the power or rights to interfere with the property and powers of the dominant class. No matter how you look at it, a constitution provides what are virtually totalitarian powers to a small ruling elite, who suppress the masses and particularly, the nation's indigenous people.

When military violence is no longer necessary to overthrow indigenous sovereignty, the colonizer uses more subtle and deceptive—but equally effective—conquest tactics. Such type of constitutional colonialism was evident in the capture of Indian land through treaty agreements. Chiefs throughout Canada signed surrender treaties that they truly did not understand, but nevertheless, signed for small personal benefits. *Treaty Six* and other land treaties were among the Indians' worse defeats. Signed in 1876, *Treaty Six* states that "the Plains and Wood Cree Tribes of Indian inhabiting the district hereinafter described and defined do hereby cede, release, surrender and yield up to the government of the Dominion of Canada for Her Majesty the Queen forever, all their rights, titles and privileges whatsoever to the lands included within the following limits."[10] This tract of land "embraced an area of one hundred and twenty-one thousand square miles" in Saskatchewan.[11] The treaty is unmistakably clear, using four verbs to explicitly define the Aboriginals' surrender of land and their rights to the land. Indians who hunted and trapped for survival became "subject to such regulations as made by her government of Canada."[12] Thereafter, Indians had to have an imperial agent's permission before they could hunt a rabbit. *Treaty Six* and others like it became part of the Canadian Constitution.

Through the surrender of virtually all their land, Indians were confined to reserves; they were segregated and suppressed into an apartheid system. This is not to say that Indians were stupid, but the common people certainly put too much trust in their chiefs. They also knew that the Mounted Police were always close in the background. And yet the myth that "these nations [Britain and Indian] entered into relations on a basis of equality and mutual respect" continues to be propagated by the state's bureaucrats and the popular media.[13] What a heinous myth!

The Charlottetown Accord provided no new provisions, advancements, or improvements—except for what the government called the right to self-government—for the Aboriginal people of Canada. Neither Indians, Metis, nor Inuit were to be granted new rights or claims to land, resources, or legal or civil rights. Everything was channeled into the 'right to self-government.' The term 'self-government,' as a concept for structural change of the Constitution, was left far too vague to have any objective meaning. There were no specifics to give it validity or definitive meaning. Throughout the constitutional negotiations, self-government was nothing more than a distant, blurry vision; it was consistent with the language of typical colonizer constitutions. Ottawa politicians refused to spell out what it meant by self-government. For the Aboriginal people, self-government was a meaningless term and, therefore, had no interest to them. Regardless of how much propaganda the government produced to convince us to accept their 'definition' of self-government, the concept failed to interest the masses of Aboriginals. The Charlottetown Accord may have been a media event in the urban sections of the Aboriginal world, but it had very little impact on the reserves and in the Metis and Inuit colonies.

All evidence suggests that what the government meant by self-government was a political unit similar to a municipality. Such a political structure would have actually reduced the governing authority of reserve Band Councils and Metis Local Councils—it would have meant a move to even greater oppression. Self-government would not have served the interests of Canada's general indigenous population. Today, nation-states are systematically trying to eliminate indigenous people even further, because as many colonizers see it: "Indigenous people belong to the dustbin of history. They must disappear if modern states are to flourish."[14] In my view, the present time is the most appropriate time for Indians, Metis, and Inuit to develop self-determination, whereby we take possession and control of our land, resources, and achieve political autonomy.

State-sanctioned self-government is a move toward deeper colonization and suppression by the global corporate state. A good example of how self-government operates is the case of the Sechelt Indian Band in British Columbia. Although the government and media give much praise to this band for achieving self-government, many Indians regard the Sechelt situation as a sell-out in which the Sechelt Indians received very little for surrendering much of their land. This case reveals the problems many have in understanding self-government. To many people, self-government is nothing more than the administration of local council matters. However, the council has no autonomy. Self-government means the "constitutional entrenchment of the power of the Province and the role of the Indian agent in managing reserve lands."[15] Under these conditions, self-government means a loss of land claims, and an entrenchment of colonization. In my assessment, the Sechelt brand of self-government does not constitute any change for Aboriginal people's autonomy or sovereignty. No matter how much the whiteman praises their self-government, in the end it is still colonialism. Nor are all Aboriginal people blind to this fact. Some concerned members of the Sechelt Band, who live on the reserve have complained, stating, "We got rid of the *Indian Act*, but took the Indian agent with us. The Band Council . . . [is] good at dealing with everything, but the Aboriginal people."[16]

The most important single event of the latest round of constitutional negotiations which challenged the government's position in maintaining its standard oppression of Aboriginal people, was the work of the Native Women's Association of Canada. On the colonizer's doorstop, this informed and well-organized group of Aboriginal women from across the nation was determined to counter the oppression of constitutional colonialism.

In the summer of 1991, the Aboriginal Women's Unity Coalition held a demonstration in Winnipeg to publicize spousal violence and the oppression of women perpetrated by Indian men and chiefs. The Aboriginal women claimed, "Not only are we the victims of violence at the hands of Aboriginal men, our voice as women is not valued in the male-dominated political structures."[17] Later, a group of Aboriginal women from Manitoba and Ontario reserves warned against implementing Native self-government. They said it would entrench a dictatorial brand of leadership on Indian reserves. They argued that self-government was not possible without resolving violence and sexism in Aboriginal communities. Vice-President Grace Meconse stated, "When you look at the dictatorship type of leadership at the band level, you can only assume that self-government is a dictator-type government."[18]

The national women's organization, the Native Women's Association of Canada, under the leadership of Gail Stacey-Moore, attempted to gain the right to participate in the constitutional negotiations as an equal with the Native organizations represented by four men. The women were refused. Mulroney, then Constitutional Affairs Minister Joe Clark, and their Aboriginal brothers—Ovide Mercredi, Yvon Dumont, and Ron George—all opposed the women's requests. The Native women refused to accept their traditional and subjugated position and so launched a Federal Court action demanding a seat at the constitutional table. But the oppressive tentacles of the state reached out and crushed the women's efforts to build a new world order. The court refused to let the group participate in the talks. The Native women were locked out of the Charlottetown talks—a result of the powers of the colonial patriarchy.

Traditional colonization was re-enacted in 1992. Aboriginal male leaders co-operated with the colonizer's scheming demands. Demands that would eventually deepen oppression of not only Aboriginal women, but of the general Aboriginal population as well. All of this was not unlike the actions of Indian chiefs a century earlier when they signed treaties dispossessing Indians of what was rightfully theirs. Indians have been hoodwinked by the colonizer and once again in 1992 with the Charlettown Accord, the colonizer was trying to mislead them. The Aboriginal leaders participating in the latest constitutional fiasco must have understood what they were doing. They knew that the proposed amendments to the Constitution stated that "the duly constituted legislative bodies of Aboriginal jurisdiction would be Band Council and Chiefs."[19] That is, they understood that the power structure and administration of Indian reserves and women's inequality would remain unchanged.

Many Native women, however, were unwilling to be swept into continued powerlessness and subservience. They continued to argue that the 'inherent right to self-government' had to incorporate the *Charter of Rights and Freedoms* before the constitutional amendments could be passed. Quebec Native women complained that "self-government for us is going into something we don't know about."[20] Chief Mercredi tried to sidetrack the women's demands for equal rights by claiming that everyone was fighting for the same equality for both groups. He said, "As far as I'm concerned, there's no issue here."[21] He opposed the women's position that they should be protected by the *Charter of Rights and Freedoms*. It was quite apparent that both Native male leaders and government authorities considered Aboriginal women as advocates of female emancipation. The women were perceived as being politically astute, and thus having a greater sense of decolonization. Colonizing male bureaucrats did not want the problems of having to handle Aboriginal business with Native women.

The Native Women's Association of Canada was justified in seeking the same federal recognition and support given to the four male-dominated Aboriginal groups. The association was justified in claiming that "the national and local Aboriginal leadership is male-dominated and isn't sensitive to women's needs."[22] Most of the Aboriginal organizations were created or revived as a result of the civil rights struggles of the 1960s and are guilty of having a male-dominated structure. These organizations have changed only slightly in the past thirty years. Unless Aboriginal women exert pressure, these out-dated organizations will persist, especially considering the fact that the state supports and funds them. Even if the Native Women's Association disrupt the Aboriginal population, it is much better that Aboriginal internal conflicts are resolved and that an authentic democracy is established. Attempting to mask our internal conflicts from the media only promotes further inequality, injustice, and male domination.

Aboriginal participation in the constitutional negotiations was limited to four male-dominated organizations and their leaders—Ovide Mercredi of the Assembly of First Nations, Ron George of the Native Council of Canada, Yvon Dumont of the Metis National Council, and Mary Simon of the Inuit Tapirisat of Canada. It is not known why the government selected only these particular organizations to participate in the constitutional talks. Possibly, because they were well known to politicians and bureaucrats through the funding system. After years of receiving government funding, the Aboriginal leaders were obligated to the state and, therefore, deeply compromised. It was no mystery that these Native organizations had almost no contact with the mass of peripheral Native communities—communities which held a largely negative attitude toward the constitutional proposals. Although these four organizations and their spokesmen claimed they represented Canada's Aboriginal people, in actuality they were not representatives of the Indians, Metis, and Inuit. Mercredi and his colleagues did not visit rural communities and did not involve the Aboriginal people with constitutional issues. As a result, the leaders failed to obtain grass-roots support for constitutional change. This was clearly shown in the results of the October 26, 1992 referendum in which the majority of Indians and Metis voted NO to the Charlottetown Accord.

Almost every Aboriginal organization in Canada is a bureaucratic institution and not a true community or social movement organization. Because the organizations' funding comes from the federal and provincial governments, they must adhere to the state's strict guidelines. Furthermore, steady funding has made these organizations dependent on the state for all dimensions of their activities and even attitudes. Since the constitutional negotiations were primarily a media event and not a political conference, the Aboriginal spokesmen were the most appropriate choice 'to represent' Canada's Aboriginal population. Physically, they appeared Native; they dressed in stereotypical Aboriginal costumes, and performed in traditional ceremonies. They presented a pleasing manner and appearance to the white mainstream population.

In a constitutional encounter, the government has all the power. Discussions take place in their home offices and according to their rules of order. All activities and decisions are made within the confines of the 'seats of the mighty.' The Aboriginal representatives were on alien territory and totally dependent on the state, which they were supposedly opposing. The Native masses did not support the Aboriginal leaders. The majority of Aboriginals, scattered in their distant communities, are beyond the pale of constitutional negotiations. What action or opposition could the Native leaders take when government officials denied them any or all requests? Nothing. The Native leaders were politically impotent. Furthermore, because they were selected to represent all Canadian Aboriginals, any decision imposed on the representative organizations would automatically reflect on all Native people in Canada.

All Native organizations in Canada now follow a constitutional strategy. It was encouraged by the government because it was ultimately in the interest of the government for Native people to follow this strategy; which seeks a pseudo-government for Native people. But this can only come about if Native people are provided with a solid economic base on which to build that self-government. The important question then becomes: Is a capitalist government willing to hand over sufficient resources in Canada to give Native people genuine self-government, i.e. real self-determination involving social justice and first class citizenship in Canada? The answer to this question can only be 'no.' To allow for this would mean taking those resources out of the hands of the rich and powerful class of people in Canada—and it is these same people who run the government state in Ottawa. In a constitutional battle the government has all the power: what can Native leaders threaten to do now that the government has refused to meet their demands? Since there is no politically aware mass movement, ready to take to the streets, the Native leaders have no effective bargaining power. This has been another consequence of state intervention and the constitutional strategy: Native organizations have long since ended the kind of political education and direct action politics that they used back in the late sixties. The constitutional strategy does not oblige leaders to educate their membership and it denies the masses of Metis and Indians the opportunity and the responsibility to genuinely participate in the political process, except to vote approval of the strategy whenever elections come around. Because constitutional negotiations take so long and can be indefinitely delayed by the government, forever, the government can continue to avoid its responsibilities in meeting the needs of Native people.

There are several ways which the constitutional strategy benefits the state —and at the same time goes against the interest of Metis, Inuit and Indian people. The constitutional strategy can be useful to certain Native groups in Canada—those living where resources have not yet been developed and handed over to corporations and some of those who have not signed treaties with Canada. Secondly, if an organization can follow other strategies at the same time and not put all its energies into the constitutional battle, then it retains some of its independence.

The fact is that Native organizations are putting most of their efforts into the constitutional strategy. What are the consequences of this decision? First, it divides Natives themselves into Metis, non-status Indian and status Indian. This is a classic divide-and-rule situation. Therefore, by following the constitutional strategy, Native leaders have themselves contributed to dividing their own people. Organizational power is from the power of masses of people and one cannot effectively use masses in a constitutional battle that takes place in court rooms and government conference rooms.

This last point is more important than it might appear and it leads to two final consequences of this political strategy. Unless there is broad support for progressive Native policies by whites, no government will implement such policies. In order for Metis, Indian and Inuit organizations to win significant reforms, social and economic progress, they must build alliances with other, non-Native groups fighting for similar goals. In the first place, if the Native organizations have let political education and mobilization of its membership slide, then there is nothing with which to build an alliance. Alliances are built between people and political relationships. If Native organizations are not politically active on a regular basis they cannot come together with non-Native people—it institutionalizes special status and gives a message to non-Natives that says 'Our problems are different from yours and our solutions are different.' However, in fact, the problems are the same in the end; a small number of rich people get all the benefits of the capitalist society, and the vast majority, Native and non-Native, face constant insecurity and poverty. It denies the fundamental class nature of Canadian society and therefore, divides them in their particular struggle. It was in this period that the federal government made it known to Native groups that funding would be made available for Aboriginal rights and land claims research. It was just a matter of applying for it. Such an offer was difficult to resist. First, Indians, Metis and Inuit peoples do have legitimate Aboriginal rights and land claims. But perhaps of equal importance in explaining why the offer was taken up is the fact that any other strategy was much more difficult, especially given the fact that the ability of organizations to mobilize large numbers of Native people was failing. The organizations were already becoming bureaucratic. In other words, the constitutional strategy was one which fit very well the kind of bureaucratic politics that was already the trend in comprador regimes. It did not involve the hard work of political education, democratic debate over the future, mobilizing people and confronting the governments that gave grants. It involved hiring researchers and lawyers to study the law and history and it involved negotiations between Native leaders and federal politicians. It was not really a political struggle at all.

None of this necessarily suggests a conspiracy on the part of government or insincerity on the part of Native organizations. The whole process of government intervention into democratic organizations is an insidious one; decisions are made gradually over time and the implications of these decisions are often not clear until years later.

Since economic and political conditions today are similar to the pre 1960s and require a mass organization and public action, then what explains the almost exclusive use of the constitutional strategy by Metis and Indian organizations? It is necessary to look at state intervention and the change to neocolonization to find the answer. The state, or government, altered the social forces. If these forces had been left to themselves, the situation would have naturally led to direct action by a mass movement for social change. By intervening in such a massive way in the organizations of Aboriginal people, the government was able to determine, indirectly, the kind of politics that would be practiced by the Aboriginal comprador regimes.

In the mid 1970s two features of Aboriginal political activity started to become clear. The first was the drawing away from public confrontations with government over jobs, social conditions, education, racism, etc. The organizations in this period became more like service organizations than political voices of the mass of Metis people. There was a marked decrease in the participation by the membership on a regular basis. By the late seventies, people only came out to local meetings if some sort of grant was being discussed or given out.

A survey of 626,000 Indians, Metis, and Inuit conducted in 1993, after the referendum vote found that "Native leaders are out of touch with the reality of their people."[23] Only 4,000 endorsed "self-government as a solution to community problems."[24] That is, not even one per cent of the Aboriginal people supported the state-endorsed version of self-government. In a wider perspective, the referendum results must be seen as Aboriginals' rejection of the four Aboriginal organizations and their leaders. It is not surprising that these organizations were out of touch with their people, because they did not communicate with the rural masses. In a neocolonial period, these organizations aid the state by maintaining control of the general Aboriginal population through indigenous administration of all local programs. The NO vote to the Charlottetown Accord, showed the government that the masses of Native people disagree with Ottawa's Native policies and management.

There is little disagreement that the Charlottetown Accord and its version of Aboriginal self-government are history. There are more serious questions about the daily circumstances of Canada's indigenous people that need to be resolved. The death of the Charlottetown Accord may have opened an opportune time and space for us to seize new opportunities to free ourselves from colonization.

Chapter Twelve

Neocolonialism

Following the end of World War II, Third World colonies went through a great change in their relationships with the imperial nations of the West. The most important change was in the decline of old style imperialism to the establishment of a new system, called neocolonialism. Colonialism in its imperialist form had a relationship of direct political domination. As colonies under direct control of their imperialist colonizers, they provided important resources to the mother country. By 1945, however, the colonial system had come under serious pressure from the oppressed indigenous people. The intensity of this oppression provoked resistance and revolts throughout Third World colonies.

In order for neocolonialism to come into existence, certain factors had to come together at the same time. The first thing that surfaced was dissent against the old imperial conquerors, usually England, France, Spain and Portugal. Secondly, a small group of Aboriginal elites of the ex-colony emerged as leaders, usually a petite bourgeois class. Finally, foreign multinational corporations financially invaded the colony. To the colonial masses, this combination of forces appeared as a national independence movement. However, when things had settled down, the colony and its people had achieved very little in their so-called independence. In some cases, the only changes were in personalities. The new class of Native rulers simply took over the old imperial institutions, such as parliament, the imperial bureaucracy and judicial system. No transformation was made in the structures and policies of traditional imperialism. The indigenous people continued to be equally repressed, exploited and impoverished by the same old imperial institutions.

The decline of imperialism did not mean the end of foreign domination. What had not changed was the form and structure through which this domination was exercised. The direct political control of the colonies was replaced by a more complex mechanism of indirect domination. The Western capitalist economy incorporated the Third World as a subordinate territory and a new type of economic colonialism. Third World nations could exercise their new independence only to the limit of political and cultural matters. Economically, they remained enslaved to their financial masters. By the

1960s, the major Western powers, particularly the United States, strengthened their grip over the economics of Third World countries forcing them into economic subservience. In theory, these new independent nations had all the outward trappings of national sovereignty; but, in reality their economic and political system was directed by foreign multinational corporations.

Foreign multinational corporations manoeuvred a newly developed Native class to command colonial governments. These new governments did not rule in the interest of the indigenous people. Instead, they governed in the interest of foreign corporations and the Native petite bourgeois. As a result, the colonial population was still under repressive imperial rule; often much more repressive and brutal than the old imperial colonizer. This new Aboriginal class of rulers, however, was not completely in control of the colony. They were only intermediaries between the indigenous masses and the multinational corporations. Imperialism was now managed by the new indigenous bourgeois class. Although many colonies had won the war, and thus political independence, they did not win freedom of their economy.

During this period of colonial change the United States emerged as the new leader of the imperialist world. The old imperialist system was an obstacle to the expansionist aims of the U.S., therefore, promoting the breakup of it. Over the next twenty-five years, most Third World colonies had obtained their national independence, but it was a pseudo-liberation.

It is not surprising that this new repressive rule eventually stirred hostility among the national Native population. The Aboriginal collaborator class is not able to stay in power without the support of foreign military force, usually the U.S. Klare claims that "U.S. national security doctrine has consistently stressed the need to defend pro-U.S. regimes against their domestic enemies and so these programs have always included provisions for the support of internal security' agencies."[1] In reality, neocolonial rule has become largely military dictatorships. Otherwise, it is unlikely that "the working people of the colonies will continue to work, pay taxes, and die for the preservation of U.S. business interests."[2] Several Third World nations have had military dictatorships for sometime; ie. Indonesia, Philippines, Chile, Malaysia, and Peru. This fact is noted by Klare; "The supply of repressive hardware to authoritarian Third World regimes is a consistent and intentional characteristic of U.S. foreign policy, under the guise of 'national security'."[3] Furthermore "the United States has tended to back a few relatively powerful conservative regimes around the world (e.g. Iran, Israel, Indonesia) which are expected to exert local hegemony [control] to protect U.S. interests, while at the same time allowing the local [Native] governments to nationalize key sections of their economies while the transnational corporations keep control through their domination of both the world market and advanced technology."[4]

Third World nations do not enjoy independence and true freedom. They are policed by Western industrial nations, particularly by the U.S. through a network of military alliances. Such alliances have made it possible for the establishment of numerous military and intelligence bases in Third World nations. Hadjor states "that in cases where direct Western intervention is necessary, client states such as Israel and South Africa can always be counted on to intervene."[5] In many respects, neocolonialism is more powerful and efficient in maintaining oppression and control than old-style colonialism. It is argued that early imperialism with its brutal methods gave way to neocolonialism, which is more subtle and better camouflaged, but more exploitative and destructive of the material and spiritual indigenous riches, and therefore more dangerous and more difficult to expose, combat and defeat. Neocolonialism perpetuates not just economic, but also political and cultural domination. Through its control of the institutions of education, the media and communications systems, Western capitalism is in a position to subvert most aspects of Third World social life.

The success of neocolonialism was founded on the strategy of transferring power to an indigenous capitalist class and a well-groomed civil service, or bureaucracy. This new Native petite bourgeois class looked to the old colonial powers for direction and management. As a result, they followed quite closely the dictates of the foreign multinationals. This partnership between the neocolonial ruling class and foreign capital provided the link of the system. To maintain neocolonialism the Western capitalist nations found it necessary to intervene continuously and systematically in the political life of Third World nations. When indigenous governments became too radical or anti-American, the U.S. through the Central Intelligence Agency (CIA) overthrew the existing indigenous governments and installed a pro-U.S. military dictatorship. This was the case in such countries as Indonesia, Grenada, Panama, Philippines, Chile and many others. Only those countries which have succeeded in demolishing the colonial structures, and keeping the U.S. totally out of their political economy, such as Cuba and Vietnam, have managed to give real meaning to national liberation and complete independence.

The basis of neocolonialism is therefore the combined control of foreign multinational corporations with the indigenous bourgeois. They work together to manage the economic resources of the colony for their particular concerns. The advantages and gains for the local Native class are expressed through wealth, privilege and status, primarily by virtue of the military and corruption. Neocolonialism acts to prevent Third World people from exercising their democratic rights. It is an obstacle to true independence. For Third World nations to be fully liberated, they must destroy neocolonialism. However, every action against the neocolonial system, however small makes for greater independence, and eventually total liberation.

In summary, neocolonialism is a modified form of traditional colonialism and its methods and structures of domination. The transformation from colonialism to neocolonialism is a change in how the state controls the colonized economy. In traditional colonies, indigenous people did not control the economic, political, social, or cultural issues affecting their day-to-day lives. The imperial governor and the army held the decision-making powers. When the system began to collapse Third World colonies became engulfed by national liberation movements. The colonizers responded by providing certain powers to small groups of Aboriginal elites who then established different but equally effective methods of oppressing their people. The new leaders run what are Aboriginal governments, but in name only.

In sovereign nation-states such as Canada, Australia and New Zealand Aboriginal people live under conditions relatively equivalent to those in South Africa under apartied. In Canada, Indian, Metis, and Inuit communities constitute internal colonies. Internal colonies are based on four major components of colonization. The first is the method of entry. The imperialist nation invades the indigenous territory by military force. It is an unwanted invasion into foreign land. Second, the colonizer destroys the political organization, culture and economy of the Aboriginal nation, then carries out a racist colonization process that transforms the culture, values and customs of the Native society. Third, the imperial power develops a special colonial government and legal order which oppresses and subjugates the indigenous people. The European power develops a dominant/subordinate society and a pattern of racial stereotypes that stigmatizes the Native people, which serves to keep them inferiorized. The final component is racism, whereby the indigenous population is considered inferior due to biological characteristics. Together, racism and Christianity form the major basis of an apartheid system; a system common to all European imperialism. As a result of the above conditions, internal colonies are parallel to external Third World colonies. As racial, colonized people of Internal Colonies, Metis and Indians need to recognize that their situation is as critical and dangerous as any Third World nation. Canada was a colony of European imperialism that emerged with institutions and structures of racism and colonization that are very similar to most African and Asian colonies. Hence, we must view our political and economic situation from a critical Third World perspective.

During the 1950s, when the colonized had no means of supporting themselves, many Indians and Metis migrated to towns and cities. This resulted in a significant influx of unemployed, disenfranchised people entering the colonizer's midst. Realizing that it was ill-equipped to deal with thousands of unemployed Natives in a white and hostile urban environment, the government adjusted its strategy, shrewdly suppressing Natives with meagre welfare, and promises of future employment through job-training programs. These band-aid measures were designed to appease people destined to return to the job market. But for us, who had long been segregated from the mainstream economy by colonial policies, welfare only made us more dependent on the colonizer. Canada's Native people were legislated into a state of perpetual poverty. This continued relatively easily for the government until the 1960s, when our awakening political consciousness threatened the establishment. The Natives' grass-roots movement for civil rights, national liberation, and class struggle was a battle to restructure colonial administration and regain control of our lives.

Lacking neocolonial policies and experience in dealing with such a newly demanding population, the state turned to the small group of educated Native elites. Beginning in the 1960s, Canadian governments developed programs of regular meetings and conferences with Aboriginal elites. The state claimed it wanted to hear from the Aboriginal grass roots. Resolutions were passed, Metis' and Indians' expectations were raised, and recommendations were forwarded to the appropriate bureaucratic departments. However, these gatherings were just staged performances where time-worn resolutions were rehashed only to be shelved once again. The governments failed to act on almost all the proposals. The state never intended to help us; it had its own agenda. The conferences were given extensive publicity to convince whites that the state was attempting to help Natives. It appeared to the public that the government was steering away from colonial management and guiding Natives to pseudo-independence. But, neocolonialism never represents a step forward toward Aboriginal liberation; it is a more clandestine and sophisticated method of controlling indigenous people. With the help of white liberals, the state set up agencies such as Friendship Centres, Native Alcoholic Counselling Houses, job assistant programs, and education centres in towns and cities with large Native populations. These centres socialized Aboriginals to the capitalist ethic and discouraged them from participating in political activities. Like the social, educational, and alcoholism programs set up in reserves and Metis communities, these centres promoted conservative ideologies and assimilation. State programs did not help Aboriginals solve education, housing, and employment problems. Those Metis and Indians who received some benefits developed a greater dependency on the state, and their political consciousness was smothered. The state was determined to deactivate and to suppress the Native movement promoting self-determination and Aboriginal political and economic liberation.

While Western metropolitan states and their multinational corporations enforce super exploitation policies on Third World nations, they also impose suppressive administrative systems and principles on their internal colonies. Countries like Canada have applied neocolonial tactics against their domestic Aboriginals with incredible fervor. As in African or Asian neocolonial nations, Canada's indigenous people have been deliberately denied the ability to develop their own modes of production and, consequently, the means to be self-sufficient. Therefore, local Native councils do not derive their power from controlling their productive forces, e.g. sawmills. Their power is intimately and solely dependent on government funding and Aboriginal agents' patronage. Metis and Indian bourgeois are never members of the white dominant class, let alone part of the establishment. Despite their privileged status within Native communities, these elites are also marginalized by the mainstream. Many serve the colonizers' interests to maintain the privileges that come with helping the enemy.

The struggle against colonialism did not find expression in Canada's internal colonies until the period of the civil rights struggle that overtook the United States in the 1960s. Canada's indigenous people began their anti-colonial struggle in the mid-1960s. Our battle was part of the political crisis of the world, as expressed by youth and university students. We were influenced by the events south of the border and prodded by increasing racism at home, rose up against Canada's colonial administration. Racism and semi-apartheid structures were highly visible. Particularly oppressive were the state welfare officials, the police, priests, and teachers. Indians, Metis, and Inuit people were sensitive to their powerlessness and the lack of control they had over their daily lives. Aboriginals' standard of living was not increasing—instead it was decreasing drastically. Unemployment soared at 90%. Government was cutting back on welfare payments. Housing conditions were deplorable. Frustrated and fed up with these conditions, we mobilized resistance and tried to throw off the chains of colonialism. But, after a decade of struggle for self-determination, we found ourselves under 'new' control—direct colonial domination transformed into neocolonial rule.

The rise of neocolonialism followed immediately on the heels of the anti-colonial struggle that ended in the mid-1970s under heavy state intervention. It was a bitter conclusion for those of us who had struggled so hard against the system that had reduced our communities to Third World conditions. Nevertheless, we had loosened some of the oppressive controls from authoritarian Indian Affairs officials and the harsh officials of the provincial Metis administrations. Some of the more severe chains of colonization were severed. We made some gains in welfare management, the schools, and we reduced the Catholic Church's control over our people. Although the colonial state machinery was not smashed and Aboriginal people were still excluded from positions of power, there were some changes toward political independence and freedom in local administration. There was a change toward liberal democracy, but our freedom was still far off because neocolonialism 'reveals a social-democratic tendency . . . and a mixed economy development.' The establishment of social democracy in the neocolony resulted from our anticolonial struggles. Although there was also a tendency to be anticapitalist, we failed to challenge the larger framework of capitalist-imperialist relations. As a result, the newly developed system of neocolonialism remained consistent with capitalist logic.

Major structural changes were not made to the state infrastructure, but some modifications in the Aboriginal people's material conditions have occurred. Housing improved, many reserves and Metis communities now have electricity, running water, and telephones. These improvements, however, are not exclusively for Aboriginal residents. When in Aboriginal territories, white entrepreneurs and capital investors benefit from these amenities as they desire. More importantly, the state uses these amenities to impose further oppression, only in a less visible and direct way than traditional colonialism did.

The most significant change that has occurred since our struggle began in the '60s is the transformed economic conditions of the internal colonies. Private corporations in forestry, oil, uranium, water, power, and fishing have been operating within Aboriginal territory, and they have been receiving government subsidies. Likewise, grants have been given to Aboriginal entrepreneurs operating relatively large businesses. For instance, the Saskatchewan Meadow Lake Tribal Council has been granted permission to harvest a large section of the province's northwest forests. The council sells the raw logs to NorSask Forest Products. Economically, this tribal council operates as a private company, not as a tribal unit. The council clear cuts forests and pays its Indian workers low wages. This neocolonial development is made possible by the state's funding and permission to exploit the province's natural resources. Thousands of miles of paved highway and bridges have been built in Aboriginal territories during the rise of neocolonialism, but these developments are used mostly by private companies providing resources for multinational corporations. Also in northern Saskatchewan, uranium corporations make extensive use of the state's infrastructure. By binding together several economic operations in the neocolony, the state tones down class antagonism and promotes a monopolistic system, all of which fosters a conservative ideology. Thomas, claims "The economics of the periphery [neocolony] can be described as multistructured in that they combine numerous different forms of production and types of economic relations, so that monopolistic industrial and commercial corporations are never clearly dominant." [6]

The most common and definitely the worst neocolonial industry is tourism. In some Metis communities where tourism is important, the government built laundromats for the exclusive use of foreign, white tourists. Local Metis women were forbidden to use the machines, though they were prepared to pay the charges. This is the type of oppression and discrimination that invites violence. Tourism seriously exploits young Aboriginal women—prostitution and tourism go hand in hand. Tourism fosters vicious racism.

Neocolonialism is the 'indigenization' of government programs. When the federal government restructures itself into a neocolonial system, it shifts the administrative control of programs, such as welfare, job training, and maintenance of reserves and villages, to band councils or Metis village councils. Political control is taken from white bureaucrats and placed into the hands of Aboriginal elites or comprador regimes. In the early stages of neocolonialism, several top white officials in the Department of Natural Resources were removed from their posts and were replaced by elected indigenous mayors and councillors. Nevertheless, the basic repressive structure and policies remained relatively the same.

The government also provides money for Native alcoholism counselling programs, but not for political awareness programs. Service programs are designed to deal with the symptoms, not the causes of oppression, poverty, and economic inequality, because that would mean pointing a finger at the state. Instead of representing their people politically, as was originally intended, Native management has gradually taken on more and more of the government's responsibilities. Metis and Indians working in the bureaucracy create the illusion that fundamental changes are being made, and that Aboriginals could function on an equal footing in mainstream society. The state parades these councils and elites as success models for Indians and

Metis to follow; it creates a mirage of self-government. The governments place Indians and Metis in visible management positions to make them and everyone else feel like they are the authorities and managers of their local communities. Most co-opted elites see themselves as important state bureaucrats, but in reality they are only collaborators. As middle-level bureaucrats, they are merely brokers of Native power. Their judgements are never entirely their own because they see their interests as being the same as their white supervisors. They act like the white bureaucrats before them in order to maintain their positions and material benefits. Most will remain in key government positions, administering social programs and influencing Natives' political socialization as long as neocolonialism persists. In these positions, they continue to subjugate and oppress Metis, Inuit, and Indians. Furthermore, they prevent the development of political awareness and mobilization.

Early neocolonial instruments of repression came in a myriad of forms, including poorly funded 'economic development' programs designed to develop small business enterprises, such as service stations and grocery stores. The state was intent on encouraging a select few to establish small businesses. Special loans were extended and standard job qualifications were set aside. The state provided loans to Indians and Metis wanting to set up small trucking companies to serve the uranium mines and forestry industry. It was a case of giving a small share of wealth to an even smaller number of Aboriginals, and dumping the Native unemployment problem onto the local Aboriginal councils. More importantly, the state used its money to co-opt the Aboriginal collaborators. The new Indian and Metis entrepreneurs were dependent on state funds, and if they did not help the state control the Native masses, they lost their privileges. By having a small group of Aboriginals rise into the petty bourgeois class, it served to isolate them from the masses. Government grants were a highly effective way to pacify dissatisfied Natives.

The establishment also used what were clearly dishonest employment programs. After the government stopped bussing Natives to sugar beet fields, it implemented job-training programs and promised each individual a better future. Government used training programs to hire Metis and Indians at minimum wage to perform maintenance work in the provincial infrastructure. The low wages were 'justified,' according to the government, because the Aboriginals' jobs were part of training programs. The Natives were supposed to become skilled workers, after which time they would qualify for union wages. However, the government kept Indian and Metis workers on the same programs for as long as ten years without a pay increase. Non-Natives, on the other hand, were employed in the same service at considerably higher wages. The government insisted that the wage discrepancy was not based on racial differences, but on the Natives' lack of skills. In neocolonialism, the federal government makes it known that funding is available for Aboriginal programs and job creation. Many Native organizations and groups, already well on their way to becoming bureaucratic, find it is much easier to busy themselves with hiring researchers and developing trendy programs, rather than pursue the struggle for liberation.

As neocolonialism advanced through the 1960s, it gradually gained control over the Aboriginal liberation movement and stalled development of Native self-determination. Federal and provincial governments used their substantial funding to break the Natives' struggle for a progressive political ideology and collective economic base. By the 1980s, it became clear that Aboriginal puppet organizations and their leaders had defused Native activism. Collaborator organizations did not provide their people with a political voice, and there was a marked decrease in membership's participation. The state's creation of a petty bourgeois class, whether they were government officials or local Native leaders, seriously damaged the Native liberation movement. For a few million dollars, the government succeeded in subduing Native counteraction. Many of the Native elites not only abandoned political activism, but also took a stand against the liberation struggle. Neocolonialism has perpetuated Native dependency by promoting underdevelopment, economic irresponsibility, and smothering responsible leadership. The establishment's successful use of Natives to control Natives by abusing wealth and power has proven that the original Native revolutionaries were on the right track.

In today's neocolonial society, most Aboriginals live as they did before the 1960s. Alcoholism is still prevalent, welfare is once again the primary means of survival, and suicides and school dropout rates are extremely high. Rather than working together, Aboriginal elites and comprador regimes foster suspicion and internal conflicts. Those who oppose the comprador leaders are denied benefits, services, and decent housing. The collaborators and the state work hand in hand for their respective self-interests and deny the Aboriginal nation authentic self-determination.

When one talks about minorities' liberation struggles, one cannot ignore the problems of racism. The colonizer, with the help of the state media, stresses and promotes racial conflict to isolate and segregate indigenous people. Racism creates myths and stereotypes that are extremely hard to shake, because they become entrenched cultural-ideological stereotypes. Even where some racial groups have risen above their previous economic depriva-tion, the dominant culture persists in viewing them in terms of narrow cultur-al-ideological myths. For example, Indians of the Hobbema reserve have become relatively wealthy people from their oil royalties, and yet the state system still stereotypes them as impoverished and low class Indians. However, too little is said about racism's effect on people's attitudes and abil-ity to interact with people on the basis of equality.

In a study of Aboriginal communities on racism, almost three-quarters responded that racism prevents them from achieving their goals.[8] In particu-lar, the majority claimed that they were victims of employment discrimina-tion. More than 50% stated that being discriminated and stereotyped were the worst things about being Indian. Racism also coloured reserve Indians' friendships and social activities—three-quarters responded that their ability to form friendships was restricted to the confines of the reserve. Not surpris-ingly, 80% of reserve Indians reported that they had married Indians. Racism clearly circumscribes and narrows Natives' experiences. It continues to be a major force of Aboriginal oppression and isolation.

Like earlier forms of repression, neocolonialism increases racism, exploitation, and the manipulation of Aboriginal thought. Racism represents everything negative—discrimination, ghettos, poor education, low wages, denial of civil rights, imprisonment—and yet it is woven very tightly into the fabric of Canadian society. It obstructs Aboriginals' ability to develop a class consciousness. Indians, Metis, and Inuit are inclined to identify themselves first in racial terms, then in cultural terms and lastly as a economic class. The establishment has stigmatized us so effectively that we find it hard to view ourselves in a different way. Racism denigrates national minorities and hard-ens cultural boundaries between them and the dominant metropolis culture. During the Canadian Athletic Championships held in Kelowna, B.C. in August 1993, an Indian theatre group produced a play for evening entertain-ment. The young white audience hurled racial slurs and insults so viciously that the performance had to be cancelled.[9] Is Kelowna to be likened to Johannesburg? How can white liberals speak of multiculturalism and say they believe Indians and Metis are the 'same' as other Canadians?

It is important to keep in mind that true national liberation struggles are working class struggles. Therefore class and racism, the underpinning of Canada's eco-political system, must be eradicated if a liberation is ever to occur. The corporate class uses racism to subjugate an entire Aboriginal nation; it also exploits the masses of non-Native society. The state suppress-es only specific segments of society at one time so it does not lose the entire citizenry's sanction. For example, Ottawa waged war against Metis and Indians in 1885, and not against the white dissidents. Racism keeps the white proletariat separated from Aboriginals. The establishment uses it to divide and weaken the working class. It deflects people's thinking away from class consciousness, thus obstructing working class solidarity. This last point is more important than it might appear. The importance of non-Native public opinion is this: Unless there is broad non-Native support for progressive Aboriginal policies, governments will not implement change. To win significant reforms, social and economic progress, Aboriginals must build alliances with white groups fighting for similar goals. In the first place, Indian, Metis, and Inuit organizations must revive political education and Native membership, otherwise there will be nothing with which to build an alliance. Alliances are built between people, if members of Native organizations are not actively co-operative on a regular basis, they cannot come together with non-Native workers and the poor. The state's assertion that 'our problems are different from yours and therefore our solutions are different' has separated Aboriginals from whites for too long. In fact, white workers and the indigenous share many of the same economic and political problems.

Neocolonialism has made it almost impossible to unite our people in political activity to seek redress for even the most serious injustices. Aboriginal communities are so greatly fractured that in Prince Albert they let a self-proclaimed white supremacist get away with murder. Carney Nerland, a neo-Nazi and police informer, never saw a day in court after he shot and killed an Indian, Leo Lachance, in the back. Two jail guards were in Nerland's shop when he shot Lachance, but they never contacted the police. Sergeant David Demkiw of the local police force claimed "there was insufficient evidence to prove the shooting was anything but accidental."[10] Judge Gerein stated that "he found no evidence that Mr. Nerland's political or racist beliefs were motives in the killing."[11] This, however, is hard to believe after Nerland boasted, "If I'm convicted of shooting that Indian, I should get a medal and you should pin it on me."[12] Nevertheless, Judge Gerein, a policeman, and Nerland's lawyer came to a 'private arrangement' outside of the courtroom that Nerland would serve three years in jail for manslaughter, not murder. Canada's justice system still allows racial genocide.

Neocolonialism has altered the attitude and aspirations of Indian and Metis people. Federal and provincial governments have established a host of trivial programs to direct Aboriginals away from politics and deactivate those with activist leanings. Education is the master of these assimilation programs. In Regina, status Indians have their own college, which grants bachelor degrees in several disciplines but they are basically Eurocentric. There are Native Studies Departments at almost every large university in Canada. Many teacher institutes offer a special education program to train Natives to be teachers. However, when graduated, their viewpoints and attitudes are quite consistent with mainstream white supremacy stereotypes. There are also special university programs to train Aboriginals to become lawyers, administrators, and managers. All of these educational programs are designed to indoctrinate Native students with middle-class ideologies. Every program is oriented specifically toward creating a class of Aboriginal bourgeoisie to act as a bridge to the impoverished masses and to help control and oppress them. The use of an educated Native elite to help governments deal with the 'Native problem' has parallels around the world. Neo-colonialism involves the use of Metis and Indians to control other Aboriginal peoples. In general, it means giving some of the benefits of the dominant society to a small, privileged minority of Aboriginals in return for their help in making sure the majority of Natives do not cause a revolt.

Chapter Thirteen

Indigenous Collaborators in Third World Colonization

The Third World is aflame in bloodletting wars. Rivers are choked with bullet-ridden bodies. The hills and valleys are littered with sliced-up human carcasses. Masses of starving men, women and children are staggering aimlessly trying to escape; fleeing for their lives. What is the striking thing about these wars? What people are being butchered, and in what countries? Does that not tell us a lot about the nature of the global turbulence. It tells us almost everything. There are over 100 wars raging every day throughout the world. Where? Rwanda, South Africa, Somalia, Yemen, Sri Lanka, India, and on and on. The wars are in all past colonies of European imperialism. They are ex-colonies of the once powerful Arayan nations of Europe that were held in subjugation, slavery and oppression. The victims are the racial, pigmented people of nazi-like colonization. They are the residue, the 'left-overs' of hundreds of years of totalitarian imperialism. This global slaughtering is the horrid consequences of hundreds of years of colonialism. Direct, despotic imperialism was driven out of these colonies by the colonized after World War II in the early wars of liberation. The European imperialist, however, left a nation of indigenous people whose fate would inevitably end in horrifying political disaster.

Historically European nations, as colonizers disrupted or destroyed indigenous societies in almost every possible dimension. They created artificial tribal societies and unnatural administrative structures. Into these different 'tribes' were fed suspicion, distrust, hostility and even hate. For this function, colonizers used the reliable, effective weapon: Christianity. If necessary, the military exercised the essential power to choreograph the unequal power and venom among the powerless, confused 'tribes.' Throughout the long period of colonization, the imperialist masters perpetuated the fiendish game of tribal wrangling. As a result of systematic imperialist schemes, the indigenous people became political, cultural and psychological colonized creatures.

It may seem strange that all the 'blood baths' of warfare are taking place in Third World countries by Aboriginal people. But, in reality, it is not strange. It is exactly as it was intended by the Western imperialist nations which reconstructed the indigenous societies during the long period of colonization. Internal tribal wars were an intended part of decolonization. As imperial oppressors were being driven out, tribal wars would begin almost immediately. Imperialism had arranged that the colonizer would be called back to restore order because 'the savages had not learned how to govern themselves'. However, imperialist nations, including the 'glorious British Empire' was mistaken. Instead of being called back to the colonies, foreign multinational corporations moved in and took over economic management of the ex-colonies. Being interested only in the rich resources and profit, the Native people became disposable, and a new system of neocolonialism developed.

Shortly after World War II, Third World colonies began their struggle for national independence. Almost all territories in Africa were external colonies of Western Europe, but after long and fierce wars, most won national independence. However, in many cases, this hard-won autonomy was short-lived. Imperialism had been defeated, but a new type of colonialism—neocolonialism—took over. Multinational corporations and the world's new imperial power, the United States, penetrated the emerging Third World nations to create and then manipulate indigenous authoritarian regimes. Traditional colonialism, a type of direct control over other nations, was replaced by an indirect form of colonialism involving indigenous leaders collaborating with powerful nations, mostly the U.S. and its large corporations. Old imperial structures that had not been smashed were retained and used by the indigenous petite bourgeoise. As a result, 'independence' brought few major structural changes and few benefits for the masses of indigenous people. The Aboriginal military regimes simply took over the old imperial political machinery and filled the European colonizer's position. In a sense, these indigenous leaders were a new breed of colonizer.

Many Third World nations that have achieved independence have established military dictatorships which are controlled by Native elites. These comprador dictators continue to rule due to the assistance and co-operation of multinational corporations, mostly from the United States, with assistance of the Central Intelligence Agency (CIA). There is a complex combination of U.S. business, and financial interests, military, politicians, and CIA intelligence that seek the rich resources and favourable investment climate in Third World nations. Action is generated by the U.S. either to protect its vested interest—usually oil—or to open up development in the neocolony. Concern is basically for the protection and promotion of American corporations and their profits. Interest in a Third World nation is not for the benefit of the indigenous people or for its economic development. "The strategy of the

U.S.'s military power is to advance the interests of its transnational companies."[1] For this reason, the U.S. government encourages and supports comprador military dictatorships in Third World nations. It is this type of foreign support that keeps these Native dictatorships in power. Therefore, indigenous comprador regimes operate in a manner that best accommodates the interests of the U.S.; otherwise, their regime would be overthrown. As a result, Aboriginal comprador governments become very repressive, cruel, and right-wing.

In their policies to accommodate foreign corporations, comprador governments cause extreme underdevelopment and poverty in their own nation. In order to keep the indigenous people contained, the collaborator government has to have considerable military equipment, weapons and trained soldiers. "Between 1976 and 1980, ten Third World countries received $2.3 billion in military aid and arms credits from the United States."[2] Much of this military equipment was for internal use; that is, to suppress local dissent and control the Native people. According to the international news, this dissent takes the form of internal tribal wars, such as in South Africa, Rwanda, Somalia, Sri Lanka, etc. "Arms deliveries to these countries", *writes Klare,* "have included armoured cars, shotguns, tear gas, riot clubs, and other weapons unsuitable for anything other than internal political warfare."[3] These purchases of military weapons are mostly from the U.S. The total debt of the Third World nations in 1990 was $1.3 billion—an amount so enormous as to be meaningless. Most of this money is not spent on food, clothing and housing for the poor and needy people of the Third World, but for military equipment and training. "The United States stands at the supply end of a pipeline of repressive technology that extends to many of the Third World's most authoritarian regimes."[4] "The supply of repressive hardware to authoritarian Third World comprador regimes is a consistent and intentional characteristic of U.S. foreign policy."[5] Under these conditions, it is not difficult to understand reasons and factors behind tribal wars occurring in Third World nations.

By keeping the Native population fighting among themselves, it takes the focus off the central puppet Aboriginal government and its alliances, the foreign multinational corporations. This allows authoritarian governments in multinational-controlled Third World nations to be extremely suppressive. Often war occurs between two tribal/ethnic groups in the same nation, such as in Sri Lanka, Angola, Peru, and Guatemala. "U.S. involvement in repression abroad," *writes Klare,* "shows that U.S. firms and agencies are providing gun equipment, training and technical support to the police and paramilitary forces most directly involved in the torture, assassination and abuse of civilian dissidents."[6] Armament dealers from the industrialized world are selling arms to both sides of the battles. As long as tribal groups such as in Rwanda are warring among themselves they are too disorganized to challenge the Native military dictatorship and U.S. military intelligence forces. It is for these reasons that fascists dictatorships, such as General Mobotu of Zaire and other dictators are able to sustain repressive control over the Native population for 20 years and keep them so critically poor and powerless. In order to stay in power, the comprador regimes are forced to borrow money from Western industrialized nations; more precisely from the World Bank and International Monetary Fund (IMF). In order to repay their debts, the IMF and World Bank forces Third World governments to cut food supplies to the poor, reduce, or eliminate health and educational budgets. "As a result of these budget cuts, several million African children have died in the last decade from malnutrition."[7] Interest payments, alone by Third World countries are three times more than all the aid that they have received from the West. "Countries of the Third World sent to the Western nations $52 billion dollars more in debt payments than they received from the West."[8] Hence, it is the poverty-stricken Third World nations that keep the Western industrial nations wealthy. For every one dollar the West sends in aid to the Third World, it receives three dollars in return. A very profitable yield! But, at what a hideous price. On the international TV news we watch the grotesque atrocities in the ghettos of the Third World.

The U.S. developed a strategy of providing 'economic aid' to its Third World colonies. For example, the Alliance for Progress program permitted the U.S. to make generous financial grants to comprador regimes in Latin America at the sacrifice of Africa. "In 1985 the USA shipped nearly four times more aid per capita to support three of its political allies in Central America—El Salvador, Guatemala and Honduras—than it did to the entire famine region in all of Africa."[9] Massive aid is a new facet of imperialism since World War II, which has been a decisive element in keeping governments in power who respected U.S. economic interests. The indigenous comprador regimes use this aid to buy military equipment from American armament manufacturers, and these weapons are used to control the neocolony's indigenous masses. This system allows the U.S. military to stay out of public view and at the same time permits substantial financing of multinational corporations operating in neocolonies. Besides supporting private economic interests, indigenous collaboration fosters corruption and a conservative ideology. The important feature of financial aid was not only to establish corrupt comprador regimes, but to maintain them and keep the masses in a subjugated state of powerlessness. The majority of the Aboriginal population constitutes a whole universe of atomized workers, powerless and obliged to humiliate themselves before the power of the comprador. Comprador rule in neo-colonies is primarily concerned with increasing the corporate class's profits and maintaining control over the indigenous population, which is euphemistically referred to as maintaining 'law and order.' The colonizer, with the help of compradors, actually expands the state's control over Aboriginal people. Programs and projects are developed to attract the indigenous people into the easily controlled middle class. Internal colonies within nation-states, such as Canada, Australia, and South Africa are somewhat similar to Third World's struggles for self-government. Not all circumstances and practices of internal colonies are the same as those of external colonies. However, there are many similarities. Both colonies suffered the same devastation of their culture as Third World nations. The colonizer then imposed administrative rule to further subjugate Aboriginal people. Eventually, a neocolonial system was established and the indigenous people were severely colonized.

Indians, Metis and Inuit of Canada are racial indigenous people who have been colonized by British and French imperialists. We have been forced likewise, to live in colonial territories under the domination of the colonizer. The minor difference between the Natives of Rwanda, Somalia, Sri Lanka, and the Natives of Canada is that we are situated in internal colonies, in contrast to external colonies. Imperialist institutions and attitudes direct and dominate the political and social behaviour of Metis, Indians and Inuit. As Aboriginals, we are naive to believe that the Ottawa government would not treat us in a brutal authoritarian manner, if it felt inclined to do so. One has only to recall the government's atrocities against our ancestors in 1885; or against the Mohawks in 1990. A Pass Law requiring First Nations people to have written permission to leave their reserve existed until 1950. I remember when I drank beer in segregated beer parlours in Canada, because we could not go in the sections for 'whites only'. Canadian society is very clever and smooth in hiding its racist and imperial framework and nature. It is this ability for concealing this apartheid-like character that makes Canada a precarious situation for Native people. This problem is further compounded with Canada's Anglo-Saxon mainstream self-righteousness and the people's distorted belief in moral correctness on racism.

Therefore, it is crucial that as Metis, Indians and Inuit, we thoroughly understand the critical circumstances and relationships between internal colonies and the imperial centre, Ottawa. To the white mainstream society this may seem an unlikely comparison. However, from an eurocentric perspective, together with the white peoples lack of life experiences in racial, colonial ghettos, there is no sensitivity or insight into race/class and colonization. Unfortunately, Canadians have been grossly misinformed about their racial and colonial history. These historical distortions have become entrenched beliefs and attitudes to which Native people must now struggle against. As Canadians, we have been seriously indoctrinated to the belief that our national and provincial governments are compassionate, kind and just to its citizens, particularly to the Native people. In reality, however, the Canadian government has developed and followed a fairly rigid quasi-apartheid system for First Nations people through treaties, the reserve system and the *Indian Act*. Metis have been treated as semi-caste people, subjected to national wars of termination, and genocide. The Canadian government has always considered us mixed-blood colonized creatures fit only for the lowest, menial and servile tasks. Historically it was decided that we would be a separate society and unequal society from the Anglo-Saxon mainstream. It is necessary that we fully understand the position of Canadian institutions and ideology within this context. We must never forget that Louis Riel surrendered to the Ottawa government, hoping for mercy. We know, too well his fate. The Canadian government succeeded in officially dividing the Aboriginal people into several divisions. The last division was in 1987, when a grant of $60,000 was given to hold a vote that divided the Metis and non-status Indians in Saskatchewan.[10] Status Indians have further distanced themselves as separate from other Aboriginals by using the term First Nations. For these reasons, it is extremely important that all Aboriginal groups make a concentrated effort to work in solidarity. The significant point is that in the recent transition to the neocolonial period, administrative control over Aboriginal people has become a complex combination of government, bureaucracy, multinational corporations and Native collaborator organizations. We must understand that this new system has become exceedingly aggressive and exploitative, because of the corporations' greed for the rich resources on Native territories. Since governments support corporations, they are going to manoeuvre in the interest of big business; and thus, against the interests of Native people and their environment. Consequently, Native organizations, like the Metis National Council and the Assembly of First Nations will be used to perform the extra repressive control over Metis, Indians and Inuit when and where necessary.

In the period of neocolonialism, and the establishment of collaborator Native regimes, there is no question about the repressive type of administration. Indian and Metis organizations have been the red oppressor regimes for the past 20 years. They are parallel to authoritarian regimes in Third World nations, such as Chile and the Philippines. Although it may seem a far-fetched possibility in Canada's neocolonial society, it is not beyond the realm of possibility if the market system is threatened.

The crucial issue is that as Metis, Indians and Inuit people we must be acutely vigilant towards national and provincial governments in their actions and relationships with our people. We must examine most critically the governments' actions in their funding of collaborator organizations, such as the Metis National Council, the Metis Society of Saskatchewan, and all other Native organizations. We need to be suspicious of this type of unusual generosity. Repression and terrorism by Native organizations does not take place without the role of the 'unseen hand' of governments. It is time that as Aboriginal people working for nationhood we put a stop to the governments' manipulation and trifling with our political and economic lives. We must come together as a nation of race/class colonized people and map out a plan of action for genuine self-determination and autonomy in our reserves, colonies, communities and nation.

Chapter Fourteen

Metis/Indian Organizations as The New Oppressors

In May 1994 an underground newspaper, the *Metis Messenger* showed up in public places. It headlined, "The voice of the Metis people has been silent for too long. It is time to rise up and challenge the dictator leadership. The voice of the Metis masses have been silent for 20 years."[1] The liberation movements of the Metis people in the 1960s was abruptly shut down by government officials, politicians and puppet Native leaders. This happened to every Aboriginal organization in all provinces, including the First Nations, non-status Indians, and Inuit. There was no exception. Metis and Indian organizations were suddenly smothered in million dollar grants for which they did not have to give any accountability. Federal and provincial governments and their bureaucrats imposed corruption, misuse and wastefulness.

When it comes to talk on moccasin row today about Aboriginal political leaders, you won't hear a lot of pride expressed. You're likely to hear words like corruption, embarrassment and shame. According to an elderly Northern trapper, Aboriginal politicians are a pathetic joke. Those Metis leaders are declaring themselves as a nation, while they have absolutely no contact with the grass-roots people at all. The old trapper may have been speaking from folk wisdom of an elder, but there are statistics to prove his point. After the vote on the Constitutional Accord in October 1992, a survey showed that less than one percent of the Aboriginal people supported the leaders of all Native organizations across Canada.[2] They are totally out of touch with the masses. They have no creditability with the community people; yet the masses are silent. Only the puppet leaders are seen and heard. Why? Shaking as he said it, the trapper continued "Those guys are living high off the hog, making deals with thugs, doing shady who-knows-what with our money, ruining all our programs, and then they have the nerve to go back, cap-in-hand for more government money. Well, any government that would give those mafia leaders any more money should have their heads examined."[3] Twenty years ago, a group of Metis tried to force an examination of the activities of these mafia leaders and the government bureaucrats, including the Secretary of State, but everyone flatly refused to co-operate. Government officials and politicians refused to check-up on the corrupt leaders or stop the massive funding. What the trapper said is pretty common talk amongst the angry Metis. It is indeed time that the Metis became angry and demanded to put the power in the hands of the village and street people. Fear of reprisals from the comprador agents in the form of strong-arm tactics have silenced all opposition to the current movement. In truth, the fear of 'goon squad' tactics are very real. But it must be remembered that these tactics are supported by Ottawa and all the provincial governments across Canada. These leaders are puppets of the white colonial governments. That does not mean that we should be any less critical or opposed to them. Undoubtedly, the compradors are very powerful, and difficult to remove because of Ottawa's support. Examples of goon squad corruption are many if you have been involved in 'government-Aboriginal' politics. They are very effective in repression and have disastrous consequences for the rank and file Native people. The *Underground Messenger* describes the actions of a long time thug, called Ed, who is best known for his theft of funding from two Indian and Metis Friendship Centres. These crooks can smell-out funding for Aboriginal programs and manage to rip-off a nice bundle before they move-on. They have nothing to fear from governments or politicians.

It is because of this very real physical danger to the Native people that the *Messenger* has begun writing their underground news. They worry about the safety of their kids or themselves as they consider some of the Metis organizations' thugs as being violent. This is a terrible statement to make about our proud and courageous Metis nation. But these horrible conditions do exist today. We should ask why. The answers can be found only in the total political picture of the oppressive and scheming neocolonial governments, exploitative multinational corporations, and greedy Metis cheats who are willing to sell themselves for big bucks. They don't deal in small change. This is truly a very serious time for us and our nation. It is probably now or never. If we do not resolve the state-comprador dictatorship and transfer the power to local people, then we may not survive as a nation. This is exactly what governments want. They are anxious to crush the Metis as a final blow. The Ottawa ruling class has always been worried about the rebelliousness of the Metis since the spectacular days of 1870, 1885 and the 1960s. Ottawa is willing to pay high prices to hire corrupt and brutal thugs among Metis opportunists and 'hoodlums,' in order to establish a totalitarian system over the Metis, Indians and Inuit. It is in Aboriginal territory where all the valuable resources exist today.

The *Underground Messenger* says that both provincial and federal governments are now willing to assist Metis people to develop self-government.

But what kind of self government? Probably the kind in Davis Inlet, or in pre-democratic Soweto, South Africa. We must remain skeptical and suspicious of these government offers. We must never forget the dirty tricks that John A. MacDonald used on our ancestors in 1870 and 1885. But, as long as we are cautious and militant in dealing with governments, then we should explore the possibility of liberation for the Metis. But, negotiations and final decisions have to be made by the majority of Metis people in a democratic decision-making process. We have to restructure whiteman's decision-making procedure. Metis villages, urban centres and other communities should develop local collectives as the political body which makes decisions for the people, not the compradors. It must be done by consensus, and not by majority vote or by the hierarchal organization that exists today. Metis organizations today are very much like Italian political parties: neo-nazis and mafia gangs. We must turn things around and move towards self-determination. Governments have to be forced into dealing with Metis collectives on funding, developing programs and rebuilding our Aboriginal institutions. The present Metis leadership according to the *Underground Messenger* "are incompetent, liars, thieves and crooks; consequently the ship of Metis self government will surely be run around."[4]

Those Metis elites who are in the centre of Metis dictatorships know of the excessive corruption. While they falsely collect millions of dollars in corrupt tricks, many Metis families sleep in dilapidated shacks, half freezing in the winter months. These millions of dollars misspent by executive members would provide housing comfort for hundreds of Metis families. There is no conscience or justice in our Native leaders and our organizations. "Think of the thousands of Metis families who are eking out a bare existence on welfare, and living in ghettos. The hanger-on, known as the 'judge' also had his accommodation in high priced hotels paid by the Metis people", says the *Underground Messenger*, "despite the fact that by his own admission and reputation he has never worked in 20 years outside of collecting Metis Society perks and getting patronage positions."[5]

The only requirement to have a job is that the person has to be Aboriginal and be corruptible. The only requirement of the Canadian government is that Native puppets have to know how to waste and misuse millions of dollars being funded to Indian, Metis, and Inuit organizations. It is definitely not to help the impoverished Native people. Above all, it is not to educate them in any way that would raise their political awareness of their oppressed colonial situation, which would encourage them to continue to struggle in a mass movement as we did in the 1960s. The major purpose is for a small group of elite leaders to control the masses of people—keep them ignorant and confused. We have been splintered into many feuding groups, hence we can not fight the government—our real oppressor. Ottawa has conveniently turned Native organizations into repressive 'comprador regimes.' To do this, it is necessary for Native collaborators to have the right to misspend funds in whatever way they feel like. The government has not required Native leaders to be responsible or accountable for the millions of dollars they receive. The federal government may demand an occasional, auditing of the books, but that doesn't mean anything. That is part of the state corruption scheme. They have practiced this same charade for many years, but have done absolutely nothing to correct the corruption. Governments are the major players and winners in Native oppression, resources and land. We must understand how white colonizers operate to hold control over internal colonies of Aboriginal people in Canada. No Aboriginal member of parliament has yet done anything of any significance for the Indian, Metis or Inuit people. There have been many Native members of parliament and Senators over the years, but they have been totally useless in promoting any good for our people. They are part of colonial oppression.

The *Underground Messenger* suggests that hopes were raised by the Metis people for improved leadership and honest operation of programs after the 15 year tyrant leadership of the 'Regina mafia' was overthrown a couple of years ago. Over the last twenty years of the Native organization operations, bribery, graft, and greed, had become institutionalized in these organizations; and it will never change as long as the same bourgeois hierarchal structure continues to exist. The only conclusion we can draw is that the corrupt hierarchal organization based on the whiteman's customs will never function properly for our people. As long as governments give collaborators millions of dollars to play at children's games, they will play as though it was the real thing. At a meeting in Batoche in July 1995, the Metis Society, executive, and self-appointed elites held a Metis Legislative Assembly session. Not only did they have pretend MLAs, but also pretend Senators. This group of sham Metis government represents nobody, but themselves—a small group of self-appointed elites. For two days they held a mock parliamentary session, pretending it was a real assembly. They took themselves seriously, and passed certain legislation pertaining to Metis people. It was a pathetic mockery—to watch adult Metis playing children's games at the cost of million of dollars to the taxpayers. The government is pleased with itself, because it is an easy way to control and repress the Metis population. This fits the stereotypical image of the white authoritarian bureaucrat—'halfbreeds behaving as dependent, irrational children.' This is an example of how the governments controls Aboriginal people in an authoritarian way.

How did the Metis Society and Metis National Council regimes succeed in manipulating and changing the Aboriginal people? The comprador leaders spoke about democracy, and revolution but ran dictatorships. For example, to keep power within the select few, the electoral process was rigged every year. During an election, Aboriginal compradors used their influence and state money. Natives employed by the organizations were commanded to devote all their time to the campaigns and contribute in every way possible to ensure that these puppet leaders won each election. The organizations used unconstitutional, and irregular methods to win. Several ineligible voters, who were not residents of the designated area or who were simply not on the official voting list, were permitted to vote. Metis Society funds were used to rent buses for election day to bring in people who were guaranteed to vote for the compradors. The voters lists were out of date and inaccurate, and voters' identifications were not verified. If the elections were contested, comprador leaders refused to do anything. Instead, they fostered a climate of fear and terror around each election. Opposing candidates had little hope of winning. They were similar to Third World totalitarian elections.

With regard to the constitution, the Board of Directors was the decision-making body. However, the president manipulated the situation so that he controlled the Board by appointing each member as a director of a program, such as housing, Aboriginal rights, and alcohol abuse, and for which he paid them extremely high salaries. Consequently, Board members became obligated employees and accomplices of the president. The corruption spread to other groups, including the directors of regions and programs who soon learned they could gain by obeying the president's wishes. These practices are used by most Indian and Metis organizations throughout the nation. Members of the Board of Directors exercised considerable personal influence over their people in many unofficial ways. This inner clique could determine their personal wages, place other Natives on the payroll, and grant special financial benefits to those who supported them. The collaborators were relatively free to do as they pleased, to benefit and strengthen their personal positions, without fear of repercussions from governments. In fact, state bureaucrats often extended special privileges or prizes to extreme subservient and politically correct leaders. Purchasing the support of colonized people who had never had enough money to live on is easily done. Any source of income gives them a sense of false dignity, power and confidence. Any imperial government, including Canada, knows the ease with which manipulation and bribery can be used to control oppressed Aboriginal people.

However, as radical liberation leaders in 1972 we fought back against the government and tried to keep the local people politically involved in the counter-colonial movement. The major argument was over government funding and decentralization. It was argued that decentralization of policies, programs, staff and government grants should be put in force. Complete authority would be placed in Local Metis collectives. Comprador regime members fought against decentralization as it would seriously reduce their power and control over the finances. The leader went so far as to take a racist position, when he stated that '. . . he felt that our people were not ready'; that is, to administer their own programs and funds. He indicated clearly that he intended to rule in an absolute way. Particularly, he kept control of the hiring and firing of the staff. Council members who opposed him were quickly fired or 'bought-off.' That is, they were given jobs by the Metis Society. This meant that the President became their boss who had control over their salary, job, working conditions, and all the benefits that go with 'rip-offs.' He violated the constitution by allowing unauthorized persons to attend council meetings, make decisions and vote. Of course, they were his employees, thus strong supporters. He used the constitution when it was to his advantage, but violated it when it obstructed his plans. The president was administering the Metis Society as a despot. This was analogous to Marcos of the Philippines. Most of the staff had been hired under a system of patronage, nepotism and personal loyalty to the president. They worked in the form of 'goon squad' operations. They travelled as a group to local meetings, in order to disrupt them. For instance, at an area meeting in North Battleford they harassed the Metis people by vulgar speeches, shouting, intimidation and finally by physical brutality. These elite leaders often operated as brutally as early imperial oppressors. They exercised heavy-handed control over Native communities, often using violence to combat the Aboriginal movement for liberation. Accompanied by their 'hired thugs,' these leaders disrupted meetings and attacked the movement's spokespersons.

Members of the comprador regimes were not interested in developing or improving Native communities. Instead, their objectives were to suppress the masses, make corrupt deals, and to manipulate government grants. The collaborators formed a distinct group of Aboriginal leaders whose powers depended entirely on funding, state support and colonial structures. They represented a continuation of imperial oppression. In this way, they were also the state's most effective weapon against the counter-colonial movement. By using Aboriginal comprador regimes, governments can hide their colonial subjugation behind the organizations which they finance and support. The state replaced overt repression with a neocolonial system based on comprador regimes which assumed responsibility for ending the anti-colonial movement. The key to the collaborators' success was in their leadership personality, men who were eager to rise above their humble ghetto roots and who satisfied both the masses and the government. Their Aboriginal appearance favoured them among the people. The more 'Indian' the leaders looked, the more the masses accepted them; the lower the person's socioeconomic level, the greater his appeal. The government also wanted Native leaders who could communicate like white bureaucrats and receive and give commands efficiently. The collaborators understood that their main task was to use whatever methods necessary to shatter the Aboriginal anti-colonial movement. Most of them had participated in the struggle and were well acquainted with its policies and strategies. They understood the soft underbelly of our struggle.

Once in office, these elite leaders assumed the lifestyle of affluent business people. They spent extravagantly on their personal pleasures, buying luxury cars and homes, fashionable clothes, and expensive entertainment. They indulged in a routine of attending extravagant conferences, racking up huge bills on air fare, luxury hotel accommodation, alcohol, and 'per diem' allowances. Their status as Aboriginal leaders become associated with the frequency they attend conferences. Comprador leaders do not worry about their credibility because they know that they are government agents and that their support does not depend on the Native masses, but wholly on bureaucratic patronage and government funding. Their authority to administer the indigenous population is derived from the state, not from the will of the people.

National and provincial Metis and Indian organizations are repressive instruments that federal and provincial governments promoted and supported to crush the Native liberation movement of the 1960s. However, they continue to be used, as much as ever for that same purpose today, 1994. There is no doubt that the purpose of collaborator leaders is to stamp out anti-colonial activities and prevent Aboriginal self-determination. Repression and humiliation are standard methods for disintegrating a group identity and Aboriginal consciousness. Native comprador rulers operate 'with corruption and terror of almost suffocating levels.' However, they provide havens for multinational investment. This is true of Saskatchewan's Metis Society and the Metis National Council in their dealings with uranium and logging multinational corporations in Northern Saskatchewan. Open abuse of money and power reveals how the government was willing to give money to the Metis Society,

MNC and AFN as long as the organizations control their people. The general Metis and Indian population partly understand this, but are powerless to stop it, and the media refuses to report the corruption, with few exceptions. Neocolonialism allows a corrupt class of Aboriginals to profit at the expense of the majority. In the end, the state will succeed in crushing the Aboriginal movement for self-determination by dispersing and disorganizing the Native population. An Aboriginal petite bourgeois class has thwarted the growth of a Native political consciousness. It has reduced the Aboriginal masses to inertia and hopelessness. But, behind this process is the hidden hand of a repressive colonial government. In 1974 Metis people fought severely against the state in an attempt to stop government funding to the Metis organizations. In spite of our determined efforts, Ottawa and the provincial governments poured millions of dollars into Native organizations that were given the right to waste it in any way they wished, and they did not have to give an accounting of the expenditures. It was the first step towards Native totalitarianism in the neocolonial period.

There are four national organizations for the four different Aboriginal groups in Canada: the Metis National Council: the former Native Council of Canada, now called the Congress of Aboriginal Peoples, for non-status Indians, the Assembly of First Nations for status or treaty Indians, and the Inuit Tapirisat of Canada. They superimpose their powers over the provincial and local organizations. At the grass-roots level, in villages, reserves, and ghettos, these national organizations are largely unknown, or ignored, but it does not reduce their oppressiveness. This is possible because the organizations have merged with the imperial bureaucracy.

Indian and Metis organizations existed long before the 1960s; some were formed as early as the 1930s. Typically, each province and the Northwest Territories had one major organization for reserve Indians and one Metis organization. For instance, Manitoba had the Manitoba Metis Federation and, for Indians, the Assembly of Manitoba Chiefs. These organizations were relatively inactive until the 1950s, but they generally served a worthwhile purpose for the rank and file of the Indian and Metis people. The organizations spoke with a strong, united voice and obtained certain material benefits for their people. But, without funding their functions and operations were limited. Prior to the mid-seventies, there was little or no corruption. It emerged only after the federal and provincial governments provided massive funding. Government funding and corruption together allowed the state to create comprador regimes. This is not to suggest, however, that there was a government conspiracy or even that Native leaders who accepted government funds on behalf of their organizations were originally corrupt. The state did not have to be conspiratorial in nature, because it already had absolute control and its actions were legitimized by the majority of Canada's non-Native population. In any racial minority's struggle for national liberation the issues and dynamics are always complex and turbulent. When the state feels truly threatened by such movements, the colonizers may respond violently, using police or armies as in Oka. Or, colonizers may maintain control with a fictitious transfer of government powers to selected Aboriginals, such as with the pseudo-government of the Sechelt Indian reserve in B.C. Comprador regimes are insidious, but their disastrous results are often not known until years later.

As the Native national struggle advanced, it gradually encountered internal conflict. By the mid-1970s there was considerable infighting and some violence. Conflicts arose between two political groups, reactionary against revolutionary; not between two racial/tribal groups. For example, in the case of the Metis versus the Indians; A group of right-wing compradors emerged, and staged a counter-liberation struggle. This group was made up of politically-aggressive, semi-illiterate Aboriginals who held establishment beliefs. With the support of government power and funds, they formed a powerful counter-liberation force. By 1975, they succeeded in taking full control of the provincial Metis Society, deposed the radical anti-colonial leaders, and scattered their supporters. The Metis Society became a puppet of the imperial bureaucracy and multinational corporations. In 1970, the militant Metis Society which had succeeded in preventing Premier Thatcher and his multinational friends from building a pulp mill in the Aboriginal territory of Meadow Lake; and had changed, in 1975, their political position where they became a reactionary pawn organization that collaborated with and supported the neocolonial state. This new Aboriginal comprador leadership transformed the Metis Society into a counter-revolution instrument.

The struggle between the two different political groups of Metis continued for more than a year. After numerous complaints of irregularities and corruption of the right-wing Metis Society, there still remained many unanswered questions. In fact, there seemed to be some mysterious interlocking scheme in which the governments had a vested interest in perpetuating the comprador's oppressive rule over the Metis masses by dividing and disorganizing them, retarding political awareness and silencing dissidents. In the meantime the Liberal Trudeau and NDP Blakney Governments looked good, publicly by granting large sums of money to the Metis Society with no strings attached.

The Secretary of State, who granted much of the money to the Metis

Society, seemingly was protecting the collaborator president and his administration. The masses of Metis people continued to ask why, over and over.
They were enraged about the misspending of government funds that were
given in their names, but never benefitted from them. The injustice of such
'criminality' was obvious and painful to them. The police, judicial system
and government authorities have no hesitation about filling the jails with
Metis people for minor traffic and liquor offenses. The total amount of money
that was being spent on welfare for all Metis people of Saskatchewan was
probably less compared to the millions that was being poured into the coffers
of comprador offices. One does not have to speculate as to the reasons for
imposing such political and economic confusion and hardships on the Metis
people of Saskatchewan. It was a problem of transition from direct colonialism to neocolonialism within the state system. Government authorities, and
politicians were scheming with our people, to deal them out of their
resources. Through schemes of manipulation the comprador regimes ruled
over Natives and held them in a state of poverty, misery, and powerlessness.
At the same time the Federal Government gave itself an image of being con-
siderate, and benevolent towards Indians and Metis.

Ottawa claimed innocence in its complicity with the repressive actions of
the Aboriginal collaborators. Canadian bureaucrats, like the US Alliance for
Progress officials, claimed that the indigenous organizations were funded for
compassionate and humanitarian purposes. Yet, Indian and Metis 'mafia' systematically repressed their own people and used violence to crush their political activities. These Aboriginal leaders were visionless creatures of imperial
policy, aping their masters, subordinating the indigenous economy and culture to external interests and disciplining mechanisms. Collaborating Indian
and Metis leaders acted in the interests of the federal government and corporations, such as Weyerhaeuser. By 1980, the Native liberation struggle had
met defeat. The Metis Society and Metis National Council were firmly established as agencies of neocolonial control.

How did this funded comprador oppression happen to the Metis people?
Did these organizations develop through the support and direction of scheming federal and provincial governments? Was the Native liberation movement
sufficiently threatening in the 1960's that the state had to establish repressive
organizations in order to contain the struggle? Was is it necessary to grant
millions of dollars each year to organization leaders regularly for twenty years
—and still going.

In looking back at the situation, as past president of the Metis Society, I
remember the day in 1972 when a Secretary of State agent came to our office

to fill out forms for the new Metis Society president, for a grant of money of one million dollars for the Society. This was indeed a shock, as our organization had not previously received any funds from the government; nor none had ever been offered. Why the sudden generosity by the Ottawa government.? Very little explanation was given. In short time, the forms were completed and the money began arriving in the Metis Society office. In spite of the fact, that a group of Metis individuals, including myself opposed the grants of money to the point where we held a sit-in at the main office to demonstrate against these government funds, our efforts were in vain. Twenty years later, in 1994, the Metis Society is still receiving three million dollars in funding each year.

In thoughtful consideration, there had to be a threatening situation against the government in order that it grant one million dollars to the Metis organization. It certainly was not out of compassion or humanitarian purposes. The Federal Government's attitude towards the Metis has been continuous cruelty and meanness. One has only to recall 1870 and 1885, and the dispossession of our ancestors of their land following years of misery and hostile treatment. Undoubtedly, the most important reason was the Metis and Indian nationalist struggle that had been taking place since 1967. In that five year period, the Native people had waged a critical and aggressive struggle against their neo-colonial oppression. In retrospect, financial funding to Aboriginal organizations in 1972 developed because governments found it necessary to adopt a policy of containment of the Native liberation movement that was occurring. It had become a new and pressured situation because government policy had changed from direct colonial control to neocolonialism. The multinational corporations had entered the picture and considered that the Aboriginal unrest was becoming a problem. It was at this point that politicians became part of the governments' task force to bring the nationalist movement under control. Natives were refusing to remain in reserves and colonies in colonial subservience. They were moving outside of the standard structures of imperial control. The best solution to the problem, as far as the government was concerned was to develop a class of petite bourgeoise from Native communities, which would serve to bring the mass of Native people under control. The intention was to bring an elite class into mainstream society, in order to socialize them into its values. Also, this class would serve as a means of spreading the ideology and values of the dominant society throughout the colonies and reserves. Efforts were also made to bring this Native class into management and decision-making positions in the communities. For instance, Metis leaders were made managers of the Co-op stores in Native villages. Positions as mayors were filled by Metis individuals. On reserves, Indian Chiefs and Councils were given increased power. At the same time, numerous management and business training courses were offered for the 'hard core unemployed' Native workers. They were paid an allowance for attending the courses and promised jobs at the end of the program. Others were given training in how to establish a small business. Although the programs were largely 'show;' meaning that the individuals would not get jobs at the end of the course, nor would they establish a small business. Nevertheless, such courses served to de-activate the restless Native people from the quasi-liberation struggle, and hopefully socialize them into the corporate society. Social values of hard work, thrift, profit, consumerism and family values were stressed.

In the 1970s, community and economic development programs from government departments and universities were developed and implemented for Native communities. These programs involved the majority of Indians, Metis and Inuit in their communities, but not in any meaningful manner. Native individuals were involved in pseudo-decision-making positions, but nothing was changed with regard to the political and economic institutions and structures. However, these programs served to deflect the energy and activities of Aboriginal militants from the nationalist movement. In this neocolonial operation by the corporate government, Native organizations and leaders played a major role. They served as a force within Metis and Indian communities for mobilizing people in the participation and support of these programs. The funding obligated Native leaders to governments and their commands. In the same manner as the Metis Society, all other Indian and Metis organizations in Canada became tools for the establishment. They ceased being leaders of a political liberation struggle; and instead, became counter-liberation oppressors of their own people. This change took place suddenly, and without being recognized by the Native population. Simply by funding the organizations became reactionary bureaucracies of colonial control. In this manner, the federal and provincial governments turned all these Aboriginal organizations into tools of Native containment.

This neocolonial thrust by the corporate government was not the decision of a few political and corporation leaders. It was the inevitable product of the changing structure of corporate capitalism to neocolonialism. It was part of corporate penetration into the underdeveloped Native communities and territories where the hinterland resources lie, such as uranium and oil. Within these peripheral territories, the infrastructure had to be reconstructed for the benefit of the multinational corporations. As a result, costly highways, extensive communication systems, service facilities and housing had to be established. In order to accomplish these operations, it was necessary to have the co-operation and support of the Native population. For this reason, the containment of the Aboriginal people was absolutely essential. Therefore, the counter-colonial movement of the 1960s had to be crushed and contained. The most effective way to bring it under control was through the use of the established Native organizations and programs. Ten million dollars a year, or thereabouts, was a small amount for rich multinational corporations and governments in the 1970s.

Since the Native nationalist movement in Saskatchewan was more threatening to the Canadian state than in almost any other region—except for the Mohawks—we recognized that government retaliation would probably be the most severe there. However, in the 1960s, Ottawa was not able to use the naked power of the canon, machine gun, or scorched-earth tactics as it had done in 1885. The world was watching civil rights battles, not only in Canada, but throughout the Third World. The federal government had recently faced international condemnation for allowing Metis like Laureen Fontaine to starve. Therefore, government authorities were reluctant to send in the police or military to suppress us. The state had to use other methods, and it turned to the petite bourgeois Aboriginals who were willing and eager to collaborate with the enemy—the neo-colonial imperial government.

Looking back to the mid-1960s, Indians, Metis, and Inuit people throughout Canada mobilized an anti-colonial movement against the imperial government. This movement grew into a national struggle for self-determination, and drew attention from all levels of government. Most regions of Canada experienced this semi-liberation movement first hand. However, Saskatchewan was most confrontational in the struggle, and its experience was somewhat different than other areas in Canada. One of the major differences was that it was politically socialist. Also the anti-colonial struggle took the form of a revolutionary movement which supported and used militant, confrontational tactics. Saskatchewan has a history of revolutionary Aboriginal struggle. The resistance struggle of the Indians and Metis at Batoche in 1885 was based on guerrilla warfare, and was a battle against imperialism in Aboriginal territory and for Indian-Metis nationalism. The spirit of that struggle never truly died. Aboriginal leaders of the 1960s movement were direct descendants of men who had been major leaders and warriors in 1885. A certain momentum had been sustained through the years, and was kept alive by aggressive socialist Aboriginal leaders, namely Malcolm Norris, Jim Brady and Mederic MacDougall. Therefore, the 1960s movement in Saskatchewan was relatively advanced, because its members were already a politically conscious group aiming for liberation.

When the Trudeau Government granted funds to the Aboriginal organizations in 1972, apparently, it felt that such funds would co-opt Aboriginal leaders, who would bring the rebellious Native masses under control immediately, and turn them back into their traditional behaviour as submissive, inferiorized 'savages.' However, a group of militant Native people continued to struggle against the government.

It soon became clear that the state was in full control of the governing colonial apparatus of Indian, Metis and Inuit people. Also, that it was very much of an imperial system, and that Natives were still under rigid colonial control. Documents and letters from almost every government department show that Aboriginals are locked into a rigid colonized system. It was clear in 1974, as it is in 1995, that Native people will not achieve liberation, or freedom through negotiations, constitutional changes, self-government, and least of all through Aboriginal comprador regimes.

Government funding has perpetuated colonization to the extent that it has depoliticized and dispersed the Native masses. It is possible that this has been the main objective of government funding. In this sense, the colonizer has been successful. While there has been very little material change within the Aboriginal nation, there has been considerable exploitation and manipulation by the state and multinational corporations of Aboriginal people and their resources. Large corporations operate extensively and freely with the support of the state in Aboriginal territories. The sense of Aboriginal collectivism and radical counter-consciousness has disappeared. Consequently, the transition to neocolonialism has changed the political system of Native people to deeper internal colonialism.

Government ministers, bureaucrats, and politicians are fully aware of this Native 'fraud and corruption.' In 1974, twenty-one years ago, federal and provincial government authorities, including Prime Minister Chretien, then Minister of Indian Affairs, were informed in detail of the corrupt practices. But no action was ever taken to correct the problem. This practice of wasting taxpayers money has continued for twenty-one years with the approval of Liberal, Conservative and NDP governments. It has no other explanation, than the typical neocolonial, subjugation policies carried out by Third World comprador regimes with the approval of their imperial master. It, therefore, becomes necessary for the Native people to examine this 'government-Native' collaboration.

The internal corruption of the Metis Society of Saskatchewan, was not new to government authorities. A formal complaint was made earlier to the Provincial Secretary explaining the irregularities and violations against the Societies Act. It was requested that the necessary action be taken to correct these abuses. The Provincial Secretary, however, made it clear that he would not interfere with the corrupt administration. Also the Secretary of State attempted to smooth-over the whole mess by explaining that he was going to have the financial books of the Metis Society audited which would show whether there had been any misuse of government funds. Six months later, auditors were sent out to examine the books and records. However, it seemed that the auditors, were primarily concerned with being able to justify the complaints about misspending that had become public knowledge. It seemed that their efforts were less of auditing and more of rationalizing expenditures as being proper. The Provincial Prosecutor stated that it was difficult to determine whether the actions were criminal or not because of the poor bookkeeping system. Secretary of State, H. Faulkner stated that Federal Government grants given to the Metis Society could be spent by the president in any way that he wished, as long as the Board Directors approved.[6] However, all these Members were employees, and directly under the control of the president.

From records of twenty years ago, it is noted that the financial and political corruption of Native collaborators and organizations are not new. A fleet of luxury cars was rented from Jubilee Motors in Saskatoon on a regular basis. Undoubtedly, Jubilee Motors and luxury hotels made healthy profits from the Metis Society. In some cases, planes were chartered to Las Vegas and Los Angeles, where the organization's money was spent on gambling and golfing rather than on studying housing programs. Several members, many of whom were not Catholic, went to Rome to visit the Pope.[7] These abuses demonstrated the absolute disregard that the organization's leadership had for the Metis masses and their problems. The same person remained as president for fifteen years, and the 'corrupt' Metis Society was supported by a continual flow of money from both the federal and provincial governments. Also, the same type of corruption is practiced today, only that it has increased immensely.

As of May 1994, the Metis Society cannot account for more than $1 million in spending out of a $2.6 million in government funding by the federal and provincial governments.[8] There are missing documents, unrecorded expenditures, unsupported transfers and other financial irregularities. There are 300 expense reports which do not have appropriate documentation. A detailed audit of the Metis Society of Saskatchewan 'revealed that the organization's finances are in ruin.' The audit depicts an organization in financial chaos.'[9] The audit has been turned over to the provincial Justice Department for the follow up investigation. Although the auditors' report found many allegations of corruption, fraud and misuse of government funds with the financial procedures of the Metis Society of Saskatchewan, they are no different than the 'corrupt' practices of most other Native organizations in Canada. For example, the Edmonton RCMP have completed an investigation into allegations of the misuse of funds by officials of the Metis Nation of Alberta and the RCMP have made recommendations to the Alberta Department of Justice.[10] Therefore the violations and offenses reported for the MSS also apply to other Metis, Indian and Inuit organizations.

There 'was lack of documentation for such expenditures as payroll, consulting, or advances made to related organizations and projects.' The MSS executive is "unable to locate a long list of documents relating to individual expense accounts, such as consulting, payroll, office lease and various other payments. The March, 1993 year end financial statements reflect $600 thousand which we could find no support for this allocation" stated the audit report of the MSS.[11] "There were nearly 400 expense reports and payments that amounted to $150 thousand which do not have documentation to support these payments. There were over 100 expense accounts paid for meals and hotels that were never made."[12] These are only a sample of the type of financial 'rip-offs' and misuse of government funds granted to one Native comprador regime.

Corruption and misuse of government funds seemingly are common and typical to all government funded Native organizations. "The Metis National Council in Financial Ruin," headlined the *Star Phoenix* in April 1994.[13] A deficit of $308,000.00 is claimed by an audit report. The finances of the Metis National Council have been wasted by expense overruns, patronage and corruption. For a lavish two-day meeting at the deluxe Ramada Renaissance Hotel in Vancouver the Metis Council paid one quarter of a million dollars. What was accomplished at this extreme luxury and expense? Almost nothing. Those privileged Metis elites who were present, talked about self-government, but nothing new was discussed. The same old cliches were repeated, and the vagueness of self-government remained. Anyway, few members were paying serious attention. There was plenty of booze, food and partying. In a sense, the government had made a quarter million dollar grant to the Ramada Hotel. The $250,000.00 would have provided ten new frame homes for Metis families in their local villages. The Federal and Provincial Governments give the Metis National Council a few million dollars each year; supposedly for local programs, such as education, job training, etc. But, in reality, this generous funding is to keep the Metis masses contained and under control. Ottawa does not want any more Riel Rebellions. Furthermore, the state wants the rich resources on Metis territory and cheap labour for the multinational corporations.

Nearly $400,000.00 was paid to the seven directors of the MNC as honorarium, per diem ($300.00 a day for attending meetings) and advances. One director was paid $3,000.00 for attending a weekend meeting in Saskatoon, but apparently did not attend, according to the bookkeeping records. Six directors attended the funeral of the Alberta director at a cost of $6,000.00. Despite this being a private matter, the money was taken from the MNC fund. Although Yvon Dumont served only two months as a Director before being appointed Lt. Governor of Manitoba he was paid nearly $30,000.00 in honorarium and per diem expenses.[14] On these gifts of money, no income tax was paid. Hence, the MNC is breaking the Income Tax Regulations. In his new position as Lt. Governor, Mr. Dumont receives a salary of approximately one hundred thousand dollars a year, plus a free luxurious house, limousine and chauffeur. It is a very different story for the Metis working population where approximately 70% are unemployed. The Chief Administrative Officer of MNC was paid almost $300,000.00 a year for his services. He had sole signing power for cheques that were issued. Over half a million dollars was paid to four provincial Metis organizations: Alberta, Manitoba, Saskatchewan and Ontario. Very few receipts or documents were provided to account for this large sum of money. The presidents of these four provincial organizations are the same persons who are Directors on the Board of Metis National Council. It is, in a way, paying money to themselves. As a result of this auditor's report, "The Ottawa RCMP are investigating allegations of fraud at the Metis National Council." The official Auditors' Report for the Department of Justice, Canada stated that "Our examination indicated serious deficiencies in internal control over (MNC) Directors and Officers' expense accounts."[15]

In one year the Metis National Council spent $136,000.00 on office equipment. Yet, the organization has been operating for several years, in which it purchased office equipment every year. The audit report claims that "there is no ledger maintained by MNC for its fixed assets."[16] This says two things. One, that MNC officials totally disregard recording and accounting of government funds that it receives and spends. Two governments, federal and provincial, completely ignore how Native organizations and the officials spend governments grants. The last point raises a serious question, why do governments grant many millions of dollars to certain Native organizations, without requiring definite accountability. Knowing that governments used the tactic of million dollar grants to the Metis Society of Saskatchewan in 1972 to stop and strangle the liberation movement, there is reason to be suspicious of this same kind of funding. There is no political threat today from the Indian and Metis population, in terms of a liberation challenge—except for the Mohawks. Yet, governments continue to give several millions of dollars to Aboriginal organizations 'to spend however they wish' without giving any accounting of it. From personal experience as a leader in the liberation movement, I know that the million dollar funding to the Metis Society was tremendously effective in crushing the counter-colonial struggle. It was obvious to all movement leaders at the time that the federal and provincial governments had deliberately used this funding tactic as a method of killing the Native liberation movement.

The only way in which the funding serves the governments today is that it keeps the Native masses in a state of internal conflict and suppression. In this way, it prevents the possibility of a potential Aboriginal counter-colonial struggle from emerging. In this manner, the state and multinational corporations can appropriate from Indians, Metis and Inuit their resources; ie. oil, uranium, water, easily and cheaply.

Surely, after twenty years of corruption, fraud and thieving by mafia Aboriginal organizations, that Native people across Canada would smarten-up and call a halt to the operations and activities of all these Native organizations, such as the Metis National Council, Metis Society, Metis Federation of Manitoba, Alberta Metis Nation, United Native Nations, Assembly of First Nations and all other similar organizations that pretend to represent Indian and Metis people. It is absolutely necessary that the Metis population throughout the nation come together and re-organize in a collective and democratic way, from the bottom-up. Decision-making must be made from the local village level, community, street and ghetto level. Any organization must be very loosely structured, so as to prevent any one or few persons from gaining all the power. Personal power is our biggest problem. Surely we have not forgotten our past so much that we cannot create an indigenous form of a federation or self-government, which we as Aboriginal people can construct in a way that is beneficial and meaningful to all people of our nation. A structure of this kind can only be developed by the Metis masses, who share in-put into its creation and establishment. This is a political task that must be done right now; not tomorrow, or next month. There is a serous crisis in all Metis organizations in Canada. We must demand that governments stop donating $25 or more million dollars a year to these Metis 'mafia gangs' who oppress and shame us in the most brutal way. At the same time, we have to make governments understand that they have to deal with our newly organized collectives at the community level, and that the funding must be turned over to them for its administration. Without mass challenges, governments will ignore us. Our liberation can be achieved only through political action, mass movement, and to some extent revolutionary action. The structures and institutions of imperialism have to be transformed or smashed.

Chapter Fifteen

State Methods of Aboriginal Control

Command over Metis, Indians and Inuit is absolute; but, to understand this type of iron-hand rule, we need to know it in its historical setting. It is in early imperialism that the institutions and structures of colonial totalitarianism are developed. In the beginning, Aboriginal people were conquered and dominated by European military powers. Gradually, through time, the colonizer transforms the colonial state and bureaucracy into a more refined method of authoritarian control. European imperialism everywhere, followed a specific pattern of indigenous tyranny. After conquest and plunder, it was dispossession of land and seizure of natural resources. This was followed by the creation of an apartheid system. Indians were imprisoned on reserves, and a white European settlement founded on the vacated indigenous land. This type of imperial aggression and control was identical throughout the western world of aboriginal civilizations. This form of imperial repression can be seen from Newfoundland, to Haiti, to Rwanda, to South Africa, to Australia, and on. "Mechanisms of control must be put into operation," *concludes Friedreich*, "in order for the totalitarian regime to operate effectively and adequately."[1] This fact was recognized very early in history by European imperialism. It began when the first imperial boot stomped on the ground of indigenous lands. And this same harsh military-type of colonial control has persisted throughout the centuries, right down to the present day.

During the period of conquest, it was a rule of terror, torture and massive slaughter of indigenous populations. Out of the original population of fifty million Indians in the southern hemisphere, only 250,000 remain in the United States, and 350,000 in Canada.[2] Of those who survived, the majority live in circumstances that are similar to Third World conditions. The traditional Aboriginal society was crushed into a position of powerlessness and dependency. For example, the position of chief, as an official institution, was created by European colonizers and imposed on Indian society. As a puppet ruler, he commanded his people in the interest of the white master. As a result, chiefs and band councils have become an integral part of imperial authoritarian rule. Many similar distortions were imposed on Aboriginal societies in order to form despotic rule. "Use of local collaborators and mercenaries to suppress and control the domestic [aboriginal] population is a common practice."[3] King Leopold of Belgium reduced the Black African population from 20 to 10 million in two decades with Nazi- style atrocities.[4] "From the earliest days of the American colonies, indigenous people were controlled by terrorist operations."[5]

A fact of colonial rule is that a strong state is required to maintain considerable control over indigenous workers. In early Canada, British and French imperialists built structures of authoritarian rule over Metis and Indians for the purpose of providing slaves and underclass workers throughout the centuries of the fur industry. In Australia, South Africa, and other continents Aboriginal workers were used as cheap labour for the white masters' mines or plantations. When mercantilism changed to industrialism, Indian workers became irrelevant. At this stage they were rounded-up and placed in 'holding pens.'[6] This quasi-fascist practice was not because Indians were savages who were incapable of progressive development, but because railroad barons needed Native territory for their railway industry. With the creation of the Indian Act, Ottawa established a rule of absolutism over Indians in Canada. Captives could not leave the reserve without a written pass from the white Indian agent. This practice was in force until the 1950s. Indians and Metis were rigidly isolated and segregated from the mainstream of society. It was within reserves and halfbreed road allowance ghettos that a police culture of repression and terror functioned. "It is this culture," *according to Brogden,* "that fine-tunes the unifying of violence with repression that has characterized aboriginal policing for decades." [7] The regular actions of police repression are seldom seen. In this particular culture, policing operates as a subterranean process which ensure that police and authority agents will deal aggressively and, if necessary with brutality on those Natives who challenge or oppose colonial authoritarianism. However, since the 1960s anti-colonial movement by the Metis, Indians and Inuit this subterranean process has changed somewhat and police brutality has become more subdued.

Aboriginal colonial culture has many similarities to a prison culture. Members hold social and ideological values of a totalitarian culture, which fosters compliance to absolute control. Integral elements include: racism, inferiority, shame, guilt, submissiveness and fear. Isolation and segregation serve to perpetuate these values. Since Metis, Inuit and Indians were confined to their reserves and colonies, they had no means of exchanging ideas and culture with mainstream society. Hence, one's views and attitudes were fashioned by such a culture of confinement. Furthermore, such prison-like culture serves to criminalize Native resistance to imperial authoritarianism. Even to entertain notions of challenge against the oppressor makes one feel like a criminal. To act on such notions would create a community reputation as a criminal.

Looking back to my halfbreed ghetto, I recall the closed and repressive nature of the culture. The St. Louis-Batoche community was large and contained a huge population of French and English halfbreeds. There were definite boundaries, whether real or imaginary. Nevertheless, we lived strictly within these racial boundaries and associated exclusively with our 'inmate' Native population. Whenever a white person came to our house, I automatically assumed he was an authority agent with power. Typical of a colonized mentality, I was immediately fearful of what we had done wrong, and who would be punished. This is the operational process of political and legal terror of colonial totalitarianism. We submitted willingly and readily to authoritarian state rules and police. Obedience to colonial authority and police was embedded in our social conscious. It needed only one red-coat Mountie to control hundreds of colonized Metis. Such historical colonial repression has built-in controls. In spite of the fact that many Halfbreeds in our colony lived in a condition of hunger and deprivation, no one would have suggested that we should organize a protest against the state. We had been rendered submissive and harmless within the dynamics of colonial authoritarianism. We were incapable of developing a counter consciousness.

It is the policy of imperialism that "the colonial state adopts an aggressively interventionist position which establishes authoritarian statism."[8] In Canada, this occurred in the early 1860s when the British Government took initial steps to acquire the Northwest Territories. In 1868 the British Parliament transferred the Northwest Territories to the colonial government at Ottawa. To enforce this policy the British government sent General Wolseley with a regiment of several hundred mercenary troops to Red River in 1870 to crush the Metis national liberation movement. General Wolseley, an imperial caesar of the British empire, was recalled from his command duties in Africa to lead a mercenary regiment to conquer and subjugate the savages at Red River. "Authoritarian policies of the imperial state are administered with little restraint"[9] against the Indigenous population. Wolseley had to deal not only with the nationalist Metis, but, also with the angered Crees. "The Plains Cree," *argues Tobias*, "had prevented the construction of telegraph lines through their territory to emphasize that Canada had to deal with the Cree for their lands."[10] The Crees were determined, and thus acted "in a manner to extract guarantees for the preservation of Cree autonomy."[11] Because of these challenging conditions from Aboriginal people, the Euro-Canadian imperialists advanced an increasingly repressive and authoritarian state.

Imperialism requires control over the land and natural resources within Native territory during its territorial expansionist stage. This is the period of dispossession of land, and the destruction of Aboriginal economy. In Canada, this was between 1870 and 1890, the era of the buffalo. At this time Treaties were 'negotiated,' the Native mainstay of livelihood, the buffalo, was deliberately wiped out by the colonizer. Without an economic base, Indians and Metis became powerless and dependent. In actuality, this meant the liquidation of the whiteman's enemy and the elimination of any restoration of this enemy, the Natives. During this period, "Canada's principal concern in its relationship with the plains Cree was to establish control over them, and Canadian authorities were willing to and did wage war ;upon the Cree in order to achieve this control."[12] People who lose their property and resources because of changes caused by conquest or invasion are inclined to harbour negative and hostile feeling towards that regime. As a result, the lives of Natives are rigidly circumscribed by a jail-like culture in which they spend almost their entire lives.

State violence became the standard practice in Red River. As a result of the terrorizing and brutality of Wolseley's troops, many Metis families were forced into submission and silence. It was no different than any other imperial military campaign, where soldiers freely rampage against the conquered people, particularly the captive women. Ottawa's intervention and control of the Metis population after 1870 was direct totalitarianism. Therefore, democratic forms of political rule within Red River territory were ruled out. It denied Metis and Indians political participation in the Federal parliament. This was clearly shown when Louis Riel was driven from the House of Commons by white supremist Members of Parliament and the police. This Gestapo-like political behaviour occurred, even though Riel had been duly elected by the voters of Red River constituency. This action displayed arrogant powers by the industrial imperial rulers, who showed that an absolute and apartheid state was now in control. The transition from military to civilian governing of Aboriginal people is a lengthy and complex process. In most cases, it is never completed. In Canada, Indians are still under the command of the Federal Indian Affairs Department, and the Metis population is controlled by the Provincial Government Departments with the support of Metis collaborator organizations. Government funding, corruption and violence still remains a significant aspect of controlling the Native masses. The imperial state and its policing forces have been exercising absolute power over the Inuit, Indians and Metis for more than 150 years. The Royal Northwest Mounted Police was established in 1873 with the primary purpose "to control the Indian and Metis population of the North West."[13] They have continued in that role right down to the present day. In addition, there have been several thousands of Anglo imperial troops stationed in Indian/Metis territory as an occupation force. For this reason, it is not difficult for the government to continue to exercise quasi-totalitarianism over Native people without the presence of military and police. There are many mechanisms of state control, apart from police and troops. The more effective ones are: racism, isolation, segregation, subsistence economy, poverty, tribal and ethnic divisions. It is within this unique Canadian history that one must understand the excessive power and hidden authority that the imperial state has over Metis, Inuit and Indians. At the same time, it has made them seriously submissive, with a deep sense of inferiority, and vulnerable to manipulation and collaboration. The dole system of Treaty rations and colony welfare imposed on Indians, Metis and Inuit is for the benefit of the state, rather than providing for the Native population. A welfare bureaucracy is a more effective mechanism in surveillance and policing than direct state policing. It serves to generate behaviour to political conformity, subservience to ideological authority, as well as a form of terror.

It may be argued that my halfbreed community was unique, because Batoche was the site where the imperial troops of John A. Macdonald slaughtered and terrorized the Native people in their final struggle to retain possession of their homes and land. Many neighbours had ancestors who had been guerrilla warriors against the Anglo troops from Ottawa. The grandparents of many families had seen and experienced the violence, torture and killing of Metis and Indian citizens by hired white killers. Lying in the little graveyard of St. Louis are the bodies of these warriors. Instead of memories of brave Metis warriors who sacrificed their lives in the fight to maintain our nation, they are recollections of political and cultural stigma. Supposedly, they are reminders of savages who were too stupid to accept change and progress. As a nation of Metis people, we hung our heads in shame and disgrace. I did not understand at that time, that in the "take-over stage of [colonial totalitarianism], the brunt of political terror is directed against racial and ethnic outgroups."[14] Furthermore, I did not know that acts of military terror by the authoritarian state served to isolate and remove Native people whose values and attitudes didn't harmonize with those of the colonizer. In these expansionist campaigns, Aboriginal people became victims of repressive imperialist action, and submissive captives to colonial tyranny. This was the fate of the Metis and Indians in Batoche in 1885.

The atrocities of the conquering whiteman in the aftermath of the battle were nothing less than semi-fascist actions of a raging empire. The hideous public hangings in the city streets of North Battleford and Regina of brave Metis and Indian warriors were obscene. The terrifying spectacle of arrogant gallows commanding the main streets were more barbarous and heinous than any act of Aboriginal people. The mock trail of Louis Reil and several Metis warriors on charges of treason was a cruel farce that trifled with the lives of devout citizens to their nation. It was psychological warfare at its best. Its intended purpose of scaremongering was indeed effective. As defeated Metis and Indian people we crawled back to our shattered reserves and colonies, and were thankful to our imperial masters to be saved from the gallows. The use of terror by imperialist regimes are multiple: military, police, courts, criminal codes, and the judicial system in general. Law, as practiced in imperial courts, is an integral part of the system of Aboriginal control. This is clearly shown in the prison population of Canada; 60 to 80% of the inmate population is Native persons. The judicial system is an effective method of political control over Metis, Inuit and Indians. "The government, the courts and the police work in concert to provide for a system that sustains coercion as the mainstay of [Aboriginal] policing."[15] White supremacist, Carney Nerland of Prince Albert, Saskatchewan shot and killed Leo Lachance in 1991 as he walked out of Nerland's shop for no reason, other than he was an Indian. Nerland did not even appear in court for this cold-blood racist killing. A special arrangement was made with the Court of Queen's Bench, Judge, F. Gerein, and Police Officer D. Denikew whereby Nerland was allowed to serve a few months in jail on a minor charge. This was primarily to protect him from the angry Native masses.[16]

After the scorched-earth terrorist and genocide campaigns of the Ottawa regime in 1885, policing of Metis communities became considerably more repressive. This military campaign had sufficient results for full compliance and loyalty to a despotic colonial society. Little additional policing was needed for social and political control.

Extreme violence used by colonizers—that is, a particularly vicious attack on a community, a massacre, an execution, the imprisonment of leaders or the torture of a few people—serves to pacify large regions for long periods of time, and is carried out for that purpose. Violence, or the threat of it, as a political tool is basic to colonialism.[17]

Power over oppressed people can be maintained through non-decision; that is, silencing them before they are even heard. The ideas are smothered before they are even given consideration. Powers of the state can prevent threatening issues from arising within the colony. The fact of re-enforcing defeat every time Indians and Metis confront the authorities with an issue can render them powerless. Likewise, government funding to elite Indian and Metis organizations de-activates and silences the Native masses. Most of the money ends up in the hands of big corporations, such as the Hilton Hotels and major automobile companies, while the powerless Aboriginals in the reserves and colonies get almost nothing. It is misleading to think that government administration is neutral or non-partisan. Government decisions with regard to Aboriginal people usually end up giving power to the colonizer and peanuts to the Natives. Bureaucracy performs few services that benefit the colonized. Power and benefits go to those who already have authority. Command relationships, once established are self-sustaining. The state, historically develops structures, institutions and repressive patterns of power to control the indigenous population. They are never removed later, when the state develops into a more sophisticated administration. In fact, repressive state power is expanded and strengthened. The nature of present-day underdeveloped countries and their control has to be sought in the colonial past. Once the state is established, it maintains rigid colonization in almost every aspect of Aboriginal life. The struggle today for most Indians is land rights. This is an effective method of containing and controlling indigenous people. The notion is fostered that Indian people will achieve huge financial sums and a pseudo-liberation through land-title victories. As a result, Indians involve themselves in long, legal court battles that drag on for years.

The political culture of capitalism works hand in hand with the judicial system, politicians, bureaucracy and corporate leaders to harmonize racism, oppression and control. It is a carefully choreographed structure that maintains an apartheid authoritarian system over the Aboriginal population. One has only to recall Oka and Davis Inlet. During the last twenty-five years, the state has taken steps towards greater control of political ideology and cultural activities, largely through funding. This was not done out of compassion for Native people, but, out of a certain fear that Indians, Metis and Inuit were moving towards self-rule.

Aboriginal workers are kept in rigid control through the capitalist class structure. They are confined to the bottom as unskilled, seasonal quasi-proletariat. Few are unionized. Within the last ten years, class division has developed within Native communities which has resulted in greater exploitation and control. For example, in Saskatchewan the La Ronge Indian Band has developed the Kitsaki Development Corporation, a private enterprise. It includes a wide range of business activities that does $16 million worth of business annually. It is one of the largest employers in the area. The band is heavily funded by the Indian Affairs Department. It hires Indian band members for trainee and entry level positions, which pays extremely low wages.[17] The Indian business industry does not take into consideration the critical system of domination and exploitation of its own people. Seemingly, it is no different than corporate capitalism in mainstream society. So far, there is no issue of class struggle. A political consciousness of worker exploitation has not even surfaced. Aboriginal industry, to-date, is heavily dependent on external corporate capitalism, and obligated to governments. This type of relationship creates a quasi-control by Aboriginal individuals, and serves to contain any class struggle within the Native communities. For this reason, liberation is limited to nationalism and cultural autonomy, which cannot bring full self-determination. Since liberation can not be achieved through government funding and Aboriginal capitalism, we have to shut-down these corporate enterprises that control Native politics and economy. We need to shatter the bureaucracy and structures of capitalism that imprison us under colonialism.

Appendices

Footnotes

Chapter 1 - Colonization in Our Backyard

1. Easterbrook, W., *Canadian Economic History*, University of Toronto Press, 1988, p. 82.
2. Adams, H., *Prison of Grass*, Fifth House Publishers, Saskatoon, 1989, p. 23.
3. de las Casas, B., *The Terms of the Indians*, Oriole Chapbooks, New York, 1972. p.5.
4. Fell, B., America: B.C. *Ancient Settlers in the New World*, Pocket Books, New York, 1989, p. 255.
5. Heyerdahl, T. *Early Man in the Ocean*, Vintage Books, New York, 1980, p. 24.
6. Keare, M., *Supplying Repression*, Institute for Policy Studies, Washington, D.C., 1981, p. 4.
7. *Vancouver Sun*, March 1, 1994.
8. Klare, M., Ibid., p. 80.
9. Valley, P., *Bad Samaritans*, Orbis Books, New York, 1990, p. 4.
10. Ani, M., *Yurugu*, African World Press Inc., Trenton, New Jersey, 1994, p. 251.
11. Douglas, T.C., *The Treaties, Between Her Majesty, Queen Victoria and the Indians of British North America*, Provincial Committee on Minority Rights, Regina, 1961, p13.
12. Ibid. p. 16.
13. Ani, *Yunugu*, p. 317

Chapter 2 - The Poverty Grip on Metis

1. Bartlett, R. *Aboriginal Peoples & Constitutional Reform,* Institute of Intergovernmental Relations, Queens University, Kingston, 1986, p. 5.
2. *Vancouver Sun*, July 28, 1992.
3. *Poverty Report of the Metis*, H. Adams, Senate Committee Publication, Ottawa, 1969.
4. Petition to C. MacDonald, Minister of Welfare, Government of Saskatchewan, Regina, 1969. The author's private file, Vancouver, B.C.
5. Ibid.
6. Ibid.
7. Ibid.
8. Ibid.
9. Letter to Social Welfare Worker, J. Caulfield from Charles Moise, La Loche, Sask., June 26, 1969. The author's private file, Vancouver, B.C.
10. Ibid.
11. Ibid.

Chapter 3 - Eurocentricism: Myths of Aboriginal History

1. Moore, G. *The Romantic Poets*, Aurium Press, London, 1992, p. 27.
2. Kipling, R. *Kiplings' Verse*, Doubleday & Co. New York, 1939, p.13.
3. Palmer, R. *A History of the World*, A. Knopf Press, New York,1978.
4. Berkhofer, R. *The Whiteman's Indian*, Vintage Books, New York, 1979. p. 13.
5. Amin, S. *Eurocentrism*, Monthly Review Press, New York, 1989, p. 91.
6. Ibid., p. 105.
7. Naylor, R. *Canada in the European Age*, New Star Books, Vancouver, B.C. p. 27.
8. Berkhofer, Ibid. p. 116.
9. Ibid., p. 116.
10. Ibid., p. 117.
11. Ibid., p. 121.
12. Gough, K. *Anthropology: Child of Imperialism*, Monthly Review Magazine, V. 19, No. 11, April 1968.
13. Ani, M. *Yurugu*, Africa World Press, Trenton, New Jersey, 1994, p. 256.
14. Flanagan, T. *Riel and the Rebellion: 1885 Reconsidered.*, Western Producer Prairie Press, Saskatoon, 1983, p. 17.
15. Alberta Historical Review, *"Riel - A Criticism and a Response"*, Spring, 1984, Vol. 32, p. 26.

Chapter 4 - Mainstream Ideology: The Control of Colonized Minds

1. Barsamean, D. *Stenographers to Power*, Common Courage Press, Monroe, Maine, 1992, p. 6
2. Adler, N. *The Learning of Political Behaviour*, Scott, Foresman & Co. Glenview, Ill., 1970, p. 95.
3. Harris, M. *Justice Denied*, MacMillan Publishers, Toronto, 1987, cover page.
4. Adler, N. Ibid. p. 117.
5. Adler, N. *The Learning of Political Behaviour*, Scott, Foresman & Co. Glenview, Ill., 1970, p. 191.
6. Barsamean, D. Ibid., p. 12.

Chapter 5 - Indian and Metis Slavery in New France

1. Trudel, M., Horizen's Canada, *Ties That Bind*, No.18, 1985, p. 422.
2. Trudel, M., Horizen's Canada, *Ties That Bind*, No. 18, 1985 p. 422.
3. Neilson, H., Library & Historical Society, *Slavery In Old Canada*, p. 20.
4. Trudel, M.,L'esclavage au Canada Francais, La Presses de le L'Universite Laval, Quebec, 1960, p. 41.
5. Sulte, B. La Revue Canadienne 61, 1911, L'esclavage en Canada. p. 318.
6. Neilson, H., Ibid. p. 22.
7. Neilson, H., Ibid. p. 22.
8. Neilson, H. Ibid., p. 27.
9. Neilson, H., Ibid. p. 23
10. Neilson, H., Ibid. p. 23.
11. Trudel, M. *L'esclavage au Canada francais*, Le Presses de L'Universite Laval, Quebec, 1960, p. 71.
12. Neilson, H., Ibid. p. 24.
13. Trudel, M., Horizen's Canada, Ties That Bind, No. 18, 1985, p. 424.
14. Trudel, M. Ibid. p. 39.
15. Trudel, M. L'esclavage au Canada Francais, p. 157.
16. Trudel, M., Horizen's Canada, p. 425.
17. Neilson, H., Ibid. p. 28.
18. Ani, M. *Yurugu*, African World Press, Trenten, New Jersey, 1994, p. 251.
19. Ani, M. *Yurugu*, African World Press, Trenten, New Jersey, 1994, p. 251
20. Trudel, M., Horizen's Canada, p. 425.
21. Trudel, M. *L'esclavage au Canada francais*, p. 151.
22. Trudel, M.,Ibid., p. 153.
23. Trudel, M.,Ibid., p. 153.
24. Trudel, M., *ibid.,* p. 153.
25. Trudel, M., Horizons Canada, p. 424.
26. Leader Post, Regina, Dec. 7, 1990, p. C12.
27. Trudel, M., Horizons Canada, p. 424.

Chapter 6 - Speaking Out to White Oppressors

1. Melville-Ness, I. *National Conference on Indian & Northern Education Report*, University of Saskatchewan, Saskatoon, Extension Division, April 1967.
2. Ibid.
3. Ibid.
4. *Saskatchewan Teachers' Bulletin*, Saskatoon, April 1967, 33, (8).
5. Melville-Ness, Ibid.
6. Ibid.
7. Ibid.
8. Ibid.
9. Ibid.
10. *Teachers' Bulletin*, Saskatchewan Teachers' Federation, Sept. 1967.
11. *Star Phoenix*, Saskatoon, June 12, 1967.
12. Ibid.
13. Ibid.
14. *Canadian Broadcasting Corporation Times*, Toronto, June 10, 1967, p. 27.
15. *Toronto Star*, June 17, 1967, Gzowski, P. *Our Forgotten People*.
16. *Winnipeg Free Press*, July 1967.
17. *Western Producer*, Saskatoon, May 2, 1968.
18. *Star Phoenix*, May 20, 1968.
19. *Leader Post*, Regina, June 1968.
20. *Star Weekly Magazine*, May 11, 1968.
21. *Globe & Mail*, Toronto, June 27, 1969.
22. Ibid.
23. Ibid.

Chapter 7 - Metis/Indian Struggles of the 1960s

1. *Star Weekly Magazine*, Toronto, May 11, 1968.
2. Ibid.
3. *Georgia Straight*, Vancouver, March 2, 1972.
4. Ibid.
5. Ibid., May 15, 1974.
6. *Winnipeg Free Press*, Oct. 28, 1972.
7. *Time Magazine*, New York, May 19, 1967.
8. *Star Phoenix*, Saskatoon, Aug. 8, 1972.
9. Letter to D. Newsham, Barrister, Saskatoon, July 9, 1968. The author's private file, Vancouver, B.C.
10. Letter from D. Newsham to R. Thompson.

11. Letter from Attorney General, Heald, Government of Saskatchewan, Regina, Aug. 1968. The author's private file, Vancouver, B.C.
12. *Star Phoenix*, Saskatoon, Aug, 1993, p. A5.
13. Ibid., Feb. 14, 1969.
14. *Poverty Report of the Metis*, H. Adams, Senate Committee Publication, Ottawa, 1969.
15. *Leader Post*, Regina, Oct. 10, 1969.
16. Veltmeyer, H. *Canadian Clans Structure*, Paramont Press, Toronto, 1986, p. 103.
17. Ibid., p. 104.
18. Ibid., p. 97.
19. *Vancouver Sun*, April 24, 1993.
20. Nkrumah K. *Class Struggle in Africa*, International Publishers, New York, 1975, p. 12.
21. *Star Phoenix*, Feb. 23, 1970.
22. *Toronto Star*, Feb. 21, 1970.

Chapter 8 - Criticism of Metis Historiography

1. Stanley, G., *The Birth of Western Canada*, University of Toronto Press, Toronto, 1936, p. 194.
2. Canadian Journal of Native Studies, G. Laroque, *"The Metis in English Canadian Literature"*, V. 3, Nol. 1, 1983, p. 86.
3. Stanley, G., Ibid., p. 49.
4. Stanley, G., Ibid., p. 335.
5. Stanley, G., Ibid., p. 243.
6. Alberta Historical Review, *"Riel-A Criticism and a Response"*, Spring 1984, V. 32, p. 26.
7. Flanagan, T., *Riel & The Rebellion,* Western Producer Press, Saskatoon,1983, p.3.
8. Flanagan, Ibid., p. 1.
9. Flanagan, Ibid., p. 10.
10. Flanagan, Ibid., p. 10.
11. *Alberta Historical Review*, Ibid., p. 24.
12. Native Studies Review, University of Saskatchewan, Saskatoon, F. Tough *"A Review of Geraud's The Metis in the Canadian West"*, V. 5, No. 2, 1989, p. 55.
13. Ibid., p. 56.
14. Geraud, M., *The Metis in the Canadian West*, University of Alberta Press, Edmonton, 1986, p. 4.
15. Ibid., p.
16. Flanagan, Ibid., p. 1.
17. Bulhan, H., F. *Fanon of the Psychology of Oppression,* Phenium Press, New York, 1985, p. 65.

18. Shafar, F. ed. *Writers From South Africa*, TriQuarterly Books, Evanston, Ill., 1989, p. 85.

19. Sealey, B. & A. Lussier, *The Metis: Canada's Forgotten People*, Metis Federation Press, Winnipeg, 1975, p. 179.

20. Ibid., p. 181.

21. Adams, H. Ibid., p. 72.

22 Magubane, B. *The Political Economy of Race and Class*, Monthly Review Press, New York, 1979, p. 16.

23. Nkrumah, K. , Class Struggle in Africa, International Publishers, New York, 1970, p. 75.

24. Magubane, B., Ibid., p. 87.

25. Adams, H., Ibid., p. 71.

26. Friesen, G., Ibid., p. 146-49.

27. Saskatchewan Herald, Feb. 8, 1982

28. Van Houten, B. Corporate Canada, Progress Books, Toronto, 1991, p. 60.

29. Adams, H., Ibid., p. 71.

30. Stanley, G., Ibid., p. 300.

Chapter 9 - Metis History From Native Reality

1. Ryerson, S. *The Founding of Canada*, Progress Books, Toronto, 1960, p. 106.

2. Innis, H. *The Fur Trade in Canada*, University of Toronto Press, 1964, p. 67.

3. Woodcock, G. *A Social History of Canada*, Viking Press, New York, 1988, p. 108.

4. Ibid., p. 256.

5. W. Eccles, *Canada Under Louis XIV*. McClelland & Stewart, Toronto, 1964, p. 109.

6. Trudel, M. *L'esclavage: Au Canada Francais,* Les Press Universitairer, Laval, Quebec, 1960.

7. Ibid., Chapt. 3, p. 63.

8. Trudel, M. *"Ties That Bind"* Horizons Canada, 1985, No. 18, pp. 422-27.

9. Ibid.

10. Bourgeault, R. *"The Indian, the Metis and the Fur Trade"*, Studies in Political Economy, A Socialist Review, Fall, 1983, No. 12, p. 61.

11. Ibid., p. 62.

12. Ibid., p. 62.

13. Ibid., p. 68.

14. Myers, G. *History of Canadian Wealth,* James Lewis & Samuel Publishers, Toronto, 1972, p. 139.

15. Stanley, G. *The Birth of Western Canada*, University of Toronto Press, 1936, p. 47.

16. Bourgeault, R. Ibid., p. 69.

17. Adams, H. *Prison of Grass*, Fifth House Publishers, Saskatoon, 1989, p. 50.

18. Ibid., p. 54.
19. Bourgeault, R., Ibid., p. 23.
20. Friesen, G. *The Canadian Prairies*, University of Toronto Press, 1987, p. 149.

Chapter 10 - Challenge to Colonized Culture

1. Fanon, F., *The Wretched of the Earth*, Grove Press, New York, 1963, p. 41.
2. Szymanski, A., *Class Structure*, Praeger Publishers, New York, 1983, p. 261.
3. Veltmeyer, H., *Canadian Class Structure*, Garamond Press, Toronto, 1986. p. 96.
4. Blauner, R. Radical Oppression in America, Harper and Row, New York, 1972, p. 146.
5. Searle, C., Words Unchained, Zed Publishers, London, 1984, p. xxi.
6. Careless, J., *A Story of Challenge*, St. Martins Press, New York, 1974, p. 22.
7. Memo to Faculty and Staff, University of Saskatchewan, Students' Union, October 12, 1993.
8. *Star Phoenix*, Saskatoon, July 1994
9. Buhan, H., *Fanon and the Psychology of the Oppressed*, Plenum, New York, 1985, p. 115.
10. Chrisman, R., ed., *Contemporary Thought*, Bobbs-Merrill Co. New York, 1973, p. 76.
11. Frazier, F. *The Black Bourgeoise*, Collier Books Ltd., London, 1962, p. 187.
12. *Saturday Night Magazine*, Canada's Magazine, Vancouver, B.C. March 1992

Chapter 11 - Constitutional Colonialism

1. *Vancouver Sun*, October 25, 1991.
2. Bartlett, R., *Aboriginal Peoples & Constitutional Reform*,
Queen's University, Kingston, 1986, p. 11.
3. Chinwveizu, *The West & The Rest of Us*, Vintage Books, New York, 1975, p. 70.
4. *Royal Commission on Aboriginal Peoples*, Erasamus, George, Chairman, Ottawa, Feb. 13, 1992.
5. *Vancouver Sun*, March 9, 1991.
6. Ibid.
7. Ibid.
8. Beard, Charles, *An Economic Interpretation of the Constitution of the United States*, MacMillan Publishers, New York, 1935, p. 324.
9. Ibid.
10. Douglas, T.C. *The Treaties Between Her Majesty and the Indians of British North America*, Queens Printer, Regina, 1961, p. 16.
11. Ibid., p. 16.
12. Ibid., p. 16.
13. *Royal Commission*, p. 11.

14. *Cultural Survival Quarterly*, Cambridge Mass., Fall 1991, V. 15, No. 4, p. 32.
15. Bartlett, R., p. 35.
16. *Vancouver Sun*. Sept. 25, 1992, p. A23.
17. *Canadian Dimensions*, Winnipeg, March, 1992.
18. Ibid.
19. *Vancouver Sun*, Sept. 18, 1992.
20. *Globe & Mail*, Toronto, March 14, 1992.
21. Ibid.
22. *Vancouver Sun*, March 19, 1992.
23. *Vancouver Sun*, June 2, 1993.
24. Ibid.

Chapter 12 - Neocolonialism

1. Klare, M., *Supplying Repression*, Institute of Policy Studies, Washington, D.C., 1981, p. 43.
2. Szymanski, A., *The Logic of Imperialism*, Praeger Press, New York, 1983, p. 288.
3. Klare, Ibid., p. 8.
4. Szymanski, Ibid., p. 287.
5. Hadjor, K., *Dictionary of Third World Terms*, Penguin, New York, 1993, p. 216.
6. Thomas, C., *The Rise of the Authoritarian State*, Monthly Review Press, New York, 1984, p. 63.
7. *Star Phoenix*, Saskatoon, June 8, 1993.
8. *Tule River Reservation Study*, University of California, Davis, Native Studies Department, 1986.
9. *Vancouver Sun.*, August 20, 1993
10. Briarpatch Magazine, Sept. 1993. *"The Political World of Carney Norland"*.
11. Ibid.
12. Ibid.

Chapter 13 - Indigenous Collaborators In Third World Colonization

1. Klare, M. *Supplying Repression*, Institute For Policy Studies, Washington, D.C., 1981, p. 4.
2. Ibid., p. 4.
3. Ibid., p. 4.
4. Ibid., p. 7.
5. Ibid., p. 8.
6. Ibid., p. 6.
7. Vallely, P. *Bad Samaritans*, Orbis Books, Maryknoll, New York, 1990, p. 4.
8. Ibid., p. 4.
9. Ibid., p. 79.
10. Memo, Author's Private file, Vancouver, B.C.

Chapter 14 - Metis/Indian Organizations As The New Oppressors

1. *The Metis Messenger*, The True Voice of the Metis of Saskatchewan, March, 1994. An Underground Newspaper. Author's Personal File.
2. Ibid.
3. Ibid.
4. Metis Society Report, *"The Metis People and Their Problems."* July 5, 1974. Author's Personal File.
5. Letter from H. Faulkner, Secretary of State, Ottawa to Metis Society of Saskatchewan, Saskatoon, January 29, 1974. Author's Personal File.
6. Report of the Association of Metis and Non-Status Indians of Saskatchewan, Regina, Sask. 1988. Author's Personal File.
7. *Star Phoenix*, Saskatoon, Sask. April 29, 1994.
8. Deloitte & Touche Audit, Chartered Accountants, Auditors' Report of Metis Society of Sask. Ottawa, April 1994.
9. *Native Issues Monthly, Magazine*, Vancouver, B.C. May 1994, p. 59.
10. Deloitte & Touche Audit, Ibid.
11. *Star Phoenix*, Saskatoon, Sask. March 16, 1994.
12. Deloitte & Touche, Audit Report of the Metis National Council, Ottawa, March 11, 1994.

Chapter 15 - State Methods of Aboriginal Control

1. Friedreich, C. *Totalitarianism*, Harvard University Press, Cambridge, Ma. 1954, p. 35.
2. Dunbar-Ortiz, R. *Indians of the Americas*, Zed Books Ltd., London, England, 1984, p. 7.
3. Chomsky, N. *The Culture of Terrorism*, Black Rose Books, Montreal, 1988, p. 82.
4. Ibid., p. 82
5. Ibid., p. 82
6. Fleras, A. *The Nations Within*, Oxford University Press, Toronto, 1992, p. 41.
7. Brogden, M., Policing For a New South Africa, Routledge Publishers, New York, 1993, p. 41.
8. Ahire, P. Inperial Policing, Open University Press, Philadelphia, 1991, p. 24.
9. Ibid., p. 24.
10. Tobias, J., Canada's Subjugation of the Plains Cree, In Out of the Background, ed. Fisher, R. Copp Clarke Ltd., Toronto, 1988, p. 194.
11. Ibid., p. 192.
12. Ibid., p. 190.
13. Brown, Lorne, James Lewis. Samuel Publishers, Toronto, 1973. p. 10.
14. friedreich, C. Totalitarianism, 1954, p. 69.
15. friedreich, C. totalitarianism, 1954, p. 27 - 30
16. Briarpatch Magazine, Regina, September 1993.
17. Brogden, M. Policing For a New South Africa, 1993
18. Saskatoon Star Phoenix, June 30, 1994

Bibliography

Amin, Samir, *Class and Nation*, Monthly Review Press, New York, 1980.

Amin, Samir, *Eurocentrism*, Monthly Review Press, New York, 1978.

Adams, Howard, *Prison of Grass*, Fifth House, Saskatoon, 1989.

Anderson, P., *Lineage of Absolute State*, New Left Books, London, England, 1974.

Ani, Marimba, Yurugu: *A Critique of European Cultural Thought and Behaviour*, Africa World Press, New Jersey, 1994.

Armstrong, Jeannette, *Looking At the Words of Our People*, Theytus Books Ltd., Penticton, 1993.

Arendt, Hannah, *The Origins of Totalitarianism*, Allen and Unwin, London, 1958.

Bartlett, R., *Aboriginal Peoples and Constitutional Reform*, Queen's University, Kingston, Ontario, 1989.

Berkhofer, R., *The White Man's Indian: Images of the American Indian,* Vintage Books, New York, 1979.

Blaut, J.M., *The Colonizer's Model of the World*, Guilford Press, New York, 1993.

Boggs, Carl, *Gramsci's Marxism*, Pluto Press, London, England, 1976.

Bourgeault, Ron, *Five Centuries of Imperialism and Resistance*, Fernworld Publishers, Winnipeg, 1992.

Bourgeault, Ron, *"The Indians, the Metis and the Fur Trade"*, Studies in Political Economy, No. 12, Fall 1983, Ottawa.

Bourgeault, Ron, *Class, Race and Gender, Political Economy and the Fur Trade*, Master's Thesis, University of Saskatchewan, Regina, Sask., 1986.

Brown, Lorne & Carol, *An Unauthorized History of the RCMP*, James Lewis & Samuel, Toronto, 1973.

Burger, John, *The State and the World's Indigenous People*, Zed Books, London, England, 1987.

Bulhan, H., Fanon: *On the Psychology of Oppression*, Plenum Press, New York, 1985.

Bolaria, Singh, *Racial Oppression in Canada*, Garamond Press, Toronto, Ontario.

Carnoy, Martin, *Education as Cultural Imperialism*, David McKay Co., New York, 1974.

Casas de las, Barthlolome, *The Tears of the Indians*, Oriole Chapbooks, New York, 1972.

Chinweizu, *The West and the Rest of Us*, Vintage Books, New York,1975.

Chomsky, N., *Year 501: The Conquest Continues*, Black Rose Publishers, Montreal, 1993.

Chomsky, N., *The Culture of Terrorism*, Black Rose Books, Montreal, 1988.

Constantino, R., *Neocolonial Identity and Counterconsciousness*, Merlin Press, London, 1978.

Dobbin, Murray, *One-and-a-Half Men,* New Star Press, Vancouver, 1981.

Fanon, Frantz, *Black Skin, White Masks*, Grove Press, New York, 1967.

Fanon, Frantz, *The Wretched of the Earth*, Grove Press, New York, 1963.

Gedicks, Al, *Native and Environmental Struggles Against Multinational Corporations*, Black Rose Books, 1994.

Fleras, A., *Aboriginal State in Canada, United States and New Zealand,* Oxford University Press, Toronto, 1992.

Hansen, Emmanuel, Fanon: *Social and Political Thought,* Ohio State University Press, Columbus, 1977.

Harris, M., *Justice Denied,* The Law vs. Donald Marshall, McMillan Publishers, Toronto, 1986.

Hansen, E. Frantz Fanon, *Social and Political Thought,* Columbus, Ohio, 1977.

Hayter, Teresa, *Creation of World Poverty,* Pluto Press, London, 1981.

Innis, Harold, *Fur Trade in Canada,* University of Toronto Press, Toronto, 1960.

Jinadu, L.A., *Fanon and the African Revolution,* KPI Press, New York, 1986.

Jennings, Francis, *Indians, Colonialism, and Conquest,* W. Norton & Co., New York, 1975.

Jaenen, C., *The Role of the Church in New France,* McGraw Hill Publishers, New York, 1976.

Khan, Aga, *Indigenous Peoples, Quest for Justice,* Zed Books, London, 1987.

Klare, M., *Supplying Repression,* Institute for Policy Studies, Washington, D.C., 1981.

Koning, Hans, *The Conquest of America,* Monthly Review Press, New York, 1993.

Lemoine, J.M., *"Slavery in Quebec",* The Canadian Antiquarian Journal, Vol. IV, Montreal, 1876.

Li, Peter, *Ethnic Inequality in a Class Society,* Wall & Thompson Press, Toronto, 1988.

Lutz, Hartmut, *Contemporary Challenges, Conversations with Native Authors,* Fifth House, Saskatoon, 1991.

Megubane, Bernard, *Political Economy of Race and Class,* Monthly Review Press, New York, 1979.

McCulloch, Jack, *Black Soul, White Artifact: Fanon's Social Theory,* Cambridge University Press, New York, 1983.

McKague, Onmand, *Racism in Canada,* Fifth House Publishers, Saskatoon, 1991.

Miliband, R., *The State in Capitalist Society,* Weidenfield & Nicolson, London, 1969.

Memmi, Albert, *Colonizer and Colonized,* Beacon Press, Boston, 1967.

Naylor, R., *Canada in the European Age,* New Star Books, Vancouver, 1987.

Ngugi, Wa., *Decolonizing the Mind,* Heinemann, London, 1986.

Nkrumah, K., *Neocolonialism,* International Publishers, New York, 1965.

Niosi, Jorge, *Canadian Capitalism,* James Lorimer Publisher, Toronto, 1981.

Philip, M. Nourbese, *Frontiers, Writings on Racism & Culture,* The Mercury Press, Toronto, 1992.

Panitch, Leo, *The Canadian State,* University of Toronto Press, 1977.

Poulantzas, N., *Political Power and Social Class,* New Left Books, London, 1968.

Purich, Don, *The Metis,* James Lewis & Lorimer, Toronto, 1988.

Ryerson, S., *The Founding of Canada,* Progress Books, Toronto, 1960.

Race and Class: Journal for Third World Liberation, V. 35, No. 4, April 1994, London, England.

Szymanski, Albert, *The Capitalist State & The Politics of Class*, Winthrop Publishers, Cambridge, Ma., 1978.

Szymanski, Albert, *The Logic of Imperialism*, Praeger Press, New York, 1983.

Trudel, Marcel, *"Ties That Bind"*, Horizons Canada, No. 18, p. 422, 1985.

Tobias, J., *"Subjugation of the Plains Cree"*, *Out of the Background*, R. Fisher (ed) Copp Clark, Toronto, 1988.

Thomas, C., *The Rise of the Authoritarian State in Peripheral Societies*. Monthly Review Press, New York, 1986.

Wallerstein, I., *The Capitalist World Economy*, Cambridge University Press, New York, 1991.

Wallerstein, I., *World Inequality*, Black Rose Books, Montreal, 1975.

Wallace, Samuel, *Total Institutions*, Transaction Books, New Brunswick, New Jersey, 1968.

Watkins, M., *Dene Nation: The Colony Within*, University of Toronto Press, 1977.

Vorst, J., *Race, Class, Gender*, Garamond Press, Toronto, 1991.

Worsley, Peter, *The Third World*, Weidenfeld and Nicolson, London, 1967.

York, Geoffrey, *The Dispossessed, Life and Death in Native Canada*, Vintage, U.K. Press, 1990.

Zahar, R., *Fanon, Colonialism and Alienation*, Monthly Review Press, New York, 1974.